ZANE PRESENTS

Dare to be Tempted

AN EDEN DAVIS SERIES

Dear Reader:

In this first installment of her three-part series, Eden Davis introduces readers to erotica featuring female characters of a certain age and catering to "grown and sexy women." Aleesa keeps a journal while her husband, Walter, is in Afghanistan. It's not full of real-life experiences, but it's packed with fantasies.

Upon his return home, the impotent and psychologically damaged Walter discovers the journal. Aleesa had planned to present him her fantasy book, however, the lack of sparks forced her to put it aside.

When Walter reads the journal, he offers Aleesa the ultimate birthday gift: a forty-eight-hour pass to fulfill a sexual fantasy.

Many women dream of fantasies but are cautious to bring them to reality. Will Aleesa be bold enough to accept her husband's gift? And if so, how will it affect their marriage?

Eden Davis, the pen name of a critically acclaimed author, takes sensuality to the next level. Make sure that you keep an eye out for *Dare to be Seduced* and *Dare to Be Wild*, both releasing in Fall 2013.

Thank you for supporting Eden Davis' efforts and thank you for supporting one of the authors published under my imprint, Strebor Books. I try my best to bring you cutting-edge works of literature that will keep your attention and make you think long after you turn the last page.

Now sit back in your favorite chair or, better yet, chill in the bed, and be prepared to be tantalized by yet another great read.

Peace and Many Blessings,

Zane

Publisher
Strebor Books
www.simonandschuster.com

ZANE PRESENTS

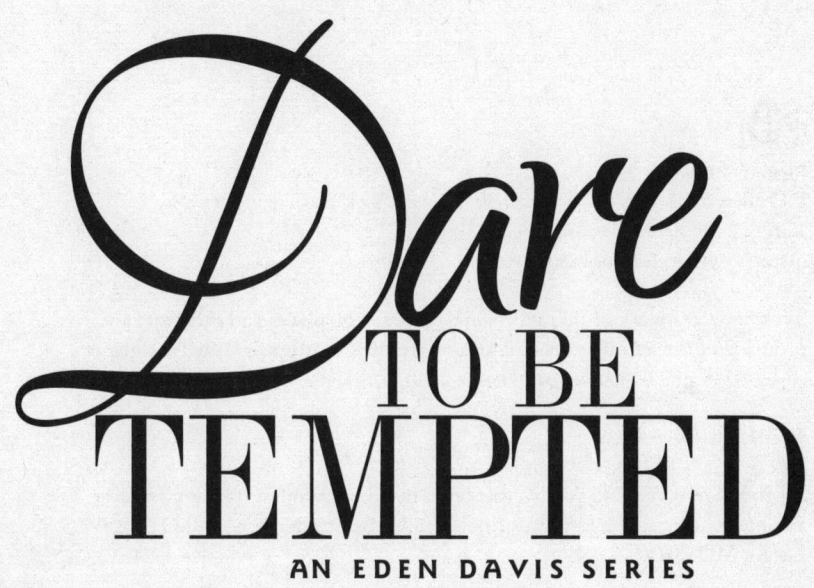

Dare to be Tempted

AN EDEN DAVIS SERIES

EDEN DAVIS

SBI

STREBOR BOOKS
NEW YORK LONDON TORONTO SYDNEY

Strebor Books
P.O. Box 6505
Largo, MD 20792
http://www.streborbooks.com

This book is a work of fiction. Names, characters, places and incidents are products of the author's imagination or are used fictitiously. Any resemblance to actual events or locales or persons, living or dead, is entirely coincidental.

© 2013 by Eden Davis

All rights reserved. No part of this book may be reproduced in any form or by any means whatsoever. For information address Strebor Books, P.O. Box 6505, Largo, MD 20792.

ISBN 978-1-4516-0914-1
ISBN 978-1-4516-0915-8 (ebook)
LCCN 2013933636

First Strebor Books trade paperback edition June 2013

Cover design: www.mariondesigns.com
Cover photograph: © Keith Saunders/Marion Designs

10 9 8 7 6 5 4 3 2 1

Manufactured in the United States of America

For information regarding special discounts for bulk purchases, please contact Simon & Schuster Special Sales at 1-866-506-1949 or business@simonandschuster.com

The Simon & Schuster Speakers Bureau can bring authors to your live event. For more information or to book an event, contact the Simon & Schuster Speakers Bureau at 1-866-248-3049 or visit our website at www.simonspeakers.com.

Dare to be Tempted is dedicated to all our courageous military families, active duty and reservists, serving in our Armed Forces. I applaud all of you who make the sacrifice to serve, in the war zone and at home. Thank you.

Acknowledgments

Welcome to the *Eden Davis Series*, hot and beautifully erotic stories written for grown and sexy women. I've wanted to write this series for a long time, because as a reader, I've had a hard time finding erotica that speaks to me and my circumstances. I'm a grown woman with a long relationship with sex, an active imagination, and a romantic, sexy side. I want to read about savvy, experienced women who (like me) are transitioning into different life stages but still quest to feel alive and sexual. I'm betting that many of you do, too. That's why The *Eden Davis Series* is about embracing a *grown* woman's naughty as well as her nice.

In this first book, you'll get to know Aleesa Davis, the wife of an Army reservist, who is dealing with her husband's return from war. Aleesa's story chronicles a rough and complicated patch in her long and loving marriage, and her grappling with her husband's intriguing concept of sexual healing. What would you do if your husband gave you a forty-eight hour pass to make one of your fantasies come true?

Even though this book tackles some provocative and difficult topics, like impotency and infidelity, I had SO much fun writing Aleesa's story. I think it was because I spent a lot of my writing time stepping out of real life and writing her hot, sexy fantasies. In my head, I pictured Idris Elba as the loving and supportive Colonel Walter Davis, and Lamman Rucker as hottie photographer Josiah Newman; both doing delightfully naughty things with Aleesa. As you can imagine, this delicious imagery kept me in top tickle mode throughout the project! I'm sure they will inspire you the same way. I'd love to hear who played the leading man roles in your head. Visit me on Twitter @EdensStories #dare2btempted and let me know.

I wrote Aleesa and Walter as a military couple because I think it's important to shed some light on the impact going to war has on our military families. Like Secretary of State John Kerry said, "It [supporting our troops] means understanding their lives both as warriors fighting for our nation, and as husbands and wives, parents, brothers and sisters, sons and daughters struggling to take care of their families." Please support our troops and their loved ones left behind in any way you can, even if it's as simple as adding them to your daily prayers.

I'd like to acknowledge my military adviser, who wishes to remain anonymous. Thank you for helping me to get things right, and giving us a glimpse of life on the battlefield. Thanks to Sara, the best agent ever; Zane, Charmaine, and everyone at Strebor Books, and my "focus group" of friends for sharing your private fantasies. And thank you, readers. Please let your friends know about *The Eden Davis Series*, and keep in touch on Facebook at Eden's Stories, and Twitter (@EdensStories).

Eden

P.S. You're going to meet Aleesa's best friend, Lena Macy, within these pages. At work, Lena is bold, ambitious and always in control, but her private life is the victim of her professional ambitions. In *Dare to be Seduced*, the workaholic goes wantonly delinquent when she loses a bet to a hot stranger who turns her on, and out, in all the right ways.

Chapter One

Aleesa took her time climbing the eight steps that led to the front door of Josiah Newman's studio. Her breaths came in short puffs, not from overexertion, as her regular workouts at the gym left her lungs plenty strong enough to take on this minor physical effort. No, it was the jangle of nerves eating through her stomach lining that was taking her breath away.

"You *need* to look hot, Lees," she coached herself. "Smokin' hot. Halle hot. Angelina hot. Tina frickin' Turner hot!"

"What am I doing?" she turned to query the cat sprawled on the stoop next door. "On what planet am I, Aleesa Raquel Davis, a fifty-two-year-old married woman, mother of two grown boys, going to get naked in front of a perfect stranger?"

The thought paralyzed her, stopping her legs two steps from the door. Continued forward motion was not an option. At least not without some serious coaxing. She reached into her pocket, pulled out her cell phone and dialed her advice guru.

"I don't think I can do this…what the hell was I thinking…that is, what were you thinking when you suggested this…how did I ever let you talk me into doing something that is so…so…so not me?" she said, as soon as she heard the tepid hello.

"Lees? Slow down," Lena Macy's groggy voice suggested, both out of concern and confusion. It was nearly 11:30 p.m. in London and she'd just drifted off into a heavy, jetlagged slumber. "Where are you? What's going on?"

"In Brooklyn. It's almost six-thirty. Six minutes before I'm supposed to strip down to my birthday suit in front of some guy whom

I've never laid eyes on. Aside from my husband, my gynecologist and that freak at the pool in Puerto Rico when Walt and I thought we were alone and decided to go skinny dipping, no man has seen me naked in ten years."

"Look, you're beautiful. For a woman two years into fifty, your body is rocking. Hell, for a woman of any age it's a killer. Now did you prepare like I told you to?"

"Yes. I'm waxed, exfoliated, and shined up like a new penny."

"Good, but I'm referring to the other…"

"Yes, I've been masturbating damn near nonstop for the past two days. I've rubbed, lubricated, vibrated, and worn my poor clit practically down to a nub. And frankly, I'm not any less nervous. I'm horny as hell and so on edge that I'm hoping with everything I've got that this photographer is Jimmy *'Good Times'* Walker ugly because if he's even the least bit sexy, I'm likely to burst out in spontaneous orgasms!"

"You are certifiable. Look, getting yourself off wasn't about calming your nerves. The idea was to make you feel sexy as hell, which you now do. Remember who you're doing this for. And why," Lena reminded her best friend.

"For Walter and the cover of his welcome home gift."

"Yes, your nasty ass journal that you've been keeping this past year. God knows, you've recorded every impure thought…" Lena paused to yawn, "and fantasy you've had since the good doctor's been in Afghanistan."

"I want him to know how much I love and missed him."

"Oh, he's going to know all right. One quick read and he's going to know that absence has not only made his woman's heart grow fonder, it's turned her into a big ole freak!"

"Seriously, Lees, it's a sweet and loving idea and deserves a great cover. I can't think of a better model, can you?"

"Maybe Sofia Vergara."

"That Colombian chick from *Modern Family*?" Lena asked, not bothering to stifle her yawn.

"Yeah, she's Walter's fantasy lover—the only woman he has my permission to have sex with. My free pass is that fine as hell French actor, Gilles something, the one who was naked in the first *Sex in the City* movie and almost won *Dancing with the Stars*."

"Oh, please, like that would ever happen. Not because some other guy, actor or not, wouldn't think you're smokin' hot, but because you and Walter are so in love and up each other's behinds, that you two don't even look at anyone else, which is pretty remarkable in this day and age."

"Oh trust me, I look, and God knows, think about it, *a lot*. I can't help it, especially since I started writing all these hot and horny fantasies. But it stops there."

"I believe you, but, Aleesa you're stalling, and I'm falling. Look, Josiah is the best in the business. He is fast becoming known in the photography world as the black and male Annie Leibovitz, for his trademark techniques with light and unusual poses.

"So between your boudoir photos and that nasty book of yours, Walter is going to be blown away by his hot-to-trot wife."

"Well, fantasy and reality are two different animals. Just because I write about all that stuff, doesn't mean I'm bold enough to actually do any of it," Aleesa reminded her friend.

"Yeah, well rest assured, you got a bit of the exhibitionist in you and a whole lot of freak! If you didn't, you wouldn't have been so eager to get your sexy on with hubby in the massage room down in Puerto Rico."

"Nobody was in the room watching us."

"That you know of! Now, I gotta get back to sleep and you have a nasty, nudie cutie photo shoot to do."

"Not nasty nude. Sexy…nice sexy," Aleesa corrected while smiling broadly at the San Juan memory.

"Yeah, well take it from me, nice can turn nasty real quick like. Now, push the doorbell, already."

"Okay, okay. Tell me I can do this, Lena."

"You. Can. Do. This. Think sexy. Be sexy. Now, I leave you with my final two words—Veuve Cliquot."

"So when in doubt, turn to alcohol?"

"Liquid courage, baby. Now ring the damn bell. Nightie-night."

"Ringing!" Aleesa said in place of goodbye, grateful that her friend, despite being a rich, powerful businesswoman, and an ocean away, was there to hold her hand. She hung up her phone and immediately pushed the doorbell.

"Think sexy. Be sexy," she muttered under her breath, repeating Lena's words. Waiting for the door to open, Aleesa closed her eyes and tried to settle her nerves by thinking sexy thoughts. Immediately, the last time she'd seen her husband's handsome, chocolate brown face came to mind. She had no problem conjuring up the memories of his surprise visit to San Juan. Their lovemaking at the spa had been mind blowing, largely because it was so unexpected and following such a long drought.

Standing there, her breasts began to tingle, as they'd done when Walt's mouth had begun its happy pilgrimage down her neck, across her shoulders and toward the large chocolate nipples he told her he'd gone to bed dreaming about. He'd given each a warm tongue massage before latching on to the left breast and sucking hard. Aleesa's hips had bucked. Walter's lips had smiled. The nipples were still Clitina's wake-up call.

"Hmm, I got it good," she informed the cat as she opened her eyes. "My man is a great step-father, an amazing friend and one kitty to another, a fanfuckingtastic husband and lover!"

The cat replied with a bored yawn and lazy stretch. "Yeah, well, you wouldn't say that if he'd licked you the way he licks me!" Aleesa sighed as her vajayjay gently clutched at the thought. After dreaming and fantasizing for so long, Walter had shown up and given her the real thing, reawakening her vagina and making her cravings stronger and more difficult to ignore. Damn, waiting for his homecoming was going to be the longest thirty-seven days of her life.

She intended to make the time go fast by staying busy. In addition to her demanding job as the Vice President of Marketing for the Sports Fan Network, she had big plans in store for the Colonel's return. If his Caribbean visit had been sexually spectacular, his welcome home was going to be downright epic. And today's errand was the first step toward making it so.

The sound of shuffling of feet approaching the door halted the conversation between her and the pussy next door. And as the door cracked open, she took a deep breath, knowing that there was no turning back.

"You must be Aleesa." His buttery words floated between perfect white teeth framed in dimples deep enough to lose your inhibitions in. "I'm Josiah. Welcome. I'm all ready for you." He opened the door wide to reveal the unlawfully good looking face and body that matched his "smooth as twelve-year-old Scotch" voice.

Aleesa swallowed a big gulp of "oh no" as her eyes went renegade and, against her wishes, thoroughly checked out the fine specimen before her. He looked to be in his early to mid-thirties and stood over six feet. He had the slim, lean musculature of a track star, and the way his jeans and untucked navy blue T-shirt clung to his body with an unspoken dare to reach out and touch, was borderline criminal. His long, thin locks were flowing free across his shoulder, giving a nonchalant sexiness to the man that left Aleesa's nerve endings perked up and on edge.

OH FUCK! OH FUCK! OH FUCK! WHY DO YOU HAVE TO BE SO FINE?!! Aleesa screamed at him in her head, all the while wishing she'd changed her clothes. Why hadn't she worn the form-fitting blue dress instead of the boho chic get-up she'd thrown on at the last minute? *Because if you'd worn the other, he'd know that you don't have any bra or panties on.*

But he knows that anyway, it occurred to her. He was the one who'd told her not to wear any so she wouldn't have elastic lines on her skin.

"You okay? Here, let me take that for you," he said, reaching for the tote bag containing her cosmetic and hair products.

"I'm fine. Thank you," Aleesa replied, embarrassed to be caught arguing with herself. She felt the butterflies in her stomach stir. Josiah was not only good looking, but apparently a gentleman as well.

"That shade of blue looks great on you," he complimented her as she stepped inside, noticing immediately how the turquoise color complemented her chestnut brown skin. Her ensemble was attractive and while fashion forward, completely covered up the body underneath. Josiah smiled to himself. His clients always seemed to fall into two camps—the wannabe *Playboy* pin-ups that arrived practically naked on his doorstep, and couldn't wait to get started; and the quiet, reserved types who required his special brand of coaching to coax the femme fatale out of them. Aleesa Davis *appeared* to fall in the latter category, but only time would tell which camp she truly belonged in.

She held the chuckle in her mouth, wondering if he could really read the thoughts running through her head. She hoped not because a few of them were totally inappropriate for a married woman, especially one who was truly in love with her husband, to be having about a man *nearly* young enough to be her son.

"Thank you." Nerves caused her voice to spike, giving her words a Minnie Mouse quality. She was even more aflutter now. Getting nude in front of a stranger was one thing, but getting nude in front of a *fine-ass* stranger whom she obviously found attractive, when she was already horny as hell, was a completely different level of intimidation.

Josiah led her down the short hallway and into a studio space that looked like it was once a living room or parlor. She followed his well-formed butt wondering if, no frantically *wishing*, that he was gay, but knowing instinctively that he was not.

"So based on the questionnaire you filled out online, I've set up three scenarios for you today," he informed her. "And as you can see, per your request, no 'cheesy red velour or whorehouse set-ups.'"

Aleesa looked around the room, checking out the white, claw-footed bathtub filled nearly to the rim with popcorn standing against a white background in one corner, and in the other, a beautiful mahogany chair with heart-shaped back, placed on a white fur carpet in front of sheer drapes. The chair's back reminded her of a woman's torso—a full bosom, tapering down to a tiny waist. Until this moment, it never occurred to her that furniture could be so sexy.

"There are only two," she said, choosing to share her observation rather than her thoughts.

"There is a small bedroom down the hall that I use for shoots as well."

"A tub of popcorn?"

"You said it was your husband's favorite snack food, so I thought we'd do something fun. Trust me; it's all going to be great. Now before we get you undressed and in front of the camera, let's talk for a minute." Josiah extended his arm, inviting her to sit on a chaise on the opposite side of the room. "Tell me a little about yourself, Ms. Davis."

"Aleesa. Well, I'm married. The mother of two grown sons—Aden and Ashri, 25 and 23. I live in Montclair, New Jersey, and work in Manhattan as the Sports Fan Network…"

"Very impressive, but tell me about you—the woman. What

gets the charming and lovely Aleesa Davis's heart racing? What kind of music do you listen to? What do you like to eat? Where's the sexiest place in the whole wide world?" Josiah asked, leaning in close like he couldn't wait to hear her voice.

Damn this boy was good! Aleesa knew that he was just doing his job—trying to get a feel for her so he could bring it out in the photographs, but damn if it didn't feel like she was on a date. The alarming thing was she didn't mind as much as she probably should.

"Well, let's see. I love the full moon, the sound of the ocean. Champagne. My favorite food isn't actually a food. It's a dessert. I absolutely love ice cream. Plain old vanilla bean ice cream. Simple, satisfying and yummy."

"Oh, I get that joke. I'm a coffee ice cream man," he added. "But I agree. I don't need any extra cookies or candy mixed in and getting in the way."

"Exactly," she concurred, feeling herself relax a bit. Josiah was a charming conversationalist.

"And let's see, musically I have pretty eclectic tastes. I'm still a lover of old school funk and R & B—Earth, Wind and Fire, The Commodores, Prince…"

"Teddy Pendergrass?"

"Absolutely. Now that boy could sing. I love me some Teddy P."

"Before or after Harold Melvin and the Blue Notes?"

Aleesa looked at Josiah with surprised eyes. Baby that he was, what could he possibly know about these old school musicians? "I'm definitely in the solo, 'Close the Door' and 'Turn Off The Lights' Teddy fan club. But like I said, I also enjoy tango music, Latin salsa, Sade. I even like some of these new kids like Usher and Ne-Yo, and especially Maxwell. He has that same kind of smooth, sexy edge that Teddy had. Somehow, they both always manage to make me feel like they're only singing to me."

"Only a true master can make a woman feel like she's the only one in the room. And hey, if you like Maxwell and Usher you should check out this British artist named Omar. I think you'd really get into him, too."

"I will," Aleesa replied. She quickly swallowed the millions of questions she was dying to ask. Ones that would clue her into his likes and dislikes, and give her more insight into him as a man. She hadn't realized until now how much she'd missed having a quiet, personal conversation with an interesting companion. But any further queries about Josiah would be unnecessary and borderline inappropriate. Besides, he wasn't interested in her. He was simply doing his job.

"And the sexiest place in the world?"

Aleesa thought for a moment, conjuring up past places she'd visited around the world. The thought that kept coming to the forefront of her memories were the rather unremarkable places she'd been when she either was inspired or was composing Walter's stories. "Hmm... that would have to be wherever I am."

Josiah's eyes registered amused surprise. "I have asked that question over a thousand times, and you're the first to say that," Josiah informed her. Her reply impressed and intrigued him. "So what brings you into my world, Aleesa?"

"Well, I wanted to do this as a, uh...you know...gift for my husband."

"Lucky man," he replied with a tone and admiring look that made her think he was speaking the truth. "Anniversary? Birthday?"

"A welcome home, actually. He's been in Afghanistan, running a dental clinic for the soldiers for the past couple of years and he'll be stateside again at the end of May, in about a month."

"Nice. So you're thinking a standard, bedroom portrait?"

"Well, no. More like a book cover."

Josiah's eyebrows lifted, the corners of his mouth registering surprise before quickly falling back into place.

"I've been keeping a book...well...more like a journal...of well, you know...thoughts..." Embarrassment blushed her cheeks and kept her from continuing.

"What kind of thoughts? Fantasies?" he queried, his interest piqued. *Still waters run deep.*

"Uh...well...yes. You know...that I've had since he's been gone. It was a way of keeping him close to me and I thought it would be a nice welcome-home surprise."

"Like I said, he's a lucky man."

"Thank you, but I'm the lucky one," she told him, truly believing her words despite being fascinated by Josiah's full and luscious upper lip. "Anyway, my friend suggested that I do a cover shot, and recommended you. So that's why I'm here...in your world."

"Welcome. I'm happy to have you," he replied, flashing his dimples at her. "So, Aleesa, tell me how far you're willing go."

"How far?"

"Robe? Lingerie? Full-on nude? Each is sexy and provocative in its own way. What's most important is your comfort level. Though, if you don't mind me asking, how risqué are your...uh...thoughts in this book?"

Aleesa could feel the flush of embarrassment mixed with arousal invade her body as she thought about the sexy and sometimes outrageous scenarios she'd written over these past months. All of her fantasies had Walter either actively participating or watching. Like the butler going down on her in the hotel in Phoenix; tying Walt up while she fucked herself on the hood of his car; masturbating in the window of the hotel directly across from Walt's Manhattan dental office; being titty and finger fucked by the guest of honor on her apartment balcony during a birthday party; having her feet licked by her favorite salesman at the Jimmy Choo store.

Aleesa felt the tingle of her clitoris back on high alert. Even recalling the fantasies turned her on. Risqué? Maybe not for the kink and fetish crowd, but for her married and maternal self, Walt's freak book was as blue as the sea, and hellishly racy.

"Your face says it all," Josiah interrupted, with a flirtatious twist to his lips. "Oh, the camera is going to love you! So, since it's for his eyes only, do we match the cover shot to the contents or give him a sexy, beauty shot to admire? Completely your call."

Aleesa said nothing. She simply bit her bottom lip as she pondered the options. Writing about sex was so freeing, even though most of the stuff she'd scribed she'd never dare try. Still the experience of opening up her sexual imagination this year had definitely made her more curious and adventurous. She now felt that both risqué *and* sexy beauty were part of her sexual personality.

"Aleesa. Don't be frightened or nervous or feel like you're being judged," Josiah said as he brought his head close to tell her. She knew he intended his voice to sound soothing, but the smooth timbre and tone of it only managed to further ruffle her feathers.

"This boudoir session is totally based on your desires. Every woman has her own idea of what sexy is, as well as what she is comfortable with. Don't worry; today will be part cute, part fun, part flirty and all sexy.

"You're safe here. I am going to take good care of you. I promise. So like you did when you wrote your book, you can drop your inhibitions and be free here as well."

Aleesa continued to chew on her bottom lip as she looked into Josiah's brown, almond-shaped eyes. As gorgeous and sexy as he was, and as horny but married as she felt, dropping her inhibitions and being free was definitely not an option.

"Let's play it by ear, and see where the evening takes us."

Chapter Two

The kitschy but cute three-panel modesty screen was the first thing that caught her eye when she walked into the large closet turned dressing room. It was a totally fitting furniture choice that looked like it belonged in some lusty Victorian lady's boudoir, as did the vanity over against the far wall. Next to the screen was a rack of satin robes of varying lengths and hues, and a shelf of shoes—sandals, mules, pumps, even a pair of thigh-high boots—all stilettos, all sexy, and all her size. There was nary a marabou trimmed slipper or clear stripper shoe to be found, she noted, happy to see that Josiah had heeded her requests for nothing cliché and bawdy.

Aleesa stepped behind the screen and changed out of her clothes. She put on the amethyst-colored kimono robe from the rack, and walked over to the makeup table to lotion up and freshen her face. She applied nearly half a bottle of nothing fancy, get the job done, heavy cream all over her body. There was absolutely nothing seductive about being ashy. While she lotioned, she tried to stretch in feline ways and think sexy thoughts, all in preparation for her on-camera performance. Thankfully, yoga had kept her lean and limber and this was one area where she had no performance anxiety.

A subtle tap on the door announced the arrival of Milo, the make-up artist Josiah had hired for the shoot. He quickly unpacked a supply of shadows, blushers, lipsticks, foundations, all contained in a multitudes of little pots, tubes and pans. Aleesa, who had exactly five items in her cosmetic case, blinked with new understanding. Well, no wonder all the celebrity girls look so damn good in all their photos! Between a dump truck worth of professionally applied cosmetics *and* airbrushing, how could they not appear better than perfect?

Twenty minutes later, wearing heavy false eyelashes and feeling a bit like a drag queen, Aleesa watched as Milo completed the transformation. Per Josiah's request, he brushed back and secured her hair with an elastic band. And because there was nothing particularly alluring about a three-inch stub, he clipped on a ten-inch ponytail for a little added sex appeal.

"There you go," he said, stepping back to admire his handiwork. "I'll go and let you get dressed. They should be finished setting up soon."

Aleesa took a minute to study her model self as soon as she was alone. She was glad Milo had pulled her hair back. She had enough to worry about, and taking hair out of the equation was pure genius. Aleesa smiled at herself in the mirror as she swung her faux locks back and forth and tried to bring to her now smoky eyes a smoldering stare. Grins turned into giggles as she gazed upon a face that looked more constipated than coquettish. She tried again, this time repeating in her head the cliché command she'd heard a million times from models and other on-camera celebrities: "make love to the camera." Aleesa rolled her eyes. This wasn't working either. Sadly, she looked more like a stroke victim than a supermodel.

Frustrated, she attempted to waylay her growing anxiety with action. Aleesa hopped up and scurried behind the screen to change into one of the three sets of lingerie she'd bought for today's shoot. In case she chickened out on the nude thing, she wanted options that made her feel and look sexy. Unconsciously, she'd gone with a rather patriotic color scheme: red lace, white satin, and black with blue sequins—each progressively more daring than the next. For her first set of shots, she decided to go with the more modest black bra with a delicate navy blue-sequined pattern on the cups and matching bikini panties. Both the top and bottom, while sexy, provided adequate coverage and made Aleesa feel more like she was wearing a bathing suit than her underwear. It was a cheap psychological trick she was trying to play on herself, hoping it would work.

She pulled on the bottoms, and still topless, she turned to the mirror to inspect herself. Her soft and curvy body, which was neither plump nor overtly toned, still had the power to turn heads, but for many reasons she couldn't see that today. Glaring back at her were all the imperfections plaguing her body and self-confidence. She couldn't see the strength and beauty in the definition of her thighs, instead zeroing in on the slight pockets of cellulite that riddled them. She was blind to the sexy curve of her shoulders and collarbone, noticing only the stretch marks that formed a map of the U.S. Interstate on her slightly protruding tummy; nor did she notice her inviting, cocoa colored nipples on her still full bosom, only that they now hung perilously close to her navel. She should have heeded her cousin Livia's warning, and dumped the yoga for cardio. Maybe then she wouldn't be standing here regretting her decision to bare it all.

"What the fuck were you thinking?" she asked the madam in the mirror. The sexy edge that had ebbed and flowed since her arrival had definitely receded. In its place was the nauseating feeling of sheer panic. When she'd gone on the Internet to view Josiah's portfolio, she'd been struck by the artistic beauty of his work. The women he'd photographed all looked alluring, seductive and young—younger than she by many years. But she was so lost in the beauty of Josiah's work and the desire to do something extra special for her man, she'd conveniently overlooked this very important fact. This boudoir stuff was a young woman's game. Not some old broad whose hotness came in flashes.

In an ironic coincidence Aleesa's thoughts were interrupted by an aggressive tapping. Even though she was standing behind the screen, she instinctively wrapped her arms around her chest to cover her bare breasts.

"Come in," she answered as she scurried to put on her top.

Aleesa heard the door open, followed by an intermingled rush of music and voices. What was up with the party atmosphere in the studio?

"I've brought you some champagne," a familiar, yet strange voice informed her. "Please feel free to enjoy, but drink only enough to take the edge off your nerves; not enough to get tipsy."

"Thank you," she said, wondering if Josiah already had champagne on hand or had run out to get it to please her. *It's not a date, you idiot. Of course he had it! Champagne and models go together!*

Aleesa pulled the robe back on and stepped out from behind the screen into Josiah's face that now had a fuzzy goatee framing those succulent lips. In his hands was a tray holding a split of bubbly bravado with a pink straw bobbing from its mouth.

Aleesa simply stared in confusion as this man, who looked exactly like Josiah but was not, placed the champagne on the vanity.

"I'm Jesse," he explained, noticing her confusion. "Josiah's twin brother and assistant. Nice to meet you, Aleesa. We're about ready. As soon as Cheri is done setting up the props, we'll get started."

Twin? Assistant? Milo? Cheri? Aleesa's panic began to boil over. She hadn't anticipated spectators. But why was she surprised? She'd been to hundreds of photo shoots for work, and there were never less than three people in the room. Why did she think hers would be different?

Because I'm supposed to be naked or at least damn near, she rumi-

had fixed it so she would be mostly covered, and where attitude and sexual suggestiveness would be the star of the show, not her body. By removing the blatant exhibitionism, he was hoping to relieve some of her angst and embarrassment. Later, when she was more comfortable in front of the camera and with him, he would begin to tap into that innate sexiness that he could see existed bubbling below the surface. Aleesa Davis was one hot woman, and he intended to bring every bit of that sex appeal out.

She sunk down into the popcorn, brushing the kernels away from her butt, so she could sit comfortably. The popcorn covered her from the waist down, leaving her upper torso exposed. Josiah's keen photographer's eye was following her every move, and periodically looking through his camera lens and the attached monitor, wanting to find the perfect visual.

"Let's add two bags," he requested. Cheri immediately brought over another huge bag of movie popcorn and poured it into the tub.

"Okay. Here's what we need to do. Aleesa, I need you to pull off your straps. Cheri, can you please tuck them into the bra. Bare looks much sexier. Now, sink down into the tub and rest up against the back and pull your knees to your chest. Great. Here's a piece of licorice—Red Vines," he said, smiling. "It makes it more personal because it's your favorite, but also it gives you something to do with your hands and mouth. So play with it a bit."

Aleesa followed his directions, hoping that she was giving him what he wanted. Josiah clicked off a few test shots and she waited as Josiah, Jesse and Cheri huddled around the monitor studying the results. She tried to relax as they adjusted everything from the lighting to the amount of popcorn between her legs to the placement of the candles glowing behind her.

"Okay, love. We are finally ready. Now I want you to relax and simply be your lovely self."

Almost on cue, Bruno Mars' melodic voice began to wash over the set. Aleesa listened as he serenaded her about being amazing just the way she was. She sat back and tried to soak in the message of his song.

"Okay, baby. Give me that big, welcome home smile...beautiful... now lower your chin..." *Click...click...click.* "Wonderful, now tilt your head to left...back to the right...yep right there..." *Click... click...click.* "When you smile, the whole world stops and stares for a while," Josiah sang in between directives as he steadily clicked away.

"Okay, left leg stretched out on the edge of the tub. Give me sexy," he requested. "Slide the candy through your lips." *Click... click...*pause. Josiah stooped down to ponder the situation. The music was upbeat and cheerful and Aleesa was doing her best to exude a saucy playfulness through her smile and eyes, but it still felt forced and unnatural. He needed her to feel sexy for real... not merely for show.

"Aleesa, the trouble is you're trying too hard. You don't need to try. Believe me when I tell you that you are an extremely sexy woman."

Aleesa smiled as her ego inflated a little bit. It had been months since her husband had told her this, and over a decade since a sexy stranger had uttered those words. Josiah's compliments and charming demeanor were doing their job. She didn't feel quite so chronologically impaired or imperfect.

"Close your eyes," Josiah told her. "Now you're sitting in the tub waiting...waiting for your husband to come home to find hot and sexy you in the tub...waiting and wanting him to join you... go with that and think about your man and how much you want him. Think about how you feel."

Horny, she answered in her head. "May I have some more champagne?" she requested.

Immediately Cheri responded with the split of champagne. Aleesa took two long sips through the straw and passed it back, as she recounted the experience of her and Walt making love in Puerto Rico.

Walt turns me over, and I get up on all fours. I wiggle my ass in his face, which I know will get a reaction out of him. And it does. He smacks my ass, letting me know that he's not playing. He wants it now, without the pomp and circumstance of playful foreplay. With one powerful thrust, his dick consumes all the space in my twat. I can feel his balls slap against my bare ass as he fucks me fast and hard. Each time his dick hits my clit, tiny tremors ripple through my crotch. I have to bite down on my lip to keep the moans and nasty string of words from escaping my mouth.

"Yes, baby. Now that's what I'm talking about…" *Click…click.* "Give it to me, baby," Josiah encouraged. "Now pick up a kernel of popcorn and lay it on the tip of your tongue. Ohh."

Aleesa did as requested but forced herself to remain in the fantasy. "Oh yes…hot!" *Click…click…click.*

His stroke goes from hard to frenzied. I can feel the sweat drip on to my ass and in my crack, tickling the sensitive nerve endings between my cheeks. "You love this big dick, don't you," Josiah roars. "Open your eyes so we can get a picture of this."

Aleesa's eyes popped open as she realized that at some point in her fantasizing, the photographer had taken her husband's place.

"Yeah, baby, now we can see all that lust in your eyes."

The fantasy burst, floating away into the room, leaving its residual lust to linger. Aleesa felt the dual emotions of arousal and humiliation tingle throughout her body. Damn, what had happened? How had she allowed Josiah to creep into her daydream? Could he or the rest of the crew tell?

"Perfect," Josiah's voice interrupted. "Whatever you were thinking about was working," he informed her. "We got some great stuff."

"Terrific," she managed to squeak out.

"Take a break and change, while we set up for the next photo."

"Really nice job, Aleesa," Jesse chimed in, giving her a decadent smile.

Aleesa nearly ran out of the studio, desperately seeking the privacy of the dressing room. She was completely mortified, and the last thing she wanted to do was embarrass herself any further. She thought about calling Lena again, but it was too late in London. There was no point in calling Livia; she was busy working on some society wedding cake, plus Milo would be knocking on the door any minute to retouch her makeup.

So what if Josiah turned up in your on-the-spot fantasy, her brave inner voice spoke to her. *It's no different than all of the other strangers in your stories who pop up to fuck you while your husband and whoever else watches. It's not real. It's make believe. So change your clothes and get on with it!*

"Mere fantasy," Aleesa repeated her thoughts, ignoring the fact that unlike the other imagined strangers, she could reach out and touch Josiah. Trying to get her head in a good space for the next set of pictures, she went behind the screen and changed into the lacy red panties and bra. She wished she'd brought a few more options, as this was definitely much more risqué than the black and blue sequined set.

"Everybody decent?" Milo's voice asked through the door.

"Come on in," Aleesa replied as she tied the robe around her near naked body, and stepped from behind the screen.

"Darling, let's touch up that beautiful face and put a few clips in that head of yours. I feel a long, luxurious mane coming on."

Aleesa sat still as Milo worked on her. She tried not to think about anything, especially Josiah Newman. She was grateful for the distraction as she listened and sipped her champagne while the makeup artist filled her head with chatter. Before she knew it, he was attaching to her feet a pair of five-inch, strappy, barely there, irresistibly sexy shoes.

"The shoes alone will have his heart racing," Milo said, giving her a wink.

"Aleesa, are you ready?" Jesse showed up at the door and inquired. He took her hand and escorted her to the studio. He led her over to the chair and white rug, and waited while she disrobed. Aleesa tried to sneak out a nervous exhale as she quickly stripped down to her lacy skivvies.

Josiah also put the squash on a sigh as he inspected his model. The red against her chocolate brown skin was dynamic and compelling. The bra was solid around the edges with flowers embroidered into the cups' sheer fabric. Empty, its color and style gave it a racy and highly provocative look. Overflowing with Aleesa's copious breasts, the look became not only provocative, but delectably dangerous.

"Lucky man," he whispered under his breath.

Aleesa could feel the appreciation in Josiah's eyes as they looked her over. She didn't feel the least bit scrutinized or judged, just admired and deep down, underneath it all, surprisingly, the guilty pleasure excited her.

Josiah led her over to the chair and took several frames of her sitting in it backwards with her chest up against the chair and her legs spread wide. "Hmmm," he murmured, clearly not satisfied.

"Do you need me to do something different?" Aleesa asked, feeling like she wasn't rising to the occasion and delivering what was needed of her.

"It's not you. This looks so...obvious. Here, come lay here," Josiah directed her to lie, face up, on the rug with her legs crossed and feet propped up on the seat. He gently fanned her faux hair out on the rug. "You look beautiful," he said, admiring the color collision of her brown skin and red lingerie against the white fur.

He snapped a few test shots before deciding the best and sexiest angle. "Separate your legs and open them...not so much...just a hint," he requested. "Yes, a hint...perfect." *Click...click.* "Now turn your head to the left." *Click...click...click.* "Yes. Baby, these are hot!"

Josiah's requests were voiced as lyrically and soulfully as a Teddy Pendergrass ballad, and had the same I-want-to-get-laid-now impact. Against her will, Aleesa could feel dampness gathering in the gap between her legs.

"I have an idea," he stooped down to tell her. "Cheri, pearls, please. The long ones."

Pearls! Aleesa smiled. She'd totally planned to incorporate pearls into their lovemaking. Having her picture taken with them on would be a forever reminder. Brilliant!

Within thirty seconds, Cheri had dropped the pearls in his hand, and Josiah had placed them around her neck. "Okay, prop yourself up on your elbows and continue to look off to the right. I'm not shooting your face in this series," he informed her, "so you can relax your face but keep energy flowing in the rest of your body."

The photographer finished his directives and knelt, his crotch nearly straddling Aleesa's head. The near proximity of his dick released a cocktail of pheromones, causing her to feel slightly flushed. Ever the professional, Josiah, his camera positioned above her body, got straight to work and shot the length of her body from above her.

His artist's eye was drawn to the juxtaposition of shape, light and texture sitting before him, while his man's eye was glued to the mouthwatering mounds of her bosom. He took a silent and invisible "holy shit" gulp as both his left and right mind melded to produce one pressing thought—how tasty are her nipples? The mere thought made his dick jump.

"Baby, you look some kind of delicious," he told her, falling back on his gift of combining personal compliments with professional coaching. "Do you mind?" he asked. Without waiting for her reply, Josiah reached out and repositioned the pearls so they fell both between her breasts and down her one side, with one pearl resting in her belly button. His action appeared innocent while at the same time very seductive. Aleesa felt her stomach tense when his fingers accidentally grazed her naked belly, causing a mini-explosion of fireworks to erupt under the skin.

"Okay, love, now gently push your pelvis up toward the ceiling...yes...that's the energy we need."

His request tipped the dominoes. Aleesa could feel her ass cheeks clench slightly as she raised her pussy skyward. This tightening informed her clit to swell, nipples to stiffen, and pussy pores to sweat. Thank God he wasn't shooting her face as she was sure it displayed the worry she felt, wondering if he could smell the scent of her arousal.

Josiah shot several dozen frames, varying her poses slightly to get the best combination of light and line. Her face was featured only in profile in this series, but the results played back on the monitor were knock-out gorgeous. "Okay, this set-up is a wrap," he announced. "Aleesa, will you join me in bed?" he quipped, with a smile.

She knew he was referring to the next set-up, but his double entendre still sent a chill down her back. She was tempted to reply with something as equally flirtatious, but the only words her brain allowed to leave her mouth were "shall I change again?"

"Not necessary, and I want to keep your hair the same. I think it will look great against the white sheets."

Milo came in to do a quick touchup, and within five minutes, she and Josiah were alone on the bed, and he was talking softly in her ear. His request made her eyes go wide with fear. She knew at some point it could happen, but knowing and doing were two different animals.

"I—I'm not sure I can…uh…I'm ready to do that," she stammered.

"Aleesa, this is purely your choice, but I promise it will be beautiful, and tasteful and a photograph that you and your husband will be proud of."

Josiah's gentle reminder that her entire reason for being there was Walt's admiration and pleasure changed her mind. And she'd come to trust the photographer and his erotic, but tasteful, styling. Aleesa decided to literally *take off* her big girl panties and go for it. Still, the decision made, her exhibitionist streak only ran so deep. How was she going to face an audience in the buff?

"Okay, but could you take the pictures without everyone else in the room?" she asked, hoping her request didn't sound like a proposition.

"Of course, if that would make you more comfortable. We'll get set up and then I'll clear the room."

Within twenty minutes, the usual buzz of activity generated by Josiah's assistants had ceased, replaced by the tantalizing sounds of the saxophone. Josiah turned his back as Aleesa slipped out of her lingerie and back into bed. She felt strange, being in a stranger's bed after nearly fifteen years of marriage. Strange, but oddly comfortable.

"Baby, can you turn on your side with the pillows under your arm? Yes, like that," Josiah said, directing her while looking through his camera's view finder.

While the photographer puttered around with his lighting and composition, Aleesa surveyed the scene from an out-of-body perspective. Naked with her private parts strategically covered but seductively displayed, she witnessed, both visually and tactilely, her glistening brown skin against the smooth, stark white, Egyptian cotton sheets. When Josiah stepped over to adjust the drape of the top sheet to better display the fullness of her breasts, Aleesa could smell the engaging scent of his musky cologne and it caused a tingling between her legs, and her breath to momentarily catch in her throat. She swallowed hard, trying to suppress her attraction. This entire scene felt like one of her freak book fantasies come to life, and the thought made her body go tight with sexual tension.

Josiah was too much of a gentleman to give any outward expression of the temptation he'd unveiled, but his inspired cock reacted with a hiccup. Without a word, he began shooting, stopping after a dozen or so frames to guide her. "I want you to relax," he told her. "Let your imagination go, baby. Go *there*." Click... click...click. "Free your mind; the rest will follow," he said, quoting the popular En Vogue song.

Laundry detergent, paper towels, toilet paper, Soft Soap and Windex, she thought, frantically going over her grocery list to distract her body and keep her mind from going places it had no business being.

"Give me sexy, baby."

His comment made her laugh.

"What?" he asked, dropping his camera to his lap.

"Nothing." There was no way that Aleesa could tell Josiah that they were obviously operating at cross purposes. While he was working hard to bring out her saucy, sexy side, she was working overtime to shut it down.

Then she felt them coming on...the nervous giggles. Her body's protective response to uncomfortable sexual attraction. They started slowly and then erupted into total, open mouth hysteria, complete with streaming tears and embarrassing snorts. The click... click...click of Josiah's camera only intensified the laugh attack.

"I guess it's time for a break," he announced, slightly amused and totally baffled. But rather than upset him, her nerves further enticed him. Posing nude in front of a stranger with a camera in a sexuality suggestive manner was no easy task. It was refreshing to see a certain girlish shyness attached to her desire to be sexually adventurous. It added a certain innocence to her frames that was seductive as hell.

"What has you so tickled?"

"I'm so sorry," Aleesa told him, feeling even more awkward and silly, as she wrapped the bed sheet around her like a coat of armor. Here she appeared to be a self-possessed, grown woman, but was acting like some giggling pubescent.

"Don't be sorry; be honest and let me know what's going on in that head of yours. You were sort of getting into the groove and then fell apart. What's up? How can I help you feel more comfortable?"

Gain a hundred pounds and lose all your teeth.

"It's embarrassing," she admitted, unable to look him in the eye.

"What? The shoot? The nudity?"

"All of it. The truth is..." Aleesa paused, wondering which words would fall out of her mouth, the honest truth or the convenient one. "The truth is I can't help wondering if I'm too old for this. Taking sexy body shots is a young woman's game. Here I am half a century old," *with stretch marks and breasts that have seen better days,* she wanted to add, but didn't, "trying to be sexy for the camera."

And convenient trumps honest.

"Aleesa, do you know why I am so good at my job?"

Because you make women cream their pants? "Your incredible use of lighting?" she ventured to guess aloud.

"That too!" He laughed. "But people say I have a way with women. And I don't mean that in any egotistical, player way. I love women. Of any age, any color, any body type. There is beauty to find and bring out in them all. I love the way women look and smell and think. I get women. I understand them. This is why I'm able to capture the very best of them on film."

"I can see that."

"I shoot dozens of women in a month's time. And after all of these years, I definitely can read a woman's comfort level and the source of her angst, and, baby, what's bothering you has nothing to do with age."

Busted! "Okay. Well, age is part of it...but you are a very good looking man and it's very unsettling." Aleesa blurted out the honest truth, sure that it wasn't the first time he'd heard that revelation.

"Thank you. I'm flattered. But stop running from it. Let's use it."

"I can't."

"Why not?"

"Because these are pictures for my husband and it feels wrong to be lying around naked in bed, attracted to a guy who isn't him. It feels like cheating."

"It's energy, baby. That's all. Sexual energy."

"Maybe, but it feels like deceitful energy. If you've been through what I have, you'd understand why fidelity is so important to me," Aleesa remarked, referring to the pain and public embarrassment her lying, whore-mongering ex-husband had put her through. It had taken her years, and the love of a good man, to learn to trust and be happy with herself again. And while she could forgive and forget many things, infidelity was an absolute deal breaker. So now, finding herself fantasizing about a real man standing right in front of her was disconcerting to say the least.

"That's the beauty of attraction," Josiah gently informed her. "It's not action unless you want it to be. You don't have to do anything with it but feel it. Feel it and use it now to make your photos smokin' hot. Feel it and use it later to turn up the heat with your husband."

Attraction is not action. Josiah's words settled into her psyche and resonated. And the more she thought about it, the more she realized that he was asking no more of her than she'd often asked of herself this past year. In order to write the contents of Walter's freak book, she'd had to free her mind and allow it to become the sexual playground where her imagination could fly and all of her temptations could be played out with no guilt or regret. While writing those stories, she'd constantly found herself turned on, usually by some stranger she'd seen, and she had used that arousal to feed her fantasies. In so many ways, his rationale made perfect sense.

"So let's squelch the giggles and use this very *mutual* attraction," he said, looking Aleesa straight in the eyes to prove the truth of his admission, "between us to capture the image of the sultry, sexy woman who will turn your lucky husband on for years to come."

Aleesa smiled in grateful consent. She appreciated Josiah's respectful acknowledgment of her husband. Hopefully, keeping Walt solidly in the forefront of this exercise would help chase away her lingering sense of disloyalty. LTC Walter Davis, a full-time oral surgeon and part-time soldier, was such a kind and loving man. But ever since his Army Reserve unit had been called up and sent to Afghanistan eighteen months ago, his professional roles had been reversed. When he and the other dentists and hygienists under his command had been sent to war, Aleesa had initially panicked, afraid that she'd lose the man who had rescued her from a life of loneliness and mistrust to the barbarism of war. But as the months rolled on and Walter had remained safe, her fear had given way to appreciation and pride for his willingness and courage to risk his own life to help others. A good man like Walt deserved a faithful and loyal wife.

"Let's do this," she said, with a wink in her voice.

Josiah replied with a devastating flash of dimples before throwing back the sheet, exposing her delectable bosom in the most inviting manner. As Maxwell sang "Bad Habits" in the background, Josiah stepped back and picked up his camera.

"Look at me, right here," he said, pointing to the corner of his left eye. Their eyes connected and a lustful current sealed their connection.

"That's it. It's in your eyes now, baby. Give it to me, Aleesa," Josiah requested. He'd made the same request at least a dozen times earlier, but since their conversation, it had taken on a new intensity. The difference in her attitude was palatable, causing a hush to fall around the room as her now smoldering poses caught fire. Giving in to her attraction and feeding off his turned up the heat in the studio one thousand fold.

Do you know what you need? A fluffer, like in the porn movies where it's someone's job to get the star all juicy and ready for the freak scene.

So, if we brought said fluffer on set, it would be his job to touch me like this?

Yeah. He'd rub your clit like that 'til it got all hard and was peeking between those pretty lower lips of yours. His job would be to kiss, finger fuck and lick your pussy into a frenzied state so that the stud...

As in the sexy, built guy with the big, rock hard dick?

Yep. Usually fluffers are for men, but today he'll get the starlet all worked up so the stud has a nice hot, juicy hole to slide into and fuck long and hard, 'til she comes.

Whose job, the fluffer or the stud, would it be to lift my titties up like this and play with my nipples until they rose up begging to be in his warm mouth?

Both the fluffer and the stud would want that job, because your tits are so fucking tasty looking.

Does the fluffer get to fuck me or does he just get to do the foreplay and pussy licking?

No, he's just the clit tease. The stud can eat your twat and rim your asshole as well but only the stud gets to pleasure you by actually fucking you.

So both the fluffer and the stud get to pleasure me. Whom do I pleasure?

The stud, but only if you want to. If you want to lay back and get serviced, that's fine, too. It's their job to make sure you get off with the utmost pleasure.

So are you volunteering for the job?

Which? Fluffer or stud?

I see the way you're looking at me. You'd love for me to give you all this good pussy, wouldn't you, picture boy? You want to be the stud, don't you?

Absolutely. I want to get all up in that hot, wet pink of yours and tear it up.

So who can be my fluffer?

My crew is full-service. Cheri? Milo? Jesse?

How about we bring your lookalike brother in here and he fluffs my pussy while you take pictures? That would really turn me on.

And then?

And then I'd like both fluffer and stud to service me. Double the pleasure. Double the fun.

"That's a wrap," Josiah announced twenty minutes and several dozen frames later.

It took a tension-laden moment for Aleesa to get out of her sex den in her head and move back into the present. She felt highly sexed, frustrated and annoyingly unfulfilled. Josiah had stopped the shoot, and her sexual musing before she had a chance to get to the good part.

Josiah sat down on the bed next to her and respectfully pulled the sheet over her naked body. He pushed her hair behind her ear, an acknowledgment of the high level of sexual tension left simmering between them. "You were magnificent."

"Thank you."

"I'm leaving tomorrow to do a job out of the country. I'll be gone for a couple of weeks but I will be in touch by month's end with a selection of photos so you can make some choices," Josiah told her. "This book is going to be hell of hot."

"Thank you," she repeated, still feeling discombobulated by their connection.

"Aleesa, I meant what I said. He's a lucky man." Josiah caressed her cheek and lightly kissed her lips before leaving the room.

Chapter Three

Livia Charles sat in the diner booth, reading her emails while she waited for Aleesa. She was five minutes early for their weekly brunch but knew she wouldn't have to wait long, as her cousin, unlike herself, was as punctual as Big Ben.

The two had been having brunch together every Sunday since Walter's deployment had coincided with Livia's divorce nearly four years ago. It had become a ritual that had gained in importance following the death of Aleesa's father (and Livia's uncle) last year. Officially, both were now orphaned, and living alone and these weekly meals provided the cousins a much needed family tie.

Livia raised her arm above the crowd and waved until Aleesa spotted her blonde, highlighted curls. Because their sibling parents had been close, Livia and Aleesa had practically been raised as sisters. And though nearly three years apart, most people mistook Livia as the older of the two, mainly because of Aleesa's pipsqueak stature. One of the many differences that kept their status as best friends and bickering sister-cousins alive and kicking.

Where Livia, with her perpetually tan complexion and honey colored hair, stood a regal and commanding five-feet-ten inches, Aleesa barely reached five-feet-four inches on her tiptoes. Depending on whose point of view, it was both a point of contention and teasing.

Looks-wise, with the help of good genetics and the fondness of the gods, time had been more than kind to the both of them. Each woman belied their combined age of one hundred and three, both in face and figure.

Looks and size weren't the only things that separately defined them. Both women were young in looks and spirit, but Aleesa had always been the more curious and less conservative of the cousins. Personality and disposition also were markedly different in both women, resulting in entirely disparate lifestyles. While Aleesa, the mother of two, had been in a stable and loving marriage for the past fifteen years, an intentionally childless Livia was once again single and content to hide out in her bakery, leaving the high drama of the dating scene to their mutual friend, Lena.

"I already ordered for you," Livia announced in lieu of a hello. The two ate the same thing every Sunday as they'd done when their families had gathered after church as kids—waffles and scrambled eggs.

"Omigod. Did hell freeze over?" Aleesa asked, referring to her cousin's early arrival.

"Girl, I couldn't wait to get here so I could find out how your naked picture taking went. Your parents, may they rest in peace, would be so proud," Livia teased.

"Yeah, and Uncle Jimmy and Aunt Rachel would also be thrilled that their quiet, cake-baking daughter has resorted to picking up little boys on the Internet. Looks like without parental supervision we've both turned into middle-aged sluts!" Aleesa observed to their mutual amusement.

"So what is up on the online dating front? I still can't believe that you finally activated your membership," she remarked, referring to the fact that for her forty-seventh birthday, after nearly two years of being divorced and not dating, Aleesa strategically gifted Livia with a membership to eHarmony.

"I was tired of waiting for the men to find me."

"How could they when you're always up to your elbows in flour and frosting? You gotta be in it to win it!"

"Which is why I finally signed on. But, Lees, it's a whole new dating world out there. Like I said, I haven't actually been on a date yet. I don't know what's up with the brothers out there, but the majority of men who contact me are white and under thirty."

"Now what could they want from an old chick like you?" Aleesa joked.

"I couldn't tell you, because most of these boys speak in code; well, they would if they actually talked. They only use the phone to text, and half the time I don't know what the hell they are saying. Do you have any idea what this means?" she said, handing Aleesa her phone.

Hey cuT. ur 6y. We shd hk up. Tlk abt it 2MOR txt ur #

"Damn. Good luck on that one."

"I thought you'd know. Aden and Ashri are both in their twenties."

"And when they email or text me, they use proper English. But that's what you get for trying to do the cougar thing and date babies as young as your godson. Why don't you pick on some men your own age?"

"That's the thing. I only contact the guys who pick me. The computer may be the new dating thing, but I'm still old-fashioned. Men are supposed to ask women out."

"And nobody over thirty is asking?"

"Nobody interesting. For the most part, they've been kind of lame or desperate. I don't know what to do. Maybe try Match.com?"

"Maybe. Or maybe this is a real 'take lemons and make lemonade' moment."

"Meaning?"

"Meaning that maybe you should look at this with a new attitude. How many times have you said, 'if I only knew then what I know now'? Well, this is your opportunity to take the wisdom of nearly fifty years and have a do over when it comes to men and sex."

"Aleesa, what the hell are you talking about?"

"I'm talking about taking these last years of your forties, and reliving your twenties."

"Okay, I have to say that's an interesting concept. But one that sounds more like you than me."

"Why?"

"Because you're the one who lost your mind once you got in your fifties and started writing porn and taking *Penthouse* shots," Livia laughingly joked.

"I happen to believe what Woody Allen said: 'sex is only dirty if you do it right'," Aleesa quipped.

The women exchanged a fist bump and giggles, as the waitress raised an amused eyebrow while she delivered their waffles and refilled their coffee. Livia used the pause in their conversation to take a good look at her cousin. Aleesa had never looked better. Her curvy, sexy body was in the best shape of her life. It was sheathed in figure flattering jeans and a simple white sweater, purposely chosen to quietly and tastefully, but powerfully, announce upon her arrival, that a grown and sexy woman had entered the room. Livia recognized her look and attitude. They were the telltale signs of a woman in the midst of a life-altering epiphany and coming into her own. Livia recognized the look because she'd been unsuccessfully searching in the mirror for months hoping to find it.

"So how did the *Penthouse* shoot go?" Livia asked, once the waitress departed.

"At first it was really hard, but after talking with Josiah, I kind of went with the flow."

"Omigod!" Livia screamed, using Aleesa's trademark expression. "Your face is all flushed and you're actually glowing. Spill it. What did you do with this guy?"

"Nothing," Aleesa replied, trying to be coy, but knowing full well her cousin was going to pull it out of her. And truthfully, she wanted to talk about it. She needed help sorting it all out.

"Don't even try it. In the fifteen years that you've been married to Walt, I have never seen your face light up like that about another man. What is going on with you? Have you broken your own rule?"

"NO, absolutely not! It's gonna take more than the perfectly dimpled face and muscled body of a chocolate god with a voice dripping in sex," Aleesa said, wearing an 'I've got a secret' smirk while training her eyes on her scrambled eggs to avoid her cousin's.

Livia lifted her fork into the air. "Aleesa Davis, I will put this fork through your hand right now if you don't tell me what happened on that shoot!"

"You know that phrase, sex on a platter? That's Josiah Newman. That boy was so yummy I wanted to eat him up! I swear, Livia, there was this spark between us that was so fucking hot. It was scary but felt hell of good, too. Can I tell you, this celibacy thing is for the birds."

"You got that right. So what happened?"

"Nothing happened, for real. Let's just say it spawned the perfect fantasy to end Walt's book."

Aleesa recounted the photo shoot for Livia, giving her every detail from the sets and props to the wardrobe and poses. She filled her in on how nervous she was about it all, some because she felt too old but mostly because Josiah Newman was so damn charming and hot.

"And to make it worse, there were two of him! Identical fineness, doubly hot! It should be illegal!"

"Damn!"

"Omigod, Livia, I was so attracted to him that it was almost paralyzing," Aleesa admitted. "It was really messing up the shoot because I felt embarrassed and kinda guilty, and it showed," Aleesa continued, telling Livia how her fantasies of Walt had turned into fantasies of Josiah, and how mortified she was...at first. But she said that after talking with Josiah, he made her see how thrilling and useful sexual attraction could be, how she gave into her attraction and used it to create some amazing photos for her husband.

"He said the attraction was mutual, but I'm sure he was just doing his job," Aleesa said.

"I don't know; for an old broad, you're pretty hot. So did you or did you not have sex with him?"

"I did not, but I am not going to lie. There was a real part of me that wanted to. I think it's because I am so sexed up and ready to pop these days that the thought of any real live, warm dick inside me right now is tempting as hell. Between the fantasies, the nude pictures..."

"Nude?"

"Art shots."

"Yeah, Vanessa Williams said that too until the *Penthouse* pictures proved otherwise," Livia joshed, referring to the first black Miss America's scandalous girl-on-girl pics that cost her the crown in the early '80's.

"No, really. All the nastiness going on in my head had nothing to do with the kind of pictures he took. The few I saw were very tasteful and beautiful and Walter is going to love them."

"When will you see the rest?"

"He's out of the country working, so I'll get the photos in a couple of weeks."

"So that's it? Mr. Hot-to-Trot Photographer Man is a ghost of seductions past? Just like that?" Livia asked with a snap of her fingers while keeping Aleesa's face in clear focus.

"Yes. I swear, nothing happened. Well...he did kiss me."

"What?"

"It wasn't a big deal. Very short, not a sex kiss, but more like a job well done kiss. But that kiss aside, after almost thirty years of having sex, that shoot was one of the most liberating, sexy experiences of my life. Yes, I was attracted to him, and sat in that bed butt naked fantasizing about having a wild threesome with him and his brother."

"Threesome? You freak!"

"We're talking identical twins here, but let's not lose the important point, which is that when it was over, I felt alive and beautiful and sexed up as hell and yet the only person I actually *wanted* to have sex with was Walt."

"Okay, so you've found a way to have your cake and eat the damn thing!"

"Exactly. Thanks to sexy-ass Josiah, I've learned that I can feel sexy and attracted to someone other than my husband and not feel guilty, but instead use that energy to make sex between me and Walt stay hot."

"When the student is ready..."

"Yep, I think it was something I was learning by doing all of this writing but Josiah was the one who made me recognize it."

"Sounds like a real Oprah 'aha' moment, but seriously, do you think it's really possible? I mean, if the chemistry between two people is that strong, don't you think eventually somebody is gonna want to make the move to the bedroom—for real?"

"Probably. If you keep tempting yourself, you're bound to give in eventually. The key is to feel the energy but from a safe distance! Because as horny as I am right now, and as sexy as that boy was, I don't know if I could keep walking away if he was constantly in my face. I've had sex exactly five times in eighteen months—all in one weekend! The one thing that helped keep me on the straight and narrow, besides the fact that I love the hell out of Walt and don't ever want to cheat on him, is knowing that he'll be home in thirty-two days."

"Poor Walter. He has no idea the size of the task awaiting him."

"He's up for it. Trust me," Aleesa proudly informed her.

"Eww. TMI."

"Oh, you wanted to know all about Josiah."

"Yeah, but he's not my cousin-in-law, and I might have to go check Josiah out and make your fantasy my reality!"

"You always were running after me, trying to pick up my discards!"

"Oh please…"

Aleesa's phone rang, interrupting their jestful teasing. She fished her cell from the bottom of her purse, only to have it stop ringing and go to voice mail. "It's Soup."

"Walt's friend?"

"Yep. Charlie Campbell. Walt asked him to call and check up on me while he was away, and he has, though lately it's been a lot more frequently."

"What does he want?"

"Only asking how I'm doing, if I've spoken to Walt, if I had any more info on when he'll be back. Neither one of us hears from him much anymore. Not since he left Jalalabad."

"Does that worry you?"

"It's hard and I worry like hell, but as long as I don't have some guy in a uniform come knocking on my door, I know he's okay."

"Well, that's nice of Soup to call."

"Yeah, but lately, I feel like he's fishing for info."

"Sounds like you aren't the only one who misses him."

"That's very true. Those two have been best friends since the third grade," Aleesa informed her.

"So are you inviting Soup and the rest of us to your welcome home party?"

Aleesa laughed. "Eventually I'll throw a party for family and friends, but *my* welcome home is an invitation only, clothing optional, party for two. Oh, and you're baking the cake!"

Chapter Four

The sultry sounds of Kem filled the studio as Josiah sat at his computer studying the results of his latest shoot. His camera had clearly fallen for the lovely and charming Mrs. Davis, hooking up with light and angle for a *ménage à trois* of photographic *amour*. The artist in him was pleased to find that each photograph managed to peel back and expose the hidden petals of her personality, capturing a flower that was as innocent as it was erotic. The friendly hound in him wanted to peel back the petals on Aleesa's much more delicate flower.

Josiah clicked through the tub of popcorn shots, proud of himself for capturing the essence of Aleesa's playful, sexy side. In most of these shots, he could still see the nervousness in her face and eyes. But there were a few frames, caught in between her obvious attempts of trying too hard, where her natural sexiness shone through. In these shots, Josiah was sure the Colonel would find his popcorn-covered Mrs. just as tasty as he did. And the faceless floor photos were smoking hot, mainly because they captured the sexual tension evident in her limbs and torso while showcasing those incredibly tempting breasts of hers. The pearls, the tasty cleavage, the inviting opening between her legs, everything about these photographs begged for reality.

Before inspecting the final bed shots, Josiah scrolled through the first two again, noting that Aleesa's photos fell into distinct "before" and "after" categories. The before group bore witness to her discomfort with exhibitionism. Fully clothed, Aleesa moved like a woman comfortable in her own skin, but disrobed, did not easily photograph like one. While inexperience in front of a camera played its part, it quickly became clear that she was a lot less comfortable with physically revealing her sexiness, than mentally reveling in it—at least in front of a stranger.

But the after group revealed an entirely different Aleesa. In the photos he'd taken once she'd escaped into her fantasy world, the change was instantly noticeable and her sexual magnetism jumped off the frame. Her face and body became relaxed yet energized, and the natural expressions on her face were as lusty and lovely as if they'd been recorded while she'd actually been having sex.

He moved on to the elegant nude photos. They were especially hot and erotic because they captured on film what had made his dick hard in reality. Each picture left the viewer wondering what was going on in Aleesa's mind that transformed her look and energy around her from simply lovely to fucking lusty with nary a touch or kiss to egg it on. In the few hours they spent together, Josiah had learned that Aleesa was a woman gifted with a rich sexual imagination. It had been his experience that the women who allowed themselves to soar in the sex dens of their minds were usually much more sexually adventurous when it came to getting busy.

But it was the series of spontaneous frames that caught Aleesa laughing in the skin she was born in that he found the lustiest of all. They were natural and real and sexy as hell, and he planned to add them to his personal collection of favorites.

Josiah could not remember photographing another client whose entire range of sexual personality had been captured on film in such an open and pleasing way. The many sides of Aleesa Davis—warm, curious, vulnerable, shy, silly, sexy, lusty, mysterious—were revealed in these photographs. And each frame drew you in and made you want to get up close and personal with the subject. It had been her comment about the sexiest place in the world being wherever she was that had captured his imagination the most. Her declaration had not been delivered with any sense of ego, nor did it sound like braggadocio.

Josiah had to wonder if her husband had tapped into and harvested this fertile ground of fuckable potential. If he had, Walter Davis was one lucky bastard. If not, he was a lame motherfucker who was leaving himself open to having his wife plucked from her pedestal. And Josiah would be first in line.

Perhaps it was her fertile imagination, but Josiah guessed it was the air of mystery surrounding Aleesa that intrigued him so. She was a successful professional woman, loving and devoted wife and mother, and apparently, an undercover sex bomb. He'd photographed and fucked a lot of women, many of them clients, all of them beautiful in their own unique way, but none had captured his libido and held his interest like this woman had. It had been nearly three weeks since the shoot and he wanted to see her again, to tap into her fantasy life and experience her passion in real time. He debated whether or not to call her and set up a face-to-face meeting, knowing that there was an opening there, but decided against it. Aleesa definitely appeared to be the personification of the mystical goddess all men claimed to want—a lady in public and a freak in the bedroom. But she was also a woman in love with her husband. And while Josiah was a man whose dick was intrigued by a mystery, and made rock hard by a challenge, he liked to think of himself a gentleman when it mattered.

Josiah sorted through the frames, eliminating many, ignoring others, and selected his favorites to make a separate contact sheet for Aleesa. He'd be a good boy and email her the contacts. If any advances were to be made, she'd have to be the one to move them forward.

The bell to Livia's bakery announced her arrival. Aleesa walked inside inhaling the warm, sugary air. Pastry shops always struck her as happy places of business. Not only were the smells consistent with happy, sugar spun memories, but the reasons people shopped there were generally happy ones, too—birthdays, weddings, anniversaries, and in her case, highly anticipated homecomings.

Havin' Your Cake was fast becoming one of the premier cake suppliers for the nation's cake aficionados. Thanks to providing the most voted-on wedding cake for the *Today Show* Throws a Wedding segment, Livia had become the darling of wedding planners, bridal bloggers and brides-to-be across the country. Most thought that Livia was an overnight success, but Aleesa and the rest of her family and friends knew that this had been a long and tedious journey. Livia, who earned her MFA at New York University, had originally set out to be an artist. She quickly learned that talented, starving and poor didn't agree with her upper-middle-class sensibilities and settled for a job with a large non-profit organization. She spent years raising money for charitable causes before deciding to pursue her second love—baking. After graduating from the Culinary Institute of America with her Bachelors in Baking and Pastry Arts, Livia combined her love of art and baking, and Havin' Your Cake was born. And just in time to fill her days after her twenty-five-year marriage to Dale Charles ended in divorce.

"Hi, Aleesa." Katie, Livia's store manager greeted her. "Livia's in her office finishing up a call. She says to come on back."

Aleesa followed Katie out of the cake room, through the kitchen and into Livia's small office. She studied the portfolio of pictures on the wall, all pastry creations baked to mark an important moment in time for her customers. There were cakes that looked like sculptures of dogs, sandcastles, pillows and crowns, high-heels and cars. There were more traditional cakes covered in edible orchids and roses and calla lilies that looked as real as the blooms created by Mother Earth. Aleesa marveled at Livia's sugary works of art, amazed by her creativity and technique.

"I've got a date!" Olivia announced, hanging up the phone and getting up to give her a hug.

"With a young'n?"

"Yeah, Jeremy. He's twenty-seven, a trader or something on Wall Street."

"White?"

"Yep. But he actually talks on the phone, sounds very nice and thinks I'm gorgeous. I figured, what the hell? Beats sitting at home."

"When dipping your toe back into the dating pool, it can't hurt to have the upper hand of age and knowledge."

"So how are you, cuz?"

"I'm good. And judging from your artwork, you're doing pretty damn well yourself. Livia, you've been kicking ass!"

"It's amazing what a little bit of publicity can do for you."

"Another reason I'm so grateful that you're fitting me in. Seriously, I do appreciate it."

"Please. You and Walt are family. And after all he's done for the country, it's the least I can do. So when exactly is this hot and horny party for two?"

"Fourteen days and counting."

"So do you have the pictures?"

"Yes. Do you think you can do one of your sculpture kind of cakes...of this if you can," Aleesa said, pulling out her favorite photo from the several Josiah had sent earlier in the week. It was one of the pictures shot from above, taken of her wearing the red lingerie and highlighting Walter's favorite part of her body—her breasts.

"Sexy, sexy!" Livia remarked, amazed and impressed by her cousin's boldness. Never during her twenty-five years of marriage had she ever considered taking boudoir photographs, and now nearly four years divorced, she still couldn't imagine taking off her clothes in front of a stranger, let alone one wielding a camera. "I think if we concentrate on this area," she said, circling Aleesa's shoulders, chest, and stomach, "we can capture the spirit you're going for. He's going to love it."

"Do you think we can include the pearls, too?" Aleesa asked. She was planning to try Lena's pearl jam trick she'd described during her relationship with the sports agent, and thought adding the pearls on the cake would be a cute tease.

"Girl, I can do anything! Plan on picking it up that morning."

"He's going to love it!"

"So while we're on the topic of parties, what's going on with our girls' getaway this year? San Francisco is coming up quick. I want to make sure we see everything."

"Don't worry; from what I understand, she's planning to hit all the tourist traps."

"I can't wait to do some chillin' on the city by the bay. I can't believe this will be my first trip to California. What do you want to see?"

"If I were going, I'd like to drive up to Carmel."

"If you were going?"

"I don't know if I'm going to make it this year."

"You have to! You can't break a six-year tradition."

"I know, but Walt will have been home only a couple of months. I'm not sure I'm going to want to leave right after he gets back."

"Don't write it off yet. Who knows; after nearly two years of being on your own, having your spouse underfoot again might not be all you remembered it to be," Livia said, only half kidding.

"Don't project the end of your marriage on mine," Aleesa countered.

"Seriously, Lees, you've got to be prepared for some kind of adjustment period. Your man is coming back from war, not some temporary assignment on a cruise ship. I'm sure there is going to be some adjusting to do on both parts.

"Whether you realize it or not, with Walt and the boys gone, you've gotten a lot more independent. You've pretty much been living life as you've wanted without worrying about anybody else. That's going to be tough to give up that freedom."

"To have my husband back safe and sound, I'd gladly give it up, believe me."

"Oh, I believe you. I just don't want you to set yourself up to be disappointed if everything isn't as hunky dory as before he left."

"It's going to take some time before things get back into a rhythm, but Walt's a dentist. He's been over there fixing teeth. It hasn't been easy, but thank God he hasn't had to deal with all the madness our regular military guys have had to deal with. We'll be fine. So stop putting all that negativity out in the Universe. You've gotta think Kohl's."

"Kohl's? As in the chain store?" Livia asked, totally puzzled by her cousin's remark.

"Expect Great Things!"

Chapter Five

Aleesa stood in front of the floor-to-ceiling mirror in the living room and took a good look at herself. She was pleased with the attractive woman dressed in the coral-colored, flowing satin gown and matching robe grinning back at her. Her excited smile, in combination with her breasts, proudly displayed in the built-in bra, would be a powerful welcoming committee. She ran her hand through her recently keratin-treated hair, trying to imagine the pleasure its silky touch would give the calloused hands of her soldier husband. From her first Brazilian wax (at Lena's insistence) to her freshly cleaned teeth and new hairdo, Aleesa was powdered, prepped and primed for Walter's return. Her outer appearance was definitely in sync with her inner feelings.

She floated over to the CD carousel and turned up the volume on Walt's favorite crooner, Al Jarreau. While Al's smooth, melodic voice serenaded her, Aleesa inspected her decorating handiwork. The room looked and felt precisely as she had pictured it in her head all these weeks—a romantic den of erotic promise. The crackling fire and flickering candles provided a warm glow and sexy ambiance. A pink, coral, and red mix of rose petals was sprinkled around the room like confetti. Their subtle fragrance, mixed with the sweet, comforting mélange of scents, bore witness to her desire to provide her beloved husband a sensual and romantic welcome.

In the kitchen, the pork tenderloin and red onion jam, as well as mashed Yukon potatoes and grilled asparagus tips—all the Colonel's favorite dishes—sat patiently on the stove, waiting to be heated up when appetites demanded. The champagne was chilling in anticipation of a celebratory toast. But it was the last course, her one of a kind decadent dessert, that was the true *pièce de resistance*.

The sweet smell beckoned her over to the dining room where she'd set up Walt's homecoming cake and special gift. Livia had done a spectacular job of recreating her favorite pose from the boudoir photo session. They'd chosen the overhead bust shot to bring to life in baked form. From her bodacious bosom, iced in a red frosted lace brassiere identical to the real thing, to the delicate flower petals sprinkled among the realistic looking frosted fur rug, the edible sculpture was a true work of art. Most impressively, it captured and recreated the unquenchable desire she'd eventually come to feel that day.

Aleesa picked up the elaborately gift-wrapped freak book and hugged it to her chest, careful not to crush the fancy bow. Walter was going to be blown away, not only by the contents of her erotic journal, but by the cover as well. Josiah Newman had expertly managed to put on film what she'd tried to capture in words—a sexy, lustful, loving woman, hungrily awaiting the return of her man.

The memory of Josiah and their mutual attraction was knocking at the front door of her mind, but Aleesa refused to allow it entry. She'd made peace with her studio flirtation and the short and sweet kiss she'd shared with the hunky photographer. Yes, the sexual current between them had been powerful, but in her mind, it was the product of a perfect storm of pent-up lust, a highly erotic environment, and a player's natural inclination to seduce. She'd filed the experience in her mental box of secret pleasures, never to be acted upon but to be trotted out from time to time when she needed a boost to her sexual confidence. Now was not the time.

Now was the time to revel in the immediate future. Aleesa checked the clock above the mantle. It was 3:37 p.m. His plane was due in to New Jersey at noon. She'd wanted to, had been fully expecting to, be at Fort Dix to give her husband a proper hero's welcome, but Walt had insisted that he'd meet her at home. It made sense, considering that a multitude of military variables and ensuing protocols made his arrival time unpredictable, so she hadn't argued the point. Allowing a couple of hours for check-in at the base, and the drive home, she was expecting Walter in less than an hour. Forty-eight minutes until the rest of her life could finally begin.

By 9:00 p.m., Aleesa had exchanged the burned-out votive candles for fresh ones. Al Jarreau had been silenced, replaced by the 1010 WIN traffic reports, and finally silence. Instead of making love to Walter as she'd imagined, she was pacing the floor, trying not to worry. Her calls to his cell phone went unanswered. So where was he? The drive from Fort Dix, New Jersey to their home in Montclair took a little over an hour. Unless there was a traffic jam on the Garden State Parkway. Or an accident.

No, she thought, pushing the idea from her head. *God would not be that cruel.*

Aleesa threw herself into Walter's favorite chair near the fireplace and wept silently, trying to release the frustration, fear and worry through her tears, so she could think straight.

A loud and shrill ring pierced the quiet. Aleesa ran to the kitchen to pick up the phone, willing it to be him, calling to let her know he was fine and minutes from home.

"Walt?"

"That's not a good sign," her friend, Lena's voice declared. "Why are you looking for Walt?"

"He's not home yet. Lena, I'm so worried. He should have been here hours ago. I'm worried sick that he's been in a car accident or something."

"Did you call the State Police?"

"No, but that's a good idea. Look, I'll call you back."

"Okay, but don't worry. I'm sure he's fine. Probably hit a mess of traffic. He'll be home soon and with all this worry, the adrenaline rush will make your welcome home celebration all the sexier."

"Right. I'll call you later."

She'd just dialed 4-1-1 to get the number of the New Jersey State Police when she heard a car pull up in front of the house. "Never mind!" she shouted into the phone as she flew to the front window. The car sitting in her driveway was unfamiliar, but she recognized Charlie "Soup" Campbell when he stepped from the car. Aleesa saw Walter's best friend go around to the back and open the trunk, pulling from its innards a folded wheelchair. He carried the chair over to the passenger's side and opened the door, revealing Walter's face. The breath began to slowly leave her body as she watched the two men argue for a moment, each equally insistent and clinging to his point. A truce must have been reached, as the talking stopped and Soup helped his friend out of the car and into the chair.

Aleesa tore herself away from the window and ran to the front door. A million questions wrapped in worry swirled around her head, as she peered through the peephole, while Charlie pushed her husband up the walkway, stopping steps away from the door. He handed Walter a walking stick and helped him to his feet. Aleesa's heart broke into a thousand pieces as she watched her man take three stilted, baby steps toward the front door before collapsing into his friend's side. Soup held him upright and rang the bell.

Aleesa counted to five, took a deep breath and tried to put on her brave face as she flipped on the lights and opened the door.

"Baby, I'm 'shome." Walter's bourbon-soaked breath assaulted her.

Aleesa stood in wide-eyed shock. She didn't know what to react to first—the wheelchair, his tardiness, or the fact that he was pissy drunk! She said nothing, instead taking a long look at her husband, noticing how his uniform hung on his thin frame and the appearance of his drawn face, before falling against him with a desperate hug. Her body weight was too much for him and the two of them fell into Soup's able arms. Aleesa shot Charlie a baffled look, her eyes full of questions and accusations. How long had he known? Why hadn't he told her what was going on? How could either one of them have kept something like this from her?

"Whoa, Lees," a wobbly Walter said with slurry words.

Aleesa quickly disengaged and stepped into the room, allowing the two men entry. Confusion and surprise robbed her of any words, plucking them from her mouth like a thief in a jewelry store. She moved aside and watched as he took unsteady steps into the living room and over to his chair. Aleesa was not sure if his unsteady nature was due to injury or inebriation. More than likely a combination of both, she concluded.

"Home schweet home," he announced, taking a look around. "Place looks great. Show do you."

Aleesa ignored his compliments and observations, but tied her robe tighter around her. "Walter, where have you been? You're hurt. What happened to you?" she asked, unable to contain the tears any longer.

"Shh. Shh, Don't cry, It's not so...baby," he said, reaching up to clumsily wipe the tears from her cheek. "Not as blad as it looks," Walter assured her, closing his eyes for a long, bourbon induced blink. "Soup, looks like we're havin'..." His words dropped off as his chin hit his chest. "...a party."

"Ah, Lees, why don't you let me help you put him to bed?" Soup suggested.

"Yeah, not a bad idea. Sleep is apparently what he needs right now," she said, not bothering to keep the annoyance out of her voice.

"Come on, buddy, let's get you to bed," he said, putting his arm around Walter and helping to lift him from the chair and into the wheelchair.

Aleesa followed them through the living room and to the other side of the house where the bedrooms were located. She slipped by them in order to open the door to the master suite.

"No. Guest shroom," Walter insisted.

"Okay, baby," she said, confused, but trying to honor his wishes. "We can sleep in the guest room if you'd like."

"Not you."

His words pierced her heart like a sniper's bullet. Aleesa stood in the entry to their bedroom, shocked into stillness. Forget that Walter had obviously been wounded and was recovering from some pretty serious injuries that she knew absolutely nothing about. Forget the fact that her sexy, welcome home celebration, which had never really begun, was ending in shambles. Forget all that because out of all those miserable things, the one thing that felt like it was wrestling the breath from her lungs was that Walter's best friend was putting him to bed in another room because he didn't want to sleep with her.

"But, honey..." she tried to protest.

"Let him sleep this off," Soup interceded. "Everything will look different in the morning."

Aleesa turned and headed toward the dresser, retrieving a pair of Walter's pajamas and taking them across the hall. "I'll wait for you in the living room," she informed Soup.

While Soup did her wifely job of caring for her husband, Aleesa paced the living room, this time not in worry but with fast blooming ire and frustration. Apparently something enormously traumatic had happened to Walter, something both he and Charlie had been hiding from her. Is this why his communications from Afghanistan had been so spotty lately? Though she hated it, she'd assumed it was part of war-time duty. Suddenly, Charlie's frequent and often cryptic calls inquiring about her well-being began to make sense. He'd been fishing to see how much she knew about what was going on. Well, before Charlie Campbell left tonight, she fully intended on getting the whole story.

"He's out like a light," Soup announced, walking into the room. The sheepish look on his face revealed his understanding that he was about to get skewered by one angry wife.

"What happened to him, Charlie? Why is he in a wheelchair?"

"I'm sure he'll tell you everything tomorrow."

"You know, don't you? When did this happen?"

"I'm sure he'll tell you everything tomorrow," Charlie repeated.

"Okay, Charlie. You and Walter have been friends since the second grade, and you'd take a bullet for him, as he would for you, so I'm not going to ask you to break his confidence, but at least tell me what happened tonight. Why is he drunk? And where the hell have you two been all night? Why didn't you bring him straight home?" She rattled off one question after another.

"Look, I wanted to bring him straight home but Walt insisted on stopping. Honestly, Lees, I don't think he knew how to face you."

"Face me? I'm his wife! I love him. Whatever happens, I'm here for him. Always. Okay? That man is my life." She stopped to take a few deep breaths and calm herself. "Charlie, I am begging you, at least give me some clue as to what I am dealing with."

"Aleesa, all I know is that something bad happened over there. A lot of his people got killed, and he got hurt. I really don't have many more details than that," Soup said, telling her a little white lie. Walt had leaned on him, telling him everything, even the shameful parts he was trying to forget, but it was not his place to tell his friend's story. Walt had to inform his wife of the details in his own time.

"I'm sure he had every intention of coming straight home. He loves you to death, girl, and has missed the hell out of you. But the closer we got, the quieter he got, until finally he told me to find a bar. He needed to get his head together before showing up to the house in the condition he was in. He knew it was going to be a shock and you'd probably be upset with him for not telling you that he'd been injured."

"Damn right, it was a shock and I am angry as hell. I've been worried sick for hours that he'd made it through this war only to get in some deadly car crash on the parkway. You could have at least insisted that he called me so I didn't worry."

"True, but he's not thinking straight. You're going to have to be gentle and patient with him. He's been through a lot, and he still has a ways to go."

"What about his injuries? How bad are they? Is there something I need to know? To do for him?"

"Apparently, the worst of it is over, and physically, he's recovering well and getting more and more strength back in his legs. In fact, the only reason he didn't walk from the car to the door was because he was drunk. I didn't want him to fall and hurt himself, so I insisted that he ride and take only the last few steps. He wanted to be on his feet when he saw you."

"That was smart of both of you."

"We're not total buffoons," he said, trying to crack a joke.

"He'll fill you in on his physical therapy and any meds he's taking tomorrow."

"You said physically he was recovering well. What about mentally, because this behavior is not the Walter Davis that I know?"

"All I can say is that war isn't pretty and it can leave some hefty scars. Even if he hadn't gotten injured, adjusting to normal life again would take some time, but honestly, Lees, whatever happened over there has really messed with his head, so be patient with him, and like I said, I'm sure he'll tell you everything when he can."

She could see she was fighting a lost battle. Charlie was not going to tell her anything more, at least not without Walter's explicit approval. "Thank you for being such a good friend, and taking care of him."

"Girl, I've always got my boy's back, and yours. So don't be afraid to call me if you need something. And I'll be checking in on both of you as well."

The two exchanged a tight hug and Aleesa stood in the threshold and watched as Charlie got in his car and drove off. She started toward her bedroom, stopped, turned and marched back into the dining room to retrieve Walter's freak book. There would be no need for this now or in the foreseeable future, not until she got to the bottom of things and understood what was going on with her husband. On her way to greet the loneliness waiting for her in the bedroom, Aleesa began blowing out the candles, and with them, her visions of her and Walter's perfect reunion.

Chapter Six

Aleesa awoke amidst the shriveled rose petals, in an empty bed. It took her a moment to get her bearings and remember why she was sleeping alone. Had it all been a nasty nightmare? After the cobwebs cleared, it all came rushing back—the waiting, the worrying, Walt arriving home late, drunk and in a wheelchair; his insistence on sleeping in the guest room.

She got up to brush her teeth and get dressed, ready to talk with her husband and learn the answers to the growing heap of unanswered queries already crowding her head. As she had done every morning for their entire marriage, Aleesa took the time to make herself as attractive as possible. She pulled on a comfortable, body-skimming maxi dress that showcased her cleavage and the toned arms she'd been working so hard in the gym to achieve. She applied just enough makeup to enhance her natural beauty, and fixed her hair into a casual tousle of soft curls. The whole look read comfortable and sexy without trying too hard. A final spritz of the sheer tropical scent of Princess by Vera Wang and she was ready to face whatever the day, and her darling husband had to bring.

Aleesa was headed toward the bedroom door when her eye caught the shine of the metallic gift wrap adorning Walter's unopened present. She sighed with disappointment as she picked it up and carried it into the closet, burying it in the back under a pile of sweaters, before going to start her day.

The door to the guest room was open. Aleesa crossed the hall and peered inside, only to find the bed empty, but for the blue heap of pajamas Walt had worn to bed. "Walt?" she called, rounding the bed and checking out the unoccupied bathroom.

"Walt?" she called out again, venturing into the center of the house. The wheelchair had been abandoned in the family room. She stepped into the kitchen. Last night's uneaten dinner was still on the stove where she'd left it, and the dismantled coffee pot, but no husband. Aleesa slid open the pocket doors separating the kitchen and dining room and stopped in her tracks.

"What the hell?" The words slid under her breath as she surveyed the mess before her. Sitting among the shriveled rose petals was the champagne bottle covered in icing, and her cake, bashed and battered into a frosted shipwreck. Clearly the dessert baked with loving intent had been destroyed with angry abandon. But why? Why had Walter ruined not only her effort, but her image?

The front door opened, and Walter, still with his cane, but much steadier on his feet than last night, walked inside. He paused after noticing his wife standing there surveying the remains of this morning's temper tantrum. Extreme embarrassment warmed his exhausted face as he clutched the top of his walking stick, willing himself not to fall.

"Why?" she asked. Her tone was as soft as a whisper as she watched a shameful and apologetic scowl traipse across his face. They both knew that her one word question was not only about the mess she was standing near, but also covered the entire spectrum of information she was currently missing and desperately seeking.

Walter, concentrating on remaining upright, ignored all her unspoken queries. The walk had taken more out of him than he had expected. He'd probably pushed himself too far, but walking was the only way he could think of to diffuse the irrational anger that had gripped him. It had started as guilt when he'd awakened and seen the extent of Aleesa's preparations for his first night home. She'd obviously gone to great lengths to plan and execute a romantic evening to celebrate his arrival. And he'd ruined it by showing up late and drunk and a fucking invalid. And then to insult the woman even further, he'd demanded to sleep alone. The hurt his rejection had put on her face last night was unbearable. But as much as his wife loved both him and sex, he knew what she would want, and in his condition, he wasn't up to giving it to her in any form or fashion.

He'd spent a miserable night alone, wanting to be with Aleesa, but not knowing how. He'd intended on making it up to her by climbing into bed with her this morning, but humiliation had snatched him by the throat when he'd tried to test out his equipment and his fucking dick still wouldn't get hard. He hadn't had an erection since the incident, and no matter how much he prayed and willed it to move this morning, it remained limp and useless. That's when he'd come out into the living room and seen the cake—a flour and sugar monument to those spectacular breasts he'd so desperately missed and had gone to bed dreaming about every night while he was away. Seeing that cake infuriated him and his fury quickly transferred to his wife. Walt was pissed off at her for being so loving and incredibly special, and for expecting him to be her goddamn trusted white knight all these years. But mostly he was mad at himself for not being able to live up to that ideal and be the man she so richly deserved. He was furious and afraid, afraid that once Aleesa learned the truth, once he unloaded the dump truck of lies he'd been living with these past five months, his life could very well end up looking like that stupid fucking cake—a messy, fucking ruin. And just like that damn dessert, he'd be the asshole responsible for destroying it.

Aleesa watched, puzzled by the flashes of anger across his face, and waited for his response. Why was he mad? What had happened to the loving husband who'd surprised her in Puerto Rico six months ago? The romantic and accommodating man who always made her feel safe, cherished and adored? The man with whom she could always talk and work out their problems with respect and dignity? The man who couldn't fall asleep without her body pressed up against his? Where was her Walt? In the few short minutes they'd actually spent together since his arrival, the husband she knew and loved had yet to surface. Had war changed him that much? Where the changes forever?

"The chair," he said, the words sounding more like a command than he intended.

"Excuse me?" Aleesa was totally taken aback by his harsh and unfamiliar tone.

"The chair. It's in the other room...please," Walt added, making an effort to soften his voice.

Finally understanding, Aleesa hurried into the family room and retrieved the chair, rolling it out into the front. Thank goodness they lived in a ranch-style home. She had no idea how she'd manage if she had stairs to contend with. She pushed the chair behind him and stood back, steadying it with her body weight as he dropped his body into the seat.

"Are you okay?" she asked, concern jumping to the forefront of her jumble of emotions.

"Yeah. Just tired. Guess I overdid it," he replied, feeling the vibration of his cell phone against his leg.

"Can I get you something?"

"Coffee? Please. I tried to make some but couldn't find all of the stuff. I guess I've been away too long to remember."

"My dear, you didn't remember before you went away," she teased, trying to keep things light.

"I guess you're right about that," he said, cracking a smile. "So you'll make coffee and then why don't we go sit by the fire and talk. I owe you some answers."

Ya think? She wanted to say but let the sarcasm die in her throat. "Sure. I'll be right back. Black, right?" Aleesa asked, checking to make sure. Everything felt different about him at the moment. Perhaps his coffee preferences had changed, too.

"Yep."

Aleesa headed toward the kitchen, but was halted when Walter reached out and gently grabbed her hand. She turned to face him, searching his eyes. The bright and lively brown eyes she'd gazed into for the past fifteen years seemed tired and sad now. Her heart broke for him because looking into her husband's eyes, it appeared that a part of him had died in Afghanistan. Instead of acting like such a spoiled brat, she needed to pull off the sexpot g-string she'd been wearing and pull on her big girl wife panties and find out what was ailing her husband and how she could help him heal.

Love flooded through her as she bent down and covered his lips with hers. At first, she was alarmed when Walter flinched and pulled back a bit, but rather than pout, she persisted. Her hand reached up to gently caress his cheek as her tongue snuck between his lips, prompting them to open. Aleesa's tongue began to dance in his mouth, and soon, under the warmth of his wife's loving kiss, Walt's resistance fell away. Aleesa felt a weight lift from her heart. This was the familiar Walt, her husband and lover, kissing her back.

"Welcome home, my love," she said after releasing his mouth and covering his sad eyes with an onslaught of butterfly kisses before going to make coffee.

Walter watched the sway of her ass walk away from him and sat very still, desperately waiting for a reaction in his shorts. Nothing. He shook his head in disgust. A few months ago, he was the luckiest bastard in the world. He had a hot wife who not only loved him but was probably hornier now than the day he'd met her. Making love was never a chore or wifely duty for Aleesa. She always came into the bedroom, or wherever the mood struck them, lusty and ready to love and be loved. Sex with his wife, even after all of these years, felt as exciting as it had the first time. One of the things he most enjoyed about her was her ability to not only give but receive pleasure. Aleesa was a sexy woman who deserved a man who could pleasure her. The man he was when he left home nearly two years ago. Not the fucking eunuch he'd now become.

His phone vibrated again, letting him know he had another text message. Walt pulled his cell from his pocket. It was Monica again. She'd have to wait.

"Who was that?" Aleesa asked, returning with two steaming cups of coffee.

"Soup. Texting me to see how I was doing," he lied, hoping it didn't show on his face.

"Do you need any help?"

"Nah, I got it," he replied, trying to keep the frustration out of his voice.

Aleesa watched as he wheeled himself over and positioned himself next to the fireplace and across from her chair. She studied his movements as he accepted the mug and sipped on his coffee. His upper body mobility was fluid and strong. Whatever injuries he'd sustained obviously affected his legs, but thank the Lord, they too seemed to be working, though not quite at full capacity. Silence brewed between them as he drank from his cup and contemplated his surroundings. "You still make the best java in the world. One of the many things I missed about home while I was in the Middle East," he said, finally speaking.

"Thank you." In the short time he'd been out of her sight, the awkwardness had returned. While brewing his coffee, she'd promised herself that she was going to be patient and do more listening than talking. But at this rate, night would fall before she got the answers she was seeking. Aleesa decided to ignore the cake debacle for the time being, and focus on the most important thing; Walter's physical and mental health.

"Baby, tell me what happened. How did you get hurt?" she gently prodded. "I mean, it's been months since we shared more than spotty communications," she said, pointing to his wheelchair.

"I'll get into all of that, I promise, but first I want to apologize for last night. I was an ass to show up late and drunk like that and I am so very sorry. You didn't deserve that. And the guest room thing; please don't take it personally; I just have a lot of problems sleeping these days," he told her, opting for the honest, though only partial truth.

"Walt, Charlie said you were afraid to face me. Is this true?" she probed.

"What else did Charlie tell you?"

"Nothing much, really. He said you'd explain in the morning. So here we are."

"Well, he's right. I was afraid to face you. I knew you'd be angry, and I felt guilty..." he paused letting silence replace the words he didn't want to say, "...about...well, everything."

"Sweetheart, why would you possibly think I'd be angry because you got wounded?"

"No, not that I got injured, but that I didn't tell you that I did... or anything else for that matter."

"Well, tell me now," Aleesa quietly insisted, resisting the urge to concur with his rationale.

Walter took a deep breath and steeled himself against the hurtful war-time memories he needed to unearth in order to fill his wife in on his life these past few months. Many remembrances were downright ugly, others shameful, but all were extremely uncomfortable.

"As you know, for nearly all of my tour I've been behind the wire in Jalalabad, running the dental clinic for the troops. I never left the base. Soldiers who needed dental care were flown in to see me."

"You never got to leave?"

"Well, honestly, considering what's on the other side, why would I want to? Besides, on the FOBs…"

"FOBs?"

"Forward Operating Bases. The big bases. There are two in Afghanistan—Jalalabad and Bagram. On both bases, they have cafeterias, a PX, gyms and laundry service, even Pizza Hut. You can take a hot shower every day and Fobbits even have Internet service in their rooms, so communicating home on the regular is not a problem."

"Fobbits being those who live on the Forward Operating Bases?"

"Yes."

"Damn, it sounds like a five-star resort in a Harry Potter book!" Aleesa teased.

"Ha ha. But compared to the combat operating posts—"

"Let me guess, COPs?" she asked, trying not to drown in the military alphabet soup.

"You're catching on," Walter told her with a smile. "The COPs are little bases located in the middle of nowhere. Anyway, shortly after I returned from R & R, my mission changed. My unit was sent out on a humanitarian mission and assigned to COP Monti near Asmar village."

"Why?"

"The trigger pullers work hard to win the hearts and minds of the local villagers in order to keep one step ahead of the Taliban. The military has promised villages women's health seminars, lessons in farming, road building, well digging, you name it, and the U.S. Army does their best to comply. Apparently, the village elder in Asmar said they needed dental care, so we were sent."

"Why didn't you tell me that you were being reassigned?"

"Honestly, Lees, there's a lot I didn't tell you about because I didn't want you to worry about me. Knowing that you were home worrying about me would've made it harder for me to do what I had to do."

"So you moved," Aleesa moved on, not sure how she felt about her husband's apparent need to protect her from everything. As her past history proved, yes, ignorance can be bliss, but once reality hits, bliss can turn into one big time pain in the ass and heart.

"Yes, we moved. And compared to a 'five-star resort' like JAF, COP Monti is a trailer park in the projects. Picture a big barn skinned in three layers of sandbags and giant T-walls. No more Internet in your room, salsa lessons, or hot showers, for that matter. There was limited electricity, five showers, so hot water didn't last, and the latrine was a fifty-five-gallon oil drum cut in half. There were four computers for 220 soldiers with Internet service that was spotty at best, and cell phones were a big no-no. Too much danger of information about military movements getting picked up by the Taliban."

"So no wonder there was so little communication," Aleesa commented. True, the information he was giving her was interesting, but she wanted to get down to the nitty-gritty, to find out how and why he came home in a wheelchair.

"It sounds really, really...I don't know...bleak. What did you do at night? I mean, how did you pass the time?"

"Guard duty. With the guys coming and going in and out of the wire so much, they needed to sleep and relax, so that left us soft skills guys to guard the base."

Aleesa felt shock grab her heart. She had no idea that Walter had been over there being a soldier warrior and dentist. "Omigod! What was that like?"

"Quiet. You kind of wait for the explosion of mortar or rockets. Eventually, you get used to it."

"I don't think I could ever get used to that, or any of it."

"You get used to the living conditions. In fact, if you feel the shock of a cold shower, smell the smells and feel the touch of the flies constantly buzzing around you, you know you're still alive. But it's hard waiting to get hit and not being able to find the guys who are engaging you. Not being able to throw a punch back at the guys punching you gets old."

"Oh, baby, I had no idea that you were in danger like that, and you're right, I would have been worried to death, but you should have told me. I could have handled it. Now, how did you get hurt and what exactly is wrong?"

"May I have more coffee, please?" he requested, trying to buy time so he could get his act together. These were the memories he'd managed to push to the dark recesses of his mind and voluntarily pulling them out to share with Aleesa felt counterintuitive. He'd done enough sharing with the shrink the military had made him talk to during his recovery. He didn't want to share any more, but Aleesa deserved to know.

The question was, how much was he ready to tell?

Chapter Seven

Aleesa spent a few more minutes than necessary refreshing both their cups. Instinctively, she understood that Walt's revelations were painful and she wanted to give him the time and the room to express them as he needed.

"Here you go."

"Thanks," he said, before taking a long sip. He was hoping the warm liquid would squash the chill he felt running through his body. "We'd been in Asmar just shy of a month. My guys, Jack, Buddy, and Monica, the hygienist, were going out on patrol to give away toothbrushes and toothpaste to the locals and to let them see we were the good guys wanting to fix their teeth. Jack and Buddy never came back." Walter's voice cracked as he recalled the memory of his lost comrades. Aleesa, feeling his pain, knelt on the floor in front of him and put her head in his lap.

"Jack and Buddy and one other soldier went over and met a group of kids playing soccer. Stepped on an IED and blew them all to smithereens," he told her while aimlessly stroking her hair. "It was miserable. Barely anything left. All the kids...gone. Three soldiers...gone. I had to identify them by their dental records."

"Omigod, sweetheart. I'm so sorry. What about Monica?" Aleesa asked through her tears.

"She was talking to some little girls down the road. She wasn't hurt but watching your friends die in front of you has a special pain all of its own. It's no fucking joke. She was absolutely crushed and inconsolable," Walter revealed, looking off into the distance.

"Aleesa, behind the wire I saw hurt guys come in and out all the time, and even though I felt for them, I didn't have the same emotional investment. It's different when you're out in the thick of all the shit. When it's your team, your guys. You're a part of it—all of it. You're not a spectator who sees the parts that come to you. You see every fucking gory piece of it. Part of me died with them that day," Walter admitted.

"How did you cope with it all, losing your friends like that?"

"Tears, prayer, alcohol, anything that makes you feel safe and alive or helps you forget, if only for that moment..." he paused as he mentally beat back the painful memories. "...because you feel alive and grateful...grateful that you weren't the one..." he admitted, as his voice trailed off. A shadow of guilt and dread spread across his face.

"Walter, don't you dare feel bad that you survived. I will thank God every day for the rest of my life that you did. But I don't understand, if you were back at Monti, how did you get hurt?"

"A couple of weeks later, we got orders to return to JAF," he revealed, happy to stop talking about his stay in Asmar, even though the puddle of memories he was about to tread into was as painful. "Some big wig general was being flown in for an emergency surgery on an infected abscess. I didn't care why; I was just happy to go back. I only had a few months left on my tour and I did not want to spend it at COP Monti. I'm not going to lie, Aleesa, I was scared shitless out there in the middle of nowhere. It's one of the reasons the combat soldiers look down on the Fobbits, because they know that most of us soft skills guys are a liability if anything pops off. But believe me, they are the best in the business.

"So the platoon assigned to escort us back to Jalalabad picked us up and we were headed down Route Stetson, the main supply route, when we got ambushed. It's the Taliban's favorite spot because it's deep in a valley where there is no communication. There were IEDs all over the place and they hit everyone there."

"Oh no. Why not use another route?"

"It's the only supply route we've got going north."

Aleesa felt an icy cold creep through her body as she imagined the carnage that he had witnessed.

"They took out the lead vehicle with a rocket. Killed everyone on board. We were in the second truck. We all jumped out of the truck, looking for cover."

"Is that how you got shot?" Aleesa jumped in. She no longer had the stomach or patience for all of the gory details. All she wanted were the facts about him.

"Yes, and no. Those brave kids fought them off 'til they retreated. I didn't actually get shot. Bullets were flying all over and I got hit by some stray shrapnel. It lodged in my lower spine and I was paralyzed."

"PARALYZED? How could I not know this? Why didn't they call me? How did you get out of there?" The questions spilled out of Aleesa's mouth nearly as fast as the tears filled her eyes.

"Once we could get moving again, they drove until they could call for a Medevac bird to come in and pick me up and take me back to Jalalabad. They stabilized me there and pushed me on to Germany."

"GERMANY! Wait, this makes no sense. You were badly wounded and flown out of Afghanistan for medical treatment, and I didn't know any of this was happening? How is this possible? I'm your wife. Why didn't anyone contact me?"

Walter took a deep breath in preparation for the onslaught that his revelation was sure to unleash. "Because I put you down on the 'do not contact' list."

"You *what?* Why would you do that?"

"Honestly, baby, it was because I never wanted you to have to experience that knock on the door. So I put Soup down on my paperwork as next of kin. I felt better leaving, knowing that if anything happened to me while I was on tour, some stranger wouldn't be breaking the news."

"You had NO right to do that, Walter. I'm your wife, your family. And wanting to spare me a stranger's visit doesn't excuse you for not telling me what was going on once you knew you were okay."

"But I wasn't okay. Not for a long while. The shrapnel left me paralyzed from the waist down. Even after they did surgery at Landstuhl, it was weeks before some of the feeling came back and I was recovered enough for further rehab. They sent me to Walter Reed."

"In Washington, D.C.? How long were you there?"

"For two months in the Warrior Transition Unit, continuing my physical therapy. I didn't fly into Fort Dix last night. Soup picked me up in D.C. and we drove up. Baby, I'm sorry. I thought I was doing the right thing by saving you the worry."

"Omigod, Walter," Aleesa cried, covering her face in both disgust and disbelief. "So when you called a few months ago, you were stateside?"

"Yes."

"You've been hours away but didn't feel the need to let me know so I could at least come down and help you with your recovery? How could you do this to me? To us?"

"I needed to concentrate on what I had to do and not be worried about you. And to be honest, Aleesa, I didn't want to see you until I was whole again...like when I left."

"And are you?"

"Damn near. The strength in my legs is coming back. I still

have a few...uh...lingering issues. I have to work on my stamina, which is why I still use the chair when I get tired, but the doctors say that in time, other than a slight limp, everything should be working good as new."

Relief flooded through Aleesa's body, washing away the frightened concern. But before Aleesa could settle into the solace, full-fledged fury came rushing forward.

"But are you...whole? Because despite your reasoning otherwise, you are not the same man who left my arms and my bed eighteen months ago. That man wouldn't have lied to me...deceived me like this. " She was unable to keep the indignation from overtaking her compassion.

Her words "the man who left my bed," clawed at the patient veneer he'd been so artfully projecting. "Lied to you? About what?" Walter asked, suddenly furious that she'd unwittingly poured alcohol in his open wounds by questioning his intent.

"Yes. Let's start with our last conversation when you said you had to hang up and get back to your unit."

"It wasn't a lie. Not really," he insisted, knowing he was standing on the proverbial thin ice wearing rusty skates. "I did have to get back to my unit; my hospital unit."

"Oh, okay, so now lying to me by omission is okay? Well, it's not. You lied to me by letting me think you were safely behind the wire filling cavities in one country, when you were really lying in a hospital bed in another, worried that you'd never walk again. You deceived me into thinking all these years that you trusted me to be your wife and partner and rock when things got tough, like I trust you to be mine. So yeah, I resent the fact that you lied and deceived me. I don't care what your intentions were. And you of all people, Walter Davis, should know how I feel about deceit."

The black cloud of fury that descended over Walt may not have been visible, but Aleesa could certainly feel its presence, and it alarmed her.

"Goddamn it! I was merely trying to save you any added grief," Walter replied, his voice booming in anger. "How dare you accuse me of lying and being deceitful when all I was trying to be was protective. After all I've been through, after everything I've seen, coming home to this kind of bullshit is not what I had in mind or what I need!" he declared.

"Well, me either. If you look around, you'd see that I had an entirely different kind of evening planned, but you chose to spend last night alone in another room, then at some point this morning, you vandalize my efforts," she lashed back.

"Yeah, I spent last night alone because every time I close my eyes, it becomes a big fucking nightmare that never ends. So I don't sleep well anymore, and once again, I was trying to protect you from having to see me like that. And yes, I noticed many things. You say I'm not the same husband. Well, you're a different wife as well."

"How so?" Aleesa replied, her voice quieted by the shame she felt for thinking of herself and not considering what hell Walter had obviously been through. Still, how would he know if she'd changed? He'd barely spent half an hour with her since he'd been back.

"First of all, the way you opened the door last night, dressed all seductive and sexy in front of my friend. And then we walked into some sort of whorehouse set-up, complete with an X-rated cake," he threw back at her, his mouth spewing hurtful words.

Aleesa felt herself wince as if she'd been struck. She had no reply as she tried to rebound from the painful sting of his angry accusations. He might have been through hell, but where was this coming from? His argument didn't make sense. Again, his response seemed out of proportion to their discussion. Thank God he hadn't seen the freak book. What insulting things would he have to say about her then?

The look on Aleesa's face was the same as last night when he'd requested to sleep in the guest room. He hated that look, especially when he was the one who put it there for reasons that had nothing to do with her. It tore at his heart and, as most things did these past few months, infuriated him.

"I'm sick and tired of being held up on this goddamn pedestal of yours!" Walter announced, grabbing the wheels of his chair and moving away from her. His abrupt actions bumped the table and caused his coffee cup to crash to the floor, putting an end to their escalating argument.

Aleesa watched him roll away into the guestroom and slam the door behind him. As she picked up the broken pieces and wiped up the floor, she heard Soup's voice in one ear, cautioning her to be patient and compassionate and consider all the trauma he'd been through recently. In the other, she heard her hurt and anger repeat the fact that his volatile anger was uncalled for, just like his violent destruction of the cake. And though their fights had been few and far between over the years, Walter had never run away from a serious argument with her. But now he seemed to be running away from her at every possible turn.

She deposited the broken glass into the kitchen trash, then picked up the phone and dialed. She needed to get out and try to make sense of all of this madness. "Meet me at Panera Bread on Prospect," she requested as soon as Lena answered the phone. "Now! It's an emergency."

Chapter Eight

"And then he stormed off, pissed as hell that I even questioned his motives. Though I was really questioning his actions," Aleesa explained to her cousin. Luckily, their favorite table, a comfortable booth located in the corner near the dessert case, was vacant. "In what possible universe would he think it would be okay not to tell me he was injured and living stateside for three months?"

"This is a tricky one, Cuz. You and Walter have always had such a great relationship. This doesn't sound like him."

"That's exactly the point I made to him."

"But, I mean we talked about this. You really didn't expect him to come back, just the same, without any battle scars at all, did you?"

Aleesa sat and pondered her cousin's question. Livia made a sage point. "Actually, yes I did," she reluctantly admitted.

"That's pretty naïve of you, don't you think?"

"I mean, I call him warrior man, but despite all of his Army reserve training, he's an oral surgeon who plays soldier on the weekend," she revealed, feeling the tears welling up in her eyes. "He only signed up for the reserves because he wanted to do something to serve his country, and they needed him because there's such a shortage of dentists and other skilled medical professionals. But honestly, even though the thought of him going to serve in Afghanistan was so frightening, when they called him up for active duty, there was a lot of comfort in knowing that he'd be on base behind that damn wire cleaning teeth and not out on the front lines getting shot at. So, yes, this was totally unexpected."

"Probably for him, too, Lees."

"He did admit to being scared shitless."

"And can you blame him?"

"No, but…"

"And, Lees, fucked up as it was, I can kind of see his point."

"He lied to me," Aleesa commented, feeling her hackles rise. "Lying is never right!"

"Think about it. When you two met, you, Aden and Ashri were still reeling from the drama from your ugly divorce and all the financial problems Bill created and you found yourself caught up in. And then that dickwad ex of yours gets arrested and convicted of embezzlement and he goes to jail and you're without alimony and trying to figure out how to make ends meet."

Aleesa hated rehashing this miserable time in her life. The expenses of their many years of upper middle class cohabitation, even with alimony, had been no match for her broadcasting salary. But once Bill got indicted and his assets were frozen, everything began to tumble like dominoes. Without his supplemental income, she had to put the boys in public school, sell the house, the cars, and anything else to help pay off debts and legal fees. By the time she met Walter, she and the boys were living in a small apartment in West Orange. They were no longer living pay check to pay check, but the three of them were still in survival mode. Walter had come in with his bigger-than-life personality and strong, able arms, swooped up her and the boys, and rescued them. He became the lover, husband and life companion that she'd always dreamed of having, and the amazing father and friend that her boys, now 23 and 25, had always deserved.

"Walter has always been your Superman. Maybe he felt like he would be letting you down if he wasn't a hundred percent when he came home."

"He did say he was tired of living on the pedestal I'd put him on," Aleesa admitted, "but I never realized I was doing that or pressuring him to be something that he wasn't."

"I'm sure you didn't, and I'm sure he probably even liked wearing the cape. He's never complained before. But the shit never hit the fan like this before either."

"Okay, I can understand all that, but I don't understand why he was so angry at me and so cruel. It wasn't like him at all. From Bill, I'd expect 'the best defense is a good offense' bullshit, but not from Walter. We've always been very honest with each other and able to talk things out."

"Seriously, Aleesa, you're gonna have to give him time. He's got a great deal to be angry about, and I'm sure he doesn't mean to direct it at you, but I'm sure he's a jumble of nerves and emotions. What he needs for you to do right now is back off and just love him."

"But, Liv, he won't let me. It's like he picked a fight out of nowhere. We didn't even sleep together last night. He slept alone, in the guestroom. He said it was because he had trouble sleeping now and was being considerate."

"Sounds plausible. The man has been through hell and back. He watched people get blown up and die around him. I'd be surprised if his sleeping habits *weren't* all messed up."

"Yes, but there's so much more." Aleesa revealed how he'd found the cake and destroyed it and his reaction and the mean-spirited words he'd spewed at her about her and the house. "I wanted to plan a sexy homecoming for him, but he saw it as whorish and sleazy. We've always had a great sex life. I haven't changed, but now all of a sudden, something's wrong with me."

"Aleesa, girl, I know you're upset and all, but connect the dots here. You haven't changed, but he has. The boy comes home barely walking and needing a wheelchair for backup. He comes in and his wife is looking like sex on a stick, and by all indications is ready to fuck the black off of him. So he wants to sleep alone... and then he wakes up to see your tits on display. He messes it up and then has a pissy attitude all morning. And what was the thing that set him off? Sex. Come on, can't you see the problem?"

"You think he's..."

"Impotent? Yeah, I would bet you a million dollars that your husband can't get it up. Why else would he be avoiding your pussy like it was booby trapped?"

"Omigod, OMIGOD! You're so right. If he was paralyzed, he must have really damaged some nerves or something. Poor Walter. This is all so...so...sad." Sad—a small, simple and direct word that captured the complexity of emotions surrounding her situation. "No wonder he needed to get drunk to come home. Walking in that door with me and everything looking like, 'come here and fuck me now,' he must have felt like shit, which is why he acted like one."

"Even Superman can't deal with a broken penis. I'm sure he's embarrassed as hell, and him knowing how much of a sex pot you are, only makes things worse. Now he's gotta worry that he'll never be able to keep you satisfied and he'll lose you. You know how men and their egos work. So of course he's pissed, and anger is his place to hide. It keeps you away from him and keeps you from wanting to have sex."

"What am going to do? I have to help him."

"I don't know, Lees. I guess you should start by finding out everything you can about impotency. Google it, and while you're at it, Google anything that has to do with soldiers coming home, depression and any other common issues. Be patient and talk to him. Let him know you still love him no matter what, and that in the big picture, sex doesn't matter."

Aleesa wiped her eyes and thought about all she'd heard and learned in the past twenty-four hours. She'd so naively thought that she and Walt would pick things up right where they'd left them and continue on with their fairytale life. She'd been so happy, her worries so few. But once again, her happiness was built on a shifting sand dune. Everything had changed. And though the circumstances were completely different than with Bill, Aleesa was still feeling let down and betrayed.

"Am I supposed to cut some Faustian bargain. I can be happy OR I can have sex. Not both?"

"No, of course not."

"Because it does matter. Damn, Livia. This sounds so horribly selfish and saying it makes me seem like a petty bitch, but sex does matter—a lot. I feel like I finally found my sexual center and now I want to explore it with my husband. And the truth matters—a lot. And right now, Walter seems unable to give me either."

"I know, but don't put that pressure on him right now. He didn't lie to you to hurt you or set out to deceive you for dishonorable purposes. He was trying to do what he's always done, love and protect you. So you need to get over that.

"And as for the other, after a bit, once you find out the extent of what you're dealing with, I'm sure there are pharmaceutical options to get things right. Cialis, Viagra, Levitra, guys have a zillion options to get their dingies hard.

"Bottom line, Aleesa: your man is a fighter," Liv said, trying to find words to make her sister-cousin smile. "If he worked his ass off so he could walk again, you best believe he'll climb a volcano barefoot if that's what it takes to fuck you again."

Aleesa allowed her lips to lift upward, but her smile was simply an acknowledgment that she'd heard her cousin's words. Believing them was a whole different matter.

WALTER DOWNED ANOTHER SHOT OF TEQUILA AND TURNED ON the television, hoping the booze and noise would drown out the self-deprecating thoughts thrashing around in his head. He had no cause to speak to Aleesa like that. It was bad enough that he'd chastised her for questioning his bullshit reasoning for not letting her know he was in the states recuperating, but to damn near call her a whore? What the fuck was wrong with him? His wife had always been a lusty *lady* and he absolutely hated himself for how his ugly words must have confused and upset her. All because he was a fucking coward...a liar...and a cheat.

Cheater...cheater...CHEATER. The word repeated and continued to grow in volume in his head until he could no longer ignore it. The unrelated and unfortunately timed sound of canned laughter mocked him, prompting him to turn off the television and throw the remote across the room.

His wife was by no means perfect. She was strongly opinionated, could be stubborn as hell, and found change difficult. She worked hard and when she was laser focused on something, the rest of the world tended to disappear. But when she came back into the world, there was no better friend or wife. She was a completely loyal and responsible partner. She didn't judge and allowed others to live their own lives as they saw fit, including her family. Despite her past personal history, Aleesa gave her sons and him all the running room they needed. To her credit, she didn't hover, nor was she jealous or unreasonably demanding. Aleesa lived and loved life, not a particular lifestyle. One of the things Walter loved most about Aleesa was that she was one of the few people he knew who definitely had her priorities in life straight.

His wife made few demands. In the early years, when their relationship began to get serious, she had only one deal breaker—no cheating. It was the one area in their marriage where she'd been crystal clear that there would be no second chances. To ensure he didn't stray, she'd turned herself into his ideal sex partner, and Walter could not come up with one realistic complaint about his wife in bed. Aleesa was always ready and willing. She initiated as often as she acquiesced. His wife loved giving and getting head. She was experimental and curious, and their lovemaking was as fun and full of smiles as it was freaky and full of surprises. And always full of love.

Then in one night, he'd managed to fuck it all up. One stupid, scary night, he had to be the hero and ruin everything.

Chapter Nine

"Lees, have you seen my navy blue Polo shirt?" Walter inquired, walking into the laundry room.

"Over there," Aleesa told him, folding towels and pointing to the desired pile with her head.

She watched as Walter, sans cane and steady on his feet, grabbed his shirt and pulled it over his head. "A little help?" she requested.

"Sure," he replied, grabbing a bath towel and starting to fold. Aleesa smiled to herself. He was doing it all wrong. They'd never fit in the linen closet like that; but she said nothing. His effort was sexy and she was too happy to once again be doing simple household chores together to complain. She felt a tingle snake down her spine and suddenly, she had another, more pressing housekeeping item to attend to.

"Come here," she requested, grabbing his shirt and gently pulling him over. "I've been wanting to do this all morning." Her lips came down on his, finishing her sentence and expressing her thoughts in a way mere words could not adequately communicate. The weight of her hungry kiss silenced any response Walter tried to make. Aleesa held Walter's face still in her hands as she traced his lips with her tongue before probing his mouth. She moved slowly and seductively, intoxicating all of her senses and liberating any inhibitions or concerns she had about his recent behavior.

"I've missed you so much," Aleesa whispered in his ear, as her fingers ran the length of his arm under his shirt, and up his torso. She lightly ran her fingers through the hair on his chest, stopping to circle his nipples round and round until they began to harden.

"Me, too."

"I want to show you something." She pulled her hand away and brought it to her own chest. Slowly, one by one, she began to undo the buttons of her blouse to reveal the fire red lace of her brassiere.

"Pretty," he said, feeling his dick jerk.

"Thank you, but my bra isn't what I wanted you to see," Aleesa admitted as she locked eyes with her husband. With her eyes, she told him how much she'd missed his touch, while her hands translated, brushing across her stomach before slipping under the cups and pulling her breasts from their lacy wrap. "I wanted to show you how I spent my nights while you were away."

Aleesa felt the cool air on her skin as she licked her index finger before circling her nipples, moving back and forth between the two. She felt them grow, becoming long and hard under her touch. "Usually, I'd take a bath and then sit either by the fire...ooh, mmm," she told him, interrupting her admission with the moans of self-seduction. "...or in the bed with a glass of wine and make love to myself, imagining you with me."

She could feel a delightfully nagging sensation in her crotch, causing her pelvis to instinctively tilt upward in search of Walt's dick. Another slow, sexy moan escaped her lips.

"I'd feel your hands on my tits, rubbing and sucking them into a frenzy," Aleesa revealed, mimicking her words with action. She pushed them together in an offering, licking her lips in a nonverbal plea for him to suck her nipples until they were hard and stiff and begging for relief. Looking at Walt watch her with eyes full of want spurred her on.

"Once they got long and I could feel them swelling in my hand, I'd pinch hard like you do," she said, taking his hands and placing them over her swelling breasts.

Walter gave them each a squeeze, thumbing each of her nips while once again relishing his wife's soft, squishy flesh in his hands. He remained silent, simply enjoying the show Aleesa was giving him and the southern rush of blood.

"Mmmmm..." the sounds of arousal escaped her throat, announcing the thrill of having his hands once again touching her.

"I love when you make them hurt because it makes Clitina begin to twitch, and when she's twitching, I feel like such a nasty slut. You like when I'm your nasty girl, don't you?"

"Yes." Walt elaborated on his reply by reaching over to the small basket near the folding table and pulling out two clothes pins. He attached one to each of her nipples, enjoying the sound of her painful pleasure, and the rise of his cock.

"Yes, baby. I spent so many nights thinking nasty, slutty thoughts about you and me," she told him while pushing her panties and yoga pants away from her hips so they slid down her legs and settled around her ankles. With her lips attached to his, she stepped out of the legs, freeing herself from their confines, and allowing her to slide her finger into the warm moistness accumulating between her legs.

"I need to be spanked," she said. Aleesa coated her clit with personal lube before taking her hand and slapping her pussy. "Spank me."

Walter reacted by slapping Aleesa's pussy with his open palm. "Ohh," she moaned, enjoying the sting to her coochie. "That feels good, baby."

The washing machine shifting into its spin cycle inspired Aleesa. "Sometimes I'd use my vibrator, but most times I used my hands, always imagining it was you touching me, spanking me and finger fucking me. But sometimes...I'd come down here and sit for a spell.

To illustrate her point, Aleesa hopped bare ass onto the washing machine. She spread her legs and pressed her pelvis down onto the cool metal. She closed her eyes as she felt the vibrations from the machine tickle her clit and and quiver deliciously throughout her body. The pulsations brought the blood rushing in, causing her bud to swell and her vaginal walls to sweat. Aleesa felt like she was going to burst if she didn't get some immediate relief.

"I would sit here and imagine you eating my pussy again. But now you're here and I don't have to fantasize anymore. Do it now, baby. Eat me. Please eat my pussy like only you can," she begged with a desire-soaked voice.

Walter locked his forearms behind Aleesa's knees and pulled her closer to the edge of the washer. With her feet on his shoulders he pressed his nose against her silky thatch of pubic hair and targeted her protruding nib with a stream of steady, warm air. The combination of his breath and the washer's vibrations caused Aleesa to grab his head and press his face deeper into her pelvis. She needed the delicious ache in her groin to be satisfied. Walt attempted to meet her need by dragging his tongue in one long, luscious stroke from the bottom of her vagina to the top of her swollen pleasure point, before gently sucking and finger fucking his wife. The spin cycle was turning faster and faster and the unrelenting pulsations were sending her over the edge. Aleesa could feel an orgasmic cyclone rushing her. She pressed her ass into the machine while at the same time raising her pelvis and practically smothering Walter's face with her vagina.

"Oh, fuck yeah. Fuck yeah. Make me cum, baby. I wanna cum hard in your face." Aleesa felt the build-up caused by technology and tongue grow until sunlight detonated within her and scattered glimmers of supreme satisfaction throughout her body. Cumming clean never felt so dirty!

Walter sucked every last bit of orgasm from her body and the washer ground to a halt. Clitina was certainly satisfied, but Aleesa's hunger went deeper—pussy deep. Only Walter's rod, pounding her pink flesh, was going to satiate her appetite.

"I need your dick, baby. I've missed your pretty hard dick so much. Please...Walt, give me my dick."

"Please...please..." Aleesa woke up feeling aroused and talking in her sleep. She reached across the bed for Walt, only then realizing that she'd been dreaming. She stuck her hand between her legs, feeling the residual moistness of her aroused vagina. It was painful to dream about sex, particularly knowing that the object of her desire was across the hall, and apparently not interested.

She looked past his unused pillow to see the green neon numbers glowing in the dark. 3:13 a.m. Aleesa turned her head and this time gazed up at the ceiling, trying to wake up and wrap her head around what had occurred this past week. Extreme loneliness lay heavy on her chest like a stone blanket. Best she could figure out, after nearly two years of being away from her, she and Walter were finally back sleeping under the same roof, but in separate beds. Her thoughts went back to her earlier conversation with Livia. Was Walter avoiding her in the bedroom because he couldn't sleep or because he couldn't fuck?

No time like the present to find out, she decided. Aleesa got up and padded across the room and into the hallway. She paused at the guest room door, her heart jumping at the sight of him. Love hugged her heart as Aleesa quietly stood by the bed and removed her nightgown before climbing into bed. She smiled, noticing that he still slept in his drawstring pajama bottoms and naked chest—a favorite look that always turned her on. Aleesa gingerly scooted toward him, adjusting her naked body so it curved around his as she put her arm around his waist. Walter, always alert, even when trying to sleep, opened his eyes but remained still. Aleesa lay there for a minute, nuzzling his neck and happily filling her nostrils with his natural odor. After so long apart, even this simple pleasure took on magnanimous proportions. Unable to stop herself, she pressed her naked tits against her husband's back. Though thinner than she remembered him, the thrill of being skin-on-skin again further aroused her. She was tired of fantasizing and dreaming about sex with her husband. She needed the real thing. Her lips, hungry for the taste of Walter's skin, began a passionate hike, starting from his neck and journeying along his spine until it reached the top of his pajama pants.

Walter stirred, but did not move, making it unclear to his wife whether he was awake or not, or whether he wished her to continue or not. Aleesa slipped her arm across his waist and down to the fly of his pants. Her wanting hand found a hard dick! She gave it a welcome back hug, stroking him from tip to testicles.

"Walt, I am so hungry for you," she whispered in his ear.

She felt a slight twitch and then nothing. Instead of happily getting harder and rising in her hand as it usually did, Walt's erection began to shrivel and get soft. His disinterest was painfully obvious.

"I'm trying to sleep," Walt said gruffly, a tear threatening to assault his cheek as he removed her hand and separated his body from hers.

Aleesa stared at his back, feeling the cold and lonely chill of rejection. She pulled her hand back and retreated to the other side of the bed. She lay there weighing her options. She and her super-sized helping of humiliation could retreat to the master suite and spend another miserable night alone, or she could refuse to let Walter freeze her out and force him into some sort of domestic cohabitation. She decided to stay.

Aleesa was sure that Walt wasn't asleep, but she was unwilling to say or do anything more to upset him. She turned over, maintaining a respectable distance from his body, and lay by his side, listening to the ebb and flow of his breathing. The trauma of what he had experienced in Afghanistan had clearly affected him, but Aleesa was at a loss as to how she could help.

She'd done as Livia had suggested and researched as much as she could about the mental and emotional ailments of men returning from war zones. Unfortunately, according to her findings, many soldiers returned with major emotional and physical damage—and major problems having sex. Post Traumatic Stress Disorder (PTSD) could cause insomnia, chronic pain, depression and anxiety, all which affected sexual ability. And apparently, with these problems, if you had one, there was a good chance that you had others. Worse, many of the medications used to treat the above problems often severely inhibited sexual function.

Perhaps the most distressing thing she'd learned was that 65 percent of soldiers who needed mental counseling would not seek it for fear of being stigmatized. That fact upset her greatly because Walt's issues were beginning to take a toll on their marriage. They needed to start talking about what was bothering him so much, and then find a way to make the boogeyman go away.

"I love you, Walter," she whispered through the darkness.

"I love you, too."

His words were like a magnet, pulling Aleesa back to his side. Sex may be out of the question tonight, but cuddling close to her man was just what the doctor ordered to comfort his broken mind and body, and soothe her wounded heart.

Chapter Ten

"How is she really doing?" Lena inquired while she and Livia sat in the Short Hills Mall courtyard waiting for Aleesa. "I've been doing so much traveling that I haven't had the chance to really dig deep and find out what's truly going on."

"Not good, and it's throwing her off big time. When have you ever known Aleesa Davis to be thirty minutes late for anything?"

"You've got a point. So it's not getting any better? He's been home nearly two months now. I thought things might have settled back into their regular routine," Lena commented.

"They haven't. She says he's being tight-lipped and acting grouchy. Physically, she says he's getting better, but they still haven't done the nasty, and he's refusing to go to counseling.

"I went by to welcome him back, and he was friendly and all, but you can tell he's not the same old Walt," Livia reported, while checking her watch again. "The boys say the same thing."

"I feel for her. She was so looking forward to him coming home, giving him that book, and getting back to their life together. I never knew a woman who missed her man so much. Maybe he needs to miss her some."

"So let's try to convince her to come to San Francisco," Livia said.

"She's still not planning to go? We leave next week."

"Not as of yesterday. I don't even know if she's mentioned it to Walt."

"Sorry I'm so late," Aleesa apologized, rushing up to join her friends. "I couldn't get myself together. So, what haven't I mentioned to Walt?"

"That you're going with us on our annual trip," Lena replied, jumping right into the matter at hand.

"I'm not..."

"Save it; we're not taking no for an answer."

"Let's walk and talk," Livia suggested, putting her arms through each of the other's, and pointing them in the direction of Neiman Marcus. "You two are supposed to be helping me find shoes to wear on this trip."

"We've been through this. Walt's only been back two months, and things aren't..." Aleesa's voice dropped.

"Which is exactly why you need to take a step back, come on vacation, and look at the whole situation from a distance," Lena chimed in, as they headed up the escalator.

As much as Aleesa adored these two women, she didn't feel up to being badgered into going on this trip. Her life already felt stressed to the max at the moment and the last thing she wanted was more pressure. "Ladies, I know you mean well, but what I really need right now is some retail therapy. Can we just do what we came for and shop? Please."

"Absolutely," Lena said. "Off to Cinderella's Closet."

The trio headed down the escalator to the ladies' shoes department. Each woman veered off to the shelved display that suited them most—-Lena to the premier designers like Jimmy Choo, Christian Louboutin, and Giuseppe Zanotti; Aleesa to the sales rack; while her cousin stayed by her side, happy to peruse the footwear, but really not sure what she should be looking for. At work, Livia spent the majority of her time wearing her unfashionable but highly comfortable chef jacket and clogs. Her off-duty look usually consisted of jeans and a white top of utilitarian style. Sexy shoes, or any clothes for that matter, weren't part of her fashion sense.

"Ohh, try these Stuart Weitzmans on," Aleesa suggested, taking a seat while handing Livia a crocheted, ankle-wrapped espadrille. "It's casual, but the wedge gives it some sexy height."

"Like I'm not tall enough."

"It's not only about height. It's about the sex appeal. If you're going to date, Liv, you've gotta make an effort!"

"I'm missing everything with all this traveling," Lena said, plopping down beside them with one silver, strappy sandal by Giuseppe Zanotti, adding her choice to the salesman's list of their requests.

"Those are gorgeous!" Aleesa cried, lusting after the jeweled and Swarovski crystal details. "They are so you. Instant attitude."

"Shoes are definitely my weakness. So, Liv, you're dating now?"

"Kind of."

"She's trolling the playgrounds online," Aleesa teased.

"Online? You?"

"A birthday present from my dear cousin," Livia explained. "I finally decided to check it out. Unfortunately, the only guys who seem to be interested so far are young."

"And White," Aleesa added. "You should definitely get those wedges, Liv. They make your feet look tiny and you look hip and fashionable for a change."

"Word to the wise, my cougar friend. Dating younger is a whole new experience. For example, these young guys know nothing of pubic hair. It's crazy. I had a date with this kid, he was like twenty-nine or something ridiculously young like that; anyway, we started to get busy. I took off my clothes and when the drawers came off, he stood there staring at me like I was a damn alien or something."

The conversation took a pause as their shoes arrived. The women, eager to hear the rest of Lena's tale, accepted the boxes and politely declined his help.

"Anyway, he kept standing there, gawking at me like I had a raccoon attached to my crotch."

"I guess he thought your *beaver* was the *real* thing," Aleesa added, between chortles.

"I asked what was wrong. He kind of stuttered some inane remark about such a hairy thatch, and judging by the crazy and confused look on his face, I knew he wasn't going to go down on me, and if he wasn't going to eat me out, what was the point? I mean, really."

"So what did you do?" Livia inquired, thinking of her own furry cooch.

"What any grown woman would do. Got dressed, kissed the hell out of him so he knew exactly what he was missing, and rolled on out of there."

"I guess you showed him," Aleesa said, still laughing. "But, um, aren't you the one who told me to get a Brazilian before Walt came home? You would have thought you were getting a kick-back, the way you raved about the J Sisters. So who showed who?"

"Okay, yes, I admit that experience provided some pertinent food for thought." Lena laughed.

"Yeah, like you needed to step up because you couldn't risk *not* getting your pussy licked," Aleesa chimed in.

"Jeezus, girl, that whole Jason episode turned you into a card carrying freak!" Livia commented.

"Look, it may not have worked out between Jason and me, but he really did turn me out in all the right ways. I learned my lesson. 'Don't let a man, no matter how fucking great the sex, cloud your good judgment.' But he also introduced me to a side of myself that I really like."

"I don't think I even like sex that much, to want to shake hands with that side of Livia."

"That's because your ex was a dud spud in the sack and you haven't been turned out yet," her cousin announced.

"So why are you trolling the Internet?" Lena asked.

"Companionship. I'm tired of being alone. I want to see a movie or go out to dinner every once and a while."

"Well, in that case, you should be hooking up with the grandpas, not the grandsons, because the young'ins—they want to fuck! In the movies *and* in the bathroom at dinner!"

Me too, Aleesa thought, but did not express. "You've got to buy these shoes. They look amazing on you," she told Livia instead. She was tired of this line of conversation. It was depressing her. She didn't need the constant reminder that she, her husband and sex were no longer bedfellows at the moment. "And I've got to try those on," she said, reaching for the Giuseppe Zanotti sandals.

"You're not slick. I know what you're doing," Lena said. "You're trying to change the subject."

"You need to talk about it," Livia said softly. "We're your girls. That's what we're here for."

"I know, but I'm trying to stay in a positive frame of mind, and talking about it makes me sad. Omigod! These are fantastic!" Aleesa said, admiring the shoe candy on her feet. She stood up and took a stroll to the mirror.

"No wonder you wear these things. They make you feel like walking sex," she said, plopping down and picking up the box. "One thousand forty-five dollars! Damn, I'd have to go on the stroll to afford them!" Her friends watched without comment, very much aware of how badly their friend was hurting, despite her show of good humor.

"Okay, okay. Here's the update, so we can move on. Physically, he's getting much stronger. He's still doing therapy, but no longer needs the chair and is using the cane less and less. He's back in the office a few hours a week, and is easing back into seeing patients."

"Have you gotten over his not telling you about everything that was going on and being in D.C. when you thought he was in the Middle East?"

"Pretty much. I hate that he didn't tell me, but I do know that he was simply trying to protect me. Still, it has left a little dent in our trust armor.

"Honestly, the hardest part has been this re-entry period. You were so right, Livia, I was totally naïve. I thought he'd come back and we'd pick up things right where we left off. But he's not the same. War has definitely changed him."

"Don't be so hard on yourself, Lees. He's a reservist. And I'm not taking anything away from the huge sacrifice you and the other reserve families are making because of this war, but you haven't lived the day-to-day life of a military wife all these years. All of the sacrifices they make year after year—the constant moving, the long deployments, the long absences—you didn't have to deal with. This is all new to you. How were you supposed to know what it would be like?" Lena pointed out the obvious that her friend wasn't seeing.

"I don't know how these military wives do it. They are heroes themselves for dealing with this all the time. Just the toll it's taken these past two years on Walt's practice, our livelihood, and on our...well; just taken its toll."

"Your marriage? Your sex life?" Livia gently probed.

"That's still not happening, and for some reason he's not interested enough in trying to get it fixed to go see a doctor. He keeps telling me it's going to take time.

"I'm trying to be patient because all the research I've done says this is a pretty common problem for returning vets."

"Are you at least sleeping in the same bed now?" Livia asked.

"Off and on. When we do, he'll let me cuddle up with him, but it always feels like he's doing me a favor rather than wanting to be close to me. I'm starting to get scared," Aleesa admitted.

"I'm sure he's keeping his distance because he doesn't want to be put in the position of disappointing you," Livia offered, commiserating with her cousin.

"I know, and my new mantra is 'think love not lust.'"

"Fuck that, because he is disappointing her," Lena declared. "There are plenty of things he can do sexually that don't involve his dick."

"Have you asked him?" Lena said, asking what Livia was thinking.

"No. I'm afraid of getting rejected again."

"Ask," Livia said.

"Demand," Lena countered. "He may be fragile emotionally and physically, but so are you. Your heart is hurt and your libido is suffering. You aren't asking for the whole enchilada, just a bite. If things are ever going to get back to normal, he's going to have to start somewhere, and it might as well be sooner than later."

ALEESA'S THOUGHTS WERE RACING AS SHE DROVE DOWN EISENHOWER Parkway on her way home. Both women had made excellent points. It was time for her to exert some kind of control over her marital situation. True, she was not the type to issue ultimatums, but there comes a time when a wife has to take a stand against her husband and fight for the things that were important to her—like their marriage.

She began to compose the list of her demands. First, she wanted the two of them to resume sleeping together on the regular, instead of sharing a bed only on the occasions when she slipped into the guest room. On the nights when the painful nightmares struck, he had sleeping medication and her arms to retreat to and find comfort in. Second, they had to introduce lovemaking back into their marriage. She was willing to redefine it to fit their current situation, but kissing, hugging, caressing, holding, oral sex and toys could and should all be classified as sex and practiced with some regularity. And third, sooner than later, he was going to have to go seek professional help and find a way to medically deal with his problem.

With her list firmly in her head, her mind spontaneously drifted on to other thoughts—namely those of Josiah Newman, their photo shoot, and his remarkable ability to make her feel wanted and desired in a very nasty, but upstanding way. Her memory, both mind and muscle, replayed the feelings and sensations their sexy encounter had produced. It was remarkable how powerful attraction without action, to coin Josiah's words, could be.

Aleesa pulled her Audi into the garage. Stepping out of the car, she experienced a surge of arousal that was surprisingly painful. *This must be what having blue balls feels like*, she mused. Goddamn, she needed, wanted, and was going to get laid. Walter was not in the house and she assumed he was taking his evening walk through the neighborhood, which gave her plenty of time to get ready.

She headed back into the master bath, peeled down to her birthday suit and stepped into the shower. She soaped up, forgoing the exfoliating qualities of the loofah or washcloth for the soft caress of hand on skin. She was wanting and wishing that it was Walter doing the touching, and was disappointed and still slightly peeved that he wasn't. Her hands continued their soapy journey south until they reached the prickly stubble between her legs. The cactus-like texture covering her mons pubis was an irritating (literally) reminder of the effort (and pain) that had gone into Walter's botched welcome home celebration.

"Think love, not lust," she reminded herself. "NO! Tonight it's about love AND lust," she said, editing her thoughts. "So think love and lust, not lividity!"

Repeating her new mantra in her head, she reached for the razor and proceeded to mow her lawn, not totally bare but enough so that it was smooth and invitingly edible. As Lena had so aptly pointed out, no need to munch carpet when what really counted was what lingered beneath.

Aleesa finished bathing, stepped out of the shower and coated herself with a skin softening concoction of fragrant oils and lotions. She dabbed a little rose oil on her newly coiffed vajayjay and nipples and then threw on her favorite slip gown and matching robe. She had achieved the look she was going for, nonchalant sex appeal.

Sensually refreshed, she pulled out her favorite vibrator, Buzz Lightyear, from the nightstand and gave him a good cleaning. Buzz had gotten her through many a night while Walter had been away, and while she hadn't envisioned using him in the capacity of main dick so soon, she hoped that with her husband's consent, Buzz and Walt could become the dynamic duo that would lift her out of this depressing sexual drought.

Aleesa heard the front door open and close, notification of Walter's return. She finished cleaning her toy and then, in one last inspiration, decided it was time to give Walt his welcome home gift. She went into the closet, burrowed under the pile of winter sweaters and pulled out the package. She refreshed the bow, put it on the bed, returned Buzz to the nightstand, and went to find her husband.

"Why are you sitting out here by yourself?" Aleesa asked, stepping out onto the patio.

"Just enjoying the stars without all the Taliban fireworks," Walter replied, looking up from the chaise. "Care to join me?"

Thrilled by his invitation, and taking it as a good omen, she settled down beside him. For several minutes, the two lay without talking, the sounds of the warm June evening providing a natural soundtrack. Aleesa felt encouraged, as the non-communication between them felt comfortable and familiar. His phone chimed, breaking the silence.

"It feels good to relax and really enjoy the quiet," he said, ignoring his cell. He knew it was Monica again, and wasn't interested in talking to her or explaining anything to his wife. "That's one of the things I hated most about nights, hell days, too, in Asmar. Even the silence was deafeningly intrusive. You were always waiting for the next mortar round or rocket attack to happen."

Aleesa snuggled closer to him in a show of support; let his words drift into the night air without comment. Since his return, Walter rarely spoke of his war experiences, and she didn't want to say the wrong thing that might cause him to clam up. She wanted him to know that she was always available to listen. Several moments passed without Walt expanding on his comment or sharing any further thoughts. It was Aleesa's voice that broke the silence.

"Baby, we need to talk," she said, before leaning over and giving him a quick kiss on the on the side of his neck. Her words made his body tense slightly. What was it about that phrase that brought out the dread in men?

Walt sighed. "I guess we do," he concurred.

"Baby, I know you've been through a lot—the war, your injury—everything, and I truly understand that it's been very hard on you, but we can't keep avoiding the obvious. You've been home nearly two months and you're still sleeping in the guest room."

"I told you, it's because I have trouble sleeping."

"I understand that, and you have me and your sleep medication to help you on the nights that you can't sleep," she said, repeating verbatim from her mental list. "But we are husband and wife. Sometimes I feel lonelier now than I did when you were in Afghanistan. I need you back in our bed, and if that means losing a little sleep, so be it."

"Okay," he surrendered. The truth is that he missed her terribly as well and was beginning to fear the widening chasm between them, a divide created by his distance.

"And, baby, we haven't made love since you've been back," she said softly, caressing his hand, understanding that she was treading on very sensitive ground. "Sweetheart, I know you're... well...having problems in that area and I want you to know it's okay. I've been doing some research on it and impotence is a very common problem for vets coming back from the war zone."

"I told you, it's temporary," he spoke through a clenched jaw. "The doctors at Walter Reed said that based on my injuries and everything else that it may take a while to be...well...fully functional." Walter could feel his defenses rising. Under the guise of scratching his nose, he withdrew his hand from hers.

"I know, but, well, two things. Even if you aren't fully functional now, we can still make love. If I remember correctly," she said, smiling, "we both have plenty of things in our individual repertoires that don't involve...you know...penetration."

"Walter, I love you so much..." She stopped, not wanting tears to intrude and make him feel guilty.

"And I love you that much back. You believe that, don't you?" Walt asked, his eyes pleading for her to believe him.

"Yes, but, baby, I want to be close to you again so bad that it actually hurts. Please, Walter, can we go inside, to our bed, and make love in whatever configuration it happens? I need you, baby. I need my husband back. Please don't say no to me."

Walter leaned over and kissed his wife with both passion and apology. His tongue spoke volumes, softly licking and nibbling her lips in remorse, before curling into a probe and exploring her warm, wet mouth like he feared his dick would never do again. His mouth on hers felt like heaven and Aleesa did not want it to end. She kissed him back with all the want and gusto she'd been saving all these lonely months.

"Come with me," Aleesa said, breaking their lip lock to request.

She stood up and waited for Walt to get to his feet, and side by side, with his arm draped over her shoulder, the two walked into their bedroom together for the first time since his return. Aleesa broke their hold and walked over to pull the comforter down on the bed.

"What's this?" Walter inquired, lifting up the gift-wrapped package from the foot of the bed.

"Something I've been meaning to give you. Come," she said, patting the bed beside her. "Open it up, and I'll read you a story."

Walter pulled one end of the ribbon, untying the bow, and then quickly tearing away the embossed gift wrap. His eyes went wide as he turned the book in his hand over to reveal its cover. There, entangled in sea of white sheets, her beautiful breasts exposed to the world and with a freshly fucked look on her face, was his wife, snuggled up in a bed he did not recognize.

"What exactly is this, Aleesa?"

His disturbed tone surprised her. This was not the reaction she'd envisioned. Love and lust, not lividity, Aleesa repeated, taking a deep, cleansing breath. "It's my welcome home gift to you," she explained in a light and loving tone. "I imagined us making love so often while you were gone, so I decided to keep a journal of all my fantasies to give to you when you got home.

"Lena suggested I take some boudoir photographs for the cover, so she helped me find a photographer to take them."

"This is a pretty racy photo. It must have been some photo session." Walter felt his jaw clench, a telling sign that his discomfort level was rising.

"Well, we wanted to match the cover to the content," she said, giving him a wink.

"We?" he asked with a raised eyebrow.

Whoa, where was this jealously coming from? She'd never given Walter the slightest reason to be jealous, and he was acting like she'd actually slept with Josiah. Could Walter somehow tell how attracted she'd been to him? Guilt tried to rear its paranoid head, but Aleesa fought it back with Josiah's words. Attraction is not action!

"Josiah Newman, the photographer. A very young guy, very professional and extremely kind and attentive to a nervous old lady like me," she told him, hoping the truth sounded less like the rationalization it felt like.

"Is this in his bedroom?"

"No, silly. It's a studio set. Walter, please."

"Well, I'm sorry, but this is hot as hell and you do look like you just had sex."

"Well, I *didn't*, but that was the point, wasn't it? To look like I did?" she said, trying to maintain her cool. "The reason I look like that, is because…well…I was fantasizing, like I've been doing with all of these stories. We took several different shots and I had them bound into the book. So in between stories, you'll find some sexy photos of your one and only; at least I hope you'll think they're sexy."

"If they're anything like this, I'm sure I will. You look hot as hell, baby, but, uh...shit, it's that...uh...fuck...I'm sorry, Lees. You look amazing, really fucking amazing. Now read me one of these stories."

Grateful that the evening and mood had not been destroyed, Aleesa cracked the freak book and turned to one of her favorite fantasies. She snuggled up against her husband and began to read.

Chapter Eleven

"Hey, baby. I'm just getting home from the Bobbi Blake's annual birthday party/fundraiser. I know it's for a good cause, and I really applaud Bobbi for turning her birthday celebration into a worthy event to help the people of Haiti, but God, it feels like it's the same old party year after year."

"Just so you know, I began each story with a little note explaining my inspiration," she stopped reading to explain.

"Nice touch," Walter replied, curious to see what thoughts had lurked inside the sexual mind of his wife while he'd been gone. He watched her face as she continued reading.

"Same Bobbi, wearing her over-the-top, look at me outfits; same Charles, ignoring his wife and trying to hit on every woman who crosses his path; and the same old folks, who are lovely people but whose conversations never seem to change."

"It does sound like them," Walter mused. "I see nothing much has changed."

Aleesa laughed lightly in response, and continued reading. "*God, I really missed you tonight. It started while I was getting dressed. I was wearing your favorite dress, the multi-toned blue halter that showcases the girls. Because you think I'm sexy in it, I always feel sexy when I'm wearing it. I missed you watching me get dressed so much this evening that I made myself cum in the closet in front of mirror, then I decided to go to the party commando in your honor.*

"*All night I was wanting you, and when you're on my mind, deliciously naughty thoughts can't be far behind. You know, that's one of the things I love most about loving you...you bring out the nasty girl in me. At fifty plus, you still make me feel like a young, hot, happy slut! And in my head, it was the bad girl prowling the party tonight...the one who in real life is happily heterosexual, but in her fantasy life is definitely bi-curious."* Aleesa paused for a moment and gave her husband a sideways look. She noticed a slight raise of his eyebrow, but other than that, it was impossible to gauge his reaction.

PARTY FAVOR

The hired butler for the evening welcomes me and takes my fur coat. I stand in the entryway, looking around and getting my social bearings. As I suspected, it's pretty much the same crowd, all decked out in their cocktail finest, the ladies showing plenty of cleavage for the men, and displaying their latest acquired bling for the ladies. I grab a drink from the waiter circulating with a tray, take a long sip and head out into the crowd of my Black and beautiful peers.

"Aleesa, welcome! Where's Walter?" Bobbi asks, appearing out of nowhere, as only a hostess with the mostess can. She is wearing a revealing black lace cocktail dress that from a distance, makes it look as if she is nude underneath. Just the impact I am sure she is going for.

"He'll be here. We had to take separate cars. He's running late in surgery," I let her know. We briefly exchange compliments and other pleasantries before her near naked self is whisked away to greet more guests.

I nibble my way through the crowd, sampling the tasty appetizers being circulated around the room. Every few feet I pause to exchange hellos with a familiar face. I stop to join the conversation of several women from the gym, but am quickly bored by their talk of young children and nanny issues. I finish my drink, pick up a fresh cocktail, and ramble over to another group who are debating a much more interesting question: Will President Obama go down as one of the greats? I listen as the die-

hard supporters defend his record, citing the insurmountable issues he is up against and the unfair, racially motivated treatment he is receiving, while the Barack detractors decree him a weak-ass, Jimmy Carter clone. The state of politics is depressing, I decide, and part ways without saying a word.

My glass is empty again, and with little food in my stomach, the alcohol has gone straight to my head, and I decide to sit for a while. I purposely claim an out of the way seat so I can enjoy my buzz, do a little people watching and wait for your arrival. It is amazing, the undercover flirting and downright seduction that goes on under the guise of a cocktail party—some between established couples, but an awful lot of it between folks who arrived with someone else on their arm.

My eyes are drawn to a woman in a one-shouldered, white cocktail dress who, without a doubt, puts all the sin in sensational. The white satin material against her bronzed skin is striking, and stands out in the sea of little black dresses littering the room. Her breasts are quite perky, so enthusiastic, in fact, that one is threatening to jump out into the room. The guy she's speaking to can't keep his eyes off of her. I can't blame him. She is absolutely smokin'!

I watch as their bodies say everything their cocktail banter isn't. She keeps playing with the single black pearl dangling between her cleavage and he answers by occasionally licking his top lip and letting the tip of his tongue linger in the corner of his mouth. She touches his arm to make a point, and to protect her as people push to get by, he puts his hand on her lower back, right above the curve of her ass. He leans his body into hers as his free hand quickly brushes against her breasts. I can tell by the look on her face that she feels his now hard dick against her thigh. She must like it because she smirks and leans into it, pelvis first. Once the partiers move along, their contact is broken but the tell-tale signs—her hard nipples poking through her bodice, his quick readjustment to hide his boner—are there.

This scene is making me hot as hell and I'm wishing you were here so I could take you into the bathroom and blow off some of this pent-up lust. She notices me watching and gives me a lip-biting wink of sisterly solidarity. I smile back and raise my glass, a thank you, I suppose, for the peep show. I notice she is missing an earring, and my eyes go to the floor. It's there. Before I can get her attention again, his Mrs. arrives and ends the show with her dirty, territorial glare, sending them all to neutral corners. Pity. I was really getting into it.

"I get up and go over and pick up the earring. I look around the room for its owner, but she's disappeared. I accept another drink from the waiter, my third and last, I promise myself. I'm already on the verge of drunk and I don't want to be asleep on the sofa when you arrive, but I swear, boredom will drive you to drink. Earring in hand, I circulate around the apartment looking for the woman in white. She's nowhere to be found.

I feel the need for air, and step across the room and out onto the balcony. It wraps around their uptown Manhattan apartment, and I travel out to the furthest edge, away from the few outdoor partiers, and into the shimmering white light. The way the city lights hit her satin dress, she looks like an angel, not quite from heaven, but not one of hell's either. Someplace in the middle where hot, sexy women are accepted but also hated and misunderstood, largely because of their scandalously delicious actions.

"Hi," I say, stepping toward her. "I've been looking for you."

She smiles this innocently wicked smile and replies, "That's the nicest thing I've heard all night. I'm Delia."

I smile, feeling a little nervous because it feels like she's flirting with me. And I like it. "Aleesa."

"So why have you been looking for me, Aleesa?"

"You...uh...dropped this," I say, dangling her crystal earring, trying not to notice her protruding nipples, and the tingling effect they were having on mine.

"Wow," she says, touching her hand to her ear. "I didn't even realize it was gone."

I'm pleased that she says nothing about the fact that I'd been watching her every move all night. That would be mortifying.

"I should do something nice for you..."

"Not necessary at all."

"...like give you some great sex."

Every part of my body, sans my feet, takes a jump back. Did my vodka-steeped ears hear what I think they just heard? Did this fabulously hot woman offer me great sex?

"...or at least a thank you kiss," she says as she smiles as she reaches up and runs her finger across my collarbone. With the practiced expertise of a sexual nomad, her lips meet mine with a soft domination that I can neither accept nor resist.

The drunk, curious me overpowers the sober, sensible me, and decides to go with the experience. For me, "intoxicated and willing" translates into "lay back and enjoy" so I assume the attitude and give into the kiss. Her lips are soft and slightly slippery. I taste a hint of mint in her gloss.

Acceptance emboldens Delia. While her lips entertain and distract me, her hands get busy. Starting at the underside of my chin, her fingers take a seductive trek down my neck, over my collarbone, and down through the valley of my breasts. Every nerve ending in the general vicinity is placed on high alert. Delia slides her wandering hand under my dress, cupping the full underside of my breast and giving it a gentle squeeze. As her thumb begins to flick my nipple, I can feel it getting harder and longer. She gives it a pinch, and without my permission, my pelvis pushes toward hers and I release a moan of pleasure into her mouth.

Delia again takes my reaction as an invitation. She pushes me up against the railing. I can hear the sounds of the city below me as she pulls my breasts from their hiding place. She rubs her fingers all around them, avoiding my nipples, which are now aching to be touched and sucked. Delia reads my agitation and smiles as she gives each a whisper stroke with the tip of her finger.

I want to take a handful of her hair and pull her mouth down to my chest, but I am too afraid to move. Delia squeezes my breasts together for closer inspection in the moonlight.

"Your tits are beautiful. Irresisit..," she begins before leaning down and taking both nipples into her mouth. She lightly licks each one of them and then starts to suck, softly at first, first one, then the other. With each tug, my clit begins to bloom, pulling and stretching, looking for attention.

She gives my right nipple a hard pinch and pain mixes with pleasure. I am surprised how much I love the feeling of a woman's soft lips and warm mouth giving me a tongue massage. Delia lifts her eyes to mine, smiling with a mouthful of tit. My breath becomes shorter and deeper as I try to forcefully mute the sounds of arousal and delight.

"You really are a nasty little bitch, aren't you?" she says. "What a slut you are...standing out here with me where anyone can see us, loving all of this titty attention."

Rather than incense me, her accusatory words excite me, and send my clitoris into an explosion of micro-orgasms.

"Touch me," she demands. I take my hand and rub it over the satin bodice, feeling her nipple as hard as mine. I push my hand inside and her stiff, elongated nip gets caught between my fingers. I squeeze it hard, eliciting an excited yelp from her. "Yeah...yeah. That feels fucking nice," she moans. "If I could, I'd rub my hot pussy against your rock hard nipples, until I came all over you, but I can't because, well, this isn't the appropriate place for such things, now is it?" she whispers as she slips her hand down my thigh and up my dress.

"But to thank you for finding my earring," she continues as her feathery caresses come in contact with the dripping moistness between my legs. "Ohh, no panties. You are a slutty little freak, aren't you? I'm going to make you cum right here in front of this nice gentleman," she says with an amused tone as she jams two fingers inside my pussy. My eyes pop open to see who she is talking about.

"Hmmm. That's fucking hot," Walter moans under his breath. His hands reach over and slide between his wife's legs. Aleesa smiled, ecstatic to have him touching her kit cat again. She reached her face toward him and they share a long sexy kiss before Walter pulls away.

"Keep reading."

I see you standing there watching this incredibly sexy woman, finger fucking me on the balcony. As you approach, I search your face, looking for any signs of disapproval or anger, but can only find lustful surprise. Delia, intent on bringing me to orgasm, ignores your presence, and I attempt to do so as well. I am too turned on by my own risqué behavior, and her sheer audacity, to stop. Plus, I am close to bursting and filling her hand with my own brand of nookie lube, so my eyes implore you to wait.

"Nookie lube?" Walter asked with an amused chuckle.

"Shut up...mmm...you have no idea how hard it is to think of names for all of this stuff," Aleesa explained, loving the feel of her slick vagina. "Now shall I go on?"

You and I lock gazes and they stay connected as Delia's hand, palm up, pumps my coochie with two fingers while her thumb rubs my swollen nib. I lean further into the railing, ignoring the hard metal digging into my back, and spread my legs wider so she can get a better angle. Delia pushes her hand deeper inside me and, with the other, reaches up and pinches my nipple hard. I pump her hand faster and harder until I feel it begin—the tingle that starts in the middle of my pleasure center and radiates out across my pelvis, hips and thighs. I can't contain the clipped yelping sounds that announce the arrival of my orgasm. My body clutches as I ride the pleasure to its very end.

Delia pulls her fingers from inside me and with a face beaming with a predator's satisfaction, licks away my nectar.

"My turn," you say. We both look at you with blank faces. "Stand right there; don't move." You issue your command with an officer's authority. You trade places with Delia, using her to shield us from any eyes that may venture out onto the balcony.

She complies, putting her hand between her own legs as you pull your dick out and put it between mine. With one feverish thrust you slide inside my fired up and frenzied hole. I can hear Delia's breath become rapid and shallow as she rubs the heel of her palm against her mound to get herself off. Her moans mingle with your grunts and your combined noises create a sexy symphony that drives the level of my lust into overdrive. I clench my vag muscles down on your dick, grab your ass cheeks and push you deeper into me.

"Oh yeah, fuck that slut," Delia hisses, as she make herself come under the stars.

I have to admit that I'm loving the shit out of all of this—the exhibitionism, the risk, the bi-curiousness of it all. It sets me off in a fucking frenzy and I buck up against you wildly as you pump me harder and faster.

'I love you, baby,' I say because it's what's on my mind and also as a prelude to an apology. You answer with a long grunt released through closed teeth. Your ass clenches and your body goes stiff as I feel you grow, swell, tighten and then burst inside me.

We collapse against each other and, for several sweet seconds, bask in the moonlight before we straighten up and steel ourselves to rejoin the party. Delia has already started back inside. We both watch her sexy ass strut until she is out of sight, and then burst into laughter.

"The end," Aleesa said, closing the book and covering his mouth with hers.

"You've got talent," Walt murmured in her mouth, as he felt his dick show signs of life. In one quick swoop, he flipped Aleesa onto her back, their faces still connected. He clumsily tussled with his pants with one hand until he was able to free his cock and shove it into his wife's greedy pussy.

"Omigod, I love you so much, baby," she told him. "Only you."

He ground his pelvis into hers and rocked back and forth. Walt fucked his wife for nearly a minute before her words made him go limp. Aleesa could feel the drop in his energy, but continued to hump him, hoping to bring his dick back to life. She reached down and tickled his balls, knowing his sac to be a prime pleasure spot, but not even that revived him.

He rolled off of her in silence, a look of defeat and humiliation painting his face.

"It's okay, baby. Really, it's okay. Look, we can use this," she said, rolling over and pulling Buzz Lightyear from the nightstand drawer. She was not prepared for his reaction.

"I'm not using some plastic dick to fuck my wife!" he screamed, pulling up his pants and moving off the bed. "And what do you think you were doing anyway? While I was in Afghanistan seeing people get killed every day, you were sitting around writing porn? Where did you learn to write this shit?"

"I took a class on erotic storytelling. And it's not porn. I thought you'd get a kick out of hearing about my fantasies, even though you weren't here."

"Why do you think I'd want to read about other people screwing my wife when I ca…couldn't? And then you decide to embarrass me by reading it to me, knowing that I…that my…"

"Every single one of them includes you. Read them, you'll see. You're in every story.

"I'm sorry, Walter. I wasn't trying to embarrass you. I wrote down all my fantasies so you'd know how much you were missed, so you'd know that you were with me and I was always thinking about you."

His angry silence was earsplitting.

"Why are you reacting like this?"

"I'm going to bed," he said, ignoring her question and walking out of the room.

ALEESA TURNED OVER ON HER SIDE, HER FACE TO THE WALL. Her body jerked slightly, responding to the sound of the guest room door slamming. The tears of frustration began slowly until they were joined by confusion, humiliation and guilt, causing the dam to break. When she broke it all down, she was able to understand all of the emotions running through her head and heart, all but the guilt. What had she done to feel guilty? Everything she'd done was because she loved and desired Walt. Why should she feel bad because she wanted and needed her husband in every possible way? Sex was supposed to be the thing that brought and kept life partners together. Why did it feel like her desire was tearing them apart? She lay on the bed sobbing, not knowing what to say or do next to help her husband, and turn her marriage around, which by every indication, felt like it was sinking fast.

Aleesa cried until there were no more tears to shed. And then she got mad. Okay, he had a problem. But it had become her problem, too, and he didn't get to freeze her out. And he didn't get decide when and if he got help. Walter needed to get counseling and medical attention. He didn't get to sit around wishing his impotence away. He needed to be proactive about getting better. And until he did, he didn't get to make her feel bad about feeling like any wife had the right.

She got out of bed, pulled on her robe, and marched across the hall to the guest room. Hers was a message that needed to be sent. Shit, she was tired of waiting and hoping. It was time that they both looked this problem squarely in the eye, and deal with it.

"Walter, I am not going to apologize for wanting to have sex with my husband," she declared, barging in without knocking, "and you need to find a way to work through this if you want to... OMIGOD!" Aleesa stood in the threshold, her eyes not believing what she was seeing. Walter, the husband who could not, or apparently would not make love to her, was in the bed loving his damn self. She'd caught him, with his hard dick in hand, beating off.

"Omigod, you bastard," she swore at him for the first time in their marriage.

Walter pulled his hand away, and looked at his wife with shame and pain-riddled eyes. "I, uh...Lees..."

"Shut up! Not even Bill made me feel as inadequate, rejected, and lonely as you have these past few weeks," she told him as the tears began to flow. "I never thought these words would leave my mouth, but I hate you right now. I can't even look at you."

"Lees...wait!" he called out after her.

Before the tears turned once again into hysterical sobs, she turned and retreated back into the master bedroom, slamming and locking the door in his face. Feeling spent and exhausted, she took one of Walt's sleeping pills in order to shut down her thoughts and fade into black for the night. She crawled back into bed, waiting for the medication to take effect. She was more confused and angry than ever. Walter had walked out on the real thing, only to take refuge in the privacy of another room so he could jack the fuck off? She didn't know what to think anymore. The only thing she did know was that, for the first time since she and Walter had set up a home together, she didn't want to be here.

She decided to do one last thing before sleep graciously allowed her an escape. She dialed Lena's number, only to get voice mail. "I'm in. It appears that I am in desperate need of a getaway. It's my turn to have a pity party."

Chapter Twelve

"I hate to say it cuz it feels like I'm cheatin' on my man, but Rory McIlroy is probably better than Tiger was at his age. He's nineteen and already ranked number seven in the world. He's going to dominate in a few years, especially if Tiger doesn't get his act together soon," Soup said, as the two sat in his favorite neighborhood sports bar watching the British Open.

"Hmm…" was Walter's only reply as he sipped his third Bass Ale. Drinking was his sorry attempt to drown his sorrows, but rather than help sink his troubles, the alcohol had kept them floating at the top.

"Okay, you're definitely not into the golf, even though it was *your* idea to come here. So what do you wanna do, man? Talk about it or sit here in silence and get drunk? I mean, either is fine with me, but know that if you do get shit-faced, I'm sending your ass home in a cab. I am not trying to feel the wrath of your wife for bringing you home drunk again."

"She's in San Francisco."

"Well, then drink up."

"She gave me a book. A book of stories she'd been keeping all the time I was away. It was my homecoming gift."

"That was thoughtful."

"Even took a writing class…"

"To keep a journal?" Soup asked, as his eyes watched McIlroy sink a thirty-foot putt, while his brain tried to figure out where his friend's conversation was going.

"She said it was her way of keeping me close to her," Walt said, his reply not driven by Soup's question, but rather thoughts playing ping-pong in his head.

"I can see that. So what's the problem, cuz you definitely sound like there's some sort of problem?"

"It was basically a book of all her sexual fantasies."

"Damn, now *that's* a gift! The only thing that could beat that are videos."

"She said that every time she thought of making love while I was away, she'd let her imagination go and then write everything down. Then she bound them all in a book with a bunch of sexy photographs."

"I repeat, what's the problem?" Charlie asked, surprised by Walt's reaction. "It was all for you, right? She didn't publish them on the Internet or anything. I mean, were they twisted or crazy freaky or something?"

"Hell, if I know. I saw the cover. She was laid out naked on some bed, looking like somebody had fucked her brains out. She read me one story and then all hell broke loose. I haven't picked it up again."

"Really?"

"Well, why the hell do I want to hear about her fantasies about fucking while I was in some fly-infested hell hole, shitting in an oil drum, and watching people die around me?"

"And you really thought she had this in mind when she put it together?"

"Probably not, but…"

"Probably not? You know Aleesa better than that. You know damn well that she only had love in her heart when she was doing all this. You need to finish reading that book."

"You're right," Walter conceded.

"You've got a damn good woman, bro."

"I know."

"So then, who and what are you really pissed at?"

Their conversation ceased as the sound of the crowd roared through the sports bar. The two friends watched the replay of Fred Couples shooting an eagle, bringing him to the top of the leaderboard. Walter took a couple of healthy swigs of beer while he let Soup's question brew in his head. His boy knew him too well to believe that Aleesa's actions were at the crux of his anxiety.

"I can't make love to my own wife," Walter admitted.

"You don't want to or can't?"

"Can't."

"Oh shit." The both took a pause as the enormity of Walt's confession sunk in.

"So, your dick won't get hard at all?"

"Semi, and not for long."

"So, I guess you're still hanging out in the guest room?"

"Yeah, but she wants me to move back into our bedroom. I told her I sleep in the other room because of the nightmares and shit, but that's really only a half-truth. I don't sleep with her because a few weeks ago, I started getting hard in my sleep."

"Okay, I'm confused. Wouldn't gettin' a woody at night be a good thing?"

"According to my doctor, it's a good sign. It means that physically things are working normal again. But every time I'm with her it won't get hard or if it does, I can't stay hard, which means..."

"It's a head thing, not a dick thing."

"Yep. So now, I'm trying to avoid having sex with her. It's too frustrating and we both end up pissed off."

"You've been through a lot. Stress will damn sure keep a dick soft," Soup offered, trying to support his boy.

"It's like a fucking Catch-22. Instead of making love to my wife being a relaxed, good time, it's now a fucking test of wills—me against my goddamn dick. It used to be that getting an erection was automatic; now it's a job and one I never know if I can do. And the really fucked-up thing is the harder I try, the softer it gets."

"I feel all fucked up," Walt interrupted. "Between the nightmare in Asmar; getting a back full of shrapnel, the surgery and physical therapy that followed; and then coming home to half a dental practice but a full array of bills, thank God Aleesa is working; things are rough. Trying to go on with a normal life when nothing about it seems normal anymore is taking its toll big time. And now I can't even get it up…"

Walter spoke without pause. Now that he'd finally given voice to his fears, discussion had given way to the need to purge. Charlie sat back and let his boy talk, empathizing with the depressing situation his friend found himself in. War was such an 'out of sight, out of mind' event for most Americans. People had no idea what a toll war injuries took on the mind and body of both the veterans and the folks that loved them.

"Aleesa's always touching and groping on me. Last week she actually *demanded* sex. I tried, but…it didn't happen. And then… later, she caught me beating off."

"So wait a minute. You can choke the chicken, but can't fuck your wife? Dog, that's not good."

"No shit. Masturbating is all good. There's no tension. No performance anxiety. No 'can I or can't I' involved. Charlie, I'm afraid if I keep screwing up, she'll walk. She already left town out of the blue with her girls. But how long before she leaves for good? Before she left, she told me that if I wanted to stay married, I needed to go talk with somebody."

"Somehow I don't think she meant me," Soup said, cracking a

smile. "But, she may have a point. Unless you want to keep living like this, you need to find out what's wrong so you can fix it."

"I know what's wrong, and I can't fix it."

"What are you talking about?"

"All the other crap—my injuries, the practice, the bills—that will all work itself out. The only thing that I can't make right is that I cheated on Aleesa. It's the one thing I promised her that I would *never* do, and I had every intention of keeping my promise. But I had one moment of weakness, and fucked everything up."

"Man, pussy has been many a great man's downfall. Hey, if you couldn't resist it, it had to be some serious poontang."

"It wasn't like that," Walter said. "I..." his words were interrupted by his ringing phone. Soup turned his attention back to the British Open while his friend picked up.

"Hello?...Are you okay?...It's really not a good time, I'm...Calm down, I know it's hard. I think about it a lot, too...I don't know when...um...it's tough...Maybe you need to talk with someone... No, I mean, a professional. If it's bothering you this much, you need more than a friend...I know...I don't know if I'll ever be the same my damn self...Okay, I have to go...I'm out...I'll try to call you soon...Okay, take care."

"That was her? Miss It Wasn't Like That?" Soup asked.

"Yeah. Monica."

"So, I don't get it. You're still fucking her? Is that why you can't fuck your wife?"

"No! It's not like that, but it's part of it."

"Then you need to explain to me what it is like, cuz, man, I am not getting it."

"It was one time. The night I lost my team." Walter took the next few moments to break down exactly what had happened that one sad, lonely night between Monica and him. Walt made it as clear as he possibly could that their sexual union had nothing to do with sex or love or even lust. It had been about one thing only—survival.

"What does she want from you?"

"She still calls and texts, mainly to talk about what happened. Not the sex so much but all the gruesome shit that went down. She doesn't have anyone else. She hadn't been married long when she got shipped over, and her asshole husband left her when she got back. She's more messed up than I am. I can't tell her to leave me alone. And I don't know that I want her to. That shit was no joke, Charlie. Monica's the only person who can understand what I went through. And so, I feel like I'm sneaking around talking to her like I'm having an affair, when it's not like that at all.

"It's so crazy, Soup. I feel sometimes like me getting injured was karma coming back to even the score."

"Okay, that's the beer talking. Look, man, don't let guilt eat at you like that. Sometimes what's wrong or right isn't that black or white."

"I feel guilty as hell. Every time Aleesa gets near me and tells me how much she loves me, it kills me."

"Walt, you got caught up in an extraordinary situation. I think that not only would Aleesa forgive you, she'd understand. Maybe not immediately, but eventually she'd know in her heart that you did not really cheat on her."

"But I did. No matter the reason. I had sex with another woman."

"Then tell her. If guilt is keeping your dick soft, it's time to come clean. Sometimes a man's gotta be a man and confess to his fuck ups."

"But that's the thing, I can't tell Aleesa I cheated because it will be the end of our marriage. It's the one thing she'll never forgive me for—not after everything she went through with Bill."

"Okay, but you're not Bill."

"Which is why I should have known better."

"Well, you need to do something. Your nuts are in a vice here, bro. If it's status quo versus the truth, sounds like everybody loses. You need to come up with a new, winning game plan."

WALTER WALKED INTO THE EMPTY HOUSE, MISSING HIS WIFE WHILE at the same time relieved to have a few days without the pressure that seemed to squeeze his heart 24/7. Her absence would give him some much needed time to come up with a solution to this disconcerting dilemma. Soup was right on two points, he and Aleesa truly loved each other, and theirs was a marriage definitely worth saving. He was also spot-on in recognizing that their relationship was dying a slow, agonizing death, and he was the one suffocating their love. Walt was terrified that if he didn't do something soon, he was going to lose her.

He wandered back into the master bedroom, feeling the presence of his wife in every nook and cranny. Other than the framed photos of the two of them scattered around the room, this did not look nor feel like the bastion of love and comfort he'd left two years ago. True, Aleesa had redecorated, but the change in décor wasn't what made the difference. The energy was different. The familiar now seemed foreign and Walt felt like a visitor. Was it because he'd been away so long and life in this room had simply gone on without him, or was guilt stealing his joy and making him feel like a stranger in his own bedroom?

Walter sat down on the bed and ran his hand across the silk duvet. So much great lovemaking had happened in this bed over the years. He could only pray that it would resume and soon. But the truth remained, until he could reconcile his guilt and disappointment with himself and his actions, nothing would be right between them again.

He fell back onto the bed, his eyes glued to the ceiling above him, searching for clues and he prayed for an epiphany. But the thoughts filling his head were of her—Monica—his hygienist, fellow soldier, and one-night affair that now threatened his life with the only lover he did not want to live life without. What he and Monica had shared that night was life-affirming and had been a much-needed distraction from all of the carnage happening around them, but it came nowhere close to the lifesaving grace his wife had been to him these past fifteen years. And as much as he and Monica had needed each other that one night, it could not compete with a lifetime of what he had and wanted to continue to have with Aleesa.

He was caught up in such a dilemma. Not telling Aleesa about his indiscretion was taking a terrible toll on his libido and sexual function. If he assuaged his culpability by telling her the truth— that he'd slept with Monica while they were in Afghanistan— perhaps it would be the psychological break necessary for him to shake the guilt and free his mind enough to be able to make love to his wife, but it would be all for naught. Walt had broken both of the promises he'd made to Aleesa that she'd never be able to get over; first the betrayal, and second the lies.

His eye caught the glossy photograph gracing the cover of his gift. Walt reached over and picked up the tome, taking time to really admire the image of his wife. She was such a beautiful woman, and even in this highly sexed image, her classy core shone through. He flipped past the pages featuring *Party Favor*, the story she'd read aloud to him, landing on yet another photo. Her body looked fantastic stretched out on a fur rug, wearing red lace lingerie and a long string of pearls. The come-hither look in her eyes drew him in, leaving him longing for the days and nights when that same look, given in person, had him scrambling to remove his clothes and jump her bones. But those times seemed a long way away.

Walter turned the page and began to read. Perhaps her words could accomplish what her touch could not.

My Sexy Colonel,

One of the interesting changes that I've had to make since you've been gone is taking control and responsibility for our life together. For the past fifteen years, I've been so used to you being the officer-in-charge, so to speak, a job that you've done with great flourish and aplomb. I've never been better taken care of, better loved, and yes, better fucked than since we've been married. I always feel safe and secure knowing that you love me. I love that you're a take-charge kind of guy, and now by default, I've become much more of a take-charge kind of girl.

Aleesa's diary of thoughts hugged his heart. How had he allowed himself to betray her? Why hadn't he been stronger? Been the man she believed him to be? "I'm so sorry, Aleesa. So very sorry," he turned back to the photo to tell her.

And one of the fantasies I've been having since you've been away is me taking complete control of you. So this one I call, "Control," and it involves you, me and the other love of your life, Lucy, who, like me (well, almost as much), is sitting around eagerly waiting for you to take her for the ride of her life! Enjoy, my love.

Control

You're in the garage polishing up that classic Benz, and I come out dressed in your camouflage jacket and heels. You ask me what I want, and I don't answer in words, but instead open the jacket wide and flash you. When you see that, but for a silk scarf draped around my neck, I am totally naked underneath the coat, you move toward me, but I stop you.

Of course, you begin to protest, but I tell you if you want to see more, you'll have to sit down in the lawn chair. My tease has piqued your interest, and happily you comply. You sit down, your greedy hands still reaching for my body. I slap them away and warn you that if you don't follow orders, you won't see what else I have in store for you. Naturally, curiosity wins and you sit down, smiling nervously, but not protesting one bit as I tie your hands to the chair with the neckties in my pocket.

Once you're all tied up and secure, I climb onto Lucy's hood and lay out, you know like that famous poster of the girl on the Porsche. Totally ignoring your presence, I slowly remove the jacket and then start playing with my breasts—lifting them up and squeezing them together. I push them up to meet my mouth and tongue down my own nipples. This, of course, gets a big reaction, and I hear you groaning. It's a sound that really turns me on, and just to mess with you, I reprimand you for looking at me and demand that you close your eyes.

You do, but we both know it's not for long, because as soon as I let out a big moan, they pop open and you watch me begin to explore the rest of me, running my hands over my body while pretending they are yours. I pull on end of the scarf, enjoying its satiny caress across my neck. A slow and seductive "ooh" escapes my lips as I pull the fabric across my nips, feeling them grow and stiffen. I continue this most pleasurable journey down my torso, waking up every nerve ending and pleasure point along the way. I spread my legs and pull the scarf to and fro, seducing my vagina with silken strokes. She responds by puffing up with lust. When I can't stand it anymore, I begin masturbating in front of you, opening my pussy wide so you can see, knowing that you're looking, even though I've told you not to.

"Yeah, stroke that kit cat. Make Clitina hard and hungry," you say, using your nicknames for my vagina and clit.

"Shut up!" Through smiling lips, I yell at you for having the audacity to not only watch me pleasure myself, but to speak about it.

This time, as punishment, I slip off the car and come over and tie the scarf over your eyes. You take in a deep breath, savoring the scent of my sex in the fabric. You protest and beg me to let you watch, but I won't allow it. I tell you that if you say another word without being spoken to first, I will stop and go inside.

I stand in front of you naked and wearing heels, rubbing and tugging and finger fucking myself into a 'she's gotta have it' state, all the while moaning, groaning and letting all the filthy words you love to hear me say stream from my mouth. I notice the crotch of your pants twitch, a telltale sign that you know how hot and horny I'm getting and are feeling the same. As wafts of my feminine scent rise and linger under your nose, I can see you're going crazy, squirming in your seat.

"Please, baby, take off this fucking scarf. Let me watch. Please, baby, don't do this. Don't torture me like this."

"Quiet!" *I command, and to make you suffer even more, I take my wet fingers and paint your lips with my kit cat juice.* "Stop talking or I won't let you taste any more of this," *I warn as I give you a real taste by sticking my finger between your lips.*

You are so relieved to do something with your mouth that you suck my finger hard, almost like a dick, and with each pull of my digit, I feel Clitina getting longer and harder. Teasing you like this is so damn stimulating. I am creaming up and getting so hot, and it's hard not to continue without making you a more active participant. My body is dying to be ravished by you, but I refuse to give up control. Not yet.

I pull my finger from your mouth and replace it with my titty. You suck on that hard just like you know how to do. As it's been trained to do by years of practice, my clit responds by twitching and quivering, and my pussy is going crazy, standing there with nothing petting it. So I pull away, urgently undo your pants and pull them down around your ankles. Your dick expectantly springs to attention, thinking he's about to get dipped, but I'm not ready to stop my cock tease and give up the coochie yet. Instead, I spread your knees and straddle your leg so I can rub up against it. I grind my clit up against that deliciously hard thigh muscle of yours. You moan loud and long as you feel my juices drip down your leg. I watch your face contort with lustful agony. To tantalize you more, I remove the blindfold so you can see what is making both of us so frenzied.

The briny smell of wet sex is permeating the garage air. As I ride faster on your leg to increase the friction, you have this look on your face that is a mix of wild lust, surprise and love. You bend down and hungrily consume my breast again, this time leaving hickey marks all around it. I scream because it hurts, but in a really good way.

"Touch my dick, baby," you beg me, despite your full mouth. I look down, see it standing tall, twitching, and waiting for some loving. The sight of your cock excites me and beckons my mouth closer. I consider stopping you so I can treat my tongue to the pleasure of your big chocolate rod, but all your sucking and biting combined with the twat rubbing, fires a rocket in my crotch and I detonate all over your leg—convulsing, bucking and unleashing a litany of profanity, before falling against your body.

As I am recovering, you, resourceful soldier that you are, manage to loosen the ties around your arms. Springing from the chair, you pick me up and toss me back gently on to the hood of the car. Within seconds, you have turned the table, tying my wrists together and pushing my arms over my head. I can feel your hard heat mesh with my wet warmth to produce a white hot coupling.

"Whose pussy is this?" you demand to know as you proceed to lovefuck me with a surprising wildness.

"It's your pussy, baby. Always yours."

"Then give me my pussy. Give me my pussy!" you repeat, roughly pounding my kit cat while brushing your dick up against Clitina until I come hard again and she begins to pulsate in ever intensifying waves around your cock. My twitches set off yours, and you pull out of my coochie, spraying me and Lucy with your jism. We collapse on the hood, *both having totally lost control, but loving every minute of it and each other.*

I miss you, baby. I'm feeling so out of control without you here. Be safe and please hurry home.

Walter closed the book and kissed the image of Aleesa on the front. He closed his eyes, willing sleep to come and the nightmares to stay away.

Chapter Thirteen

"Seven a.m.," Livia called out, while knocking nonstop on Aleesa's room door.

"Time to rise and shine," Lena chimed in.

"Okay, okay. I'm up," Aleesa said, shuffling over to open the door. "I should call hotel security and have you two hoodlums bounced."

"We're hitting the road in twenty minutes. Be downstairs or keep your tired self here while we go hang in Carmel," Lena informed her. "But trust me, there's a lot going on there that you won't want to miss—great shopping, a picnic on the beach, art galleries to browse…"

"So get up. We're going down to the restaurant to have coffee," Livia said. "See you downstairs."

Aleesa shut the door and headed back to the bathroom to finish applying her makeup. She was torn about what to do today—take a road trip with her girls or stay at the hotel and sulk about the sorry state of her marriage. San Francisco, with its foggy, overcast sky and chilled morning air, provided the perfect weather for staying in her room with the privacy sign on the door, and having a woe is me fest.

She'd been on the West Coast for three days now, and other than a quick call in the middle of the night to let Walter know she'd arrived safely, she hadn't spoken to her husband. With the time difference, combined with days and nights spent sightseeing with Livia and satisfying her tourist fix, Aleesa hadn't had a chance.

The two had resorted to brief text messages, which proved to be more about making a courtesy connection than a true marital one. Lena, espousing the absence makes the heart grow fonder theory, thought minimal contact was a good idea, but Aleesa had had enough of both absence and abstinence when it came to her husband.

"Let it go, Lees," she told herself in the mirror. "The sun is going to eventually come out and burn off all this fog, and then what? Go have fun."

Thirty minutes later, she was in the car, stretched out in the backseat, singing along with the best of Bay Area natives, Frankie Beverly and Maze. Livia was in the front seat while Lena drove them south on Highway 1, toward the lovely California hot spots of Carmel and Monterey. They drove California-style, with the top down and the heat up, enjoying the scenic coastal route.

"This is probably the most beautiful place I've ever been!" Livia shouted through the cool morning breeze so her friends could hear her. "If I wasn't so afraid of earthquakes, I could live here!"

"Girl, listen to you. You're scared of dating, scared of sex, and now scared of earthquakes. You are absolutely, without question, the most talented punk I know," Lena teased her.

"Don't talk about my cousin like that," Aleesa threw in, chuckling. "She's no punk—a chicken shit, maybe, but certainly not a punk!"

"First of all, anybody in their right mind would be afraid of earthquakes," Livia defended herself. "And if you two weren't so crazy in lust, you'd be a little bit scared of sex, too. You do know that the fastest growing HIV population is women over fifty."

"Well, speak for yourself. I'm only forty-three years old, and I always play it safe."

"And I am the poster child of safe. I'm in a committed relationship which, at the moment, is sexless," Aleesa interjected, trying to keep her voice lighthearted and upbeat.

"Like most marriages in America," Livia threw in for support. "But yours is only temporary."

"From your mouth to God's ears," Aleesa said, giving her backseat thoughts a voice. "By the way, did I mention that Walter *can* get erection? I've seen it. I caught him masturbating."

"How can you masturbate if you have limp dick syndrome?" Lena inquired.

"Apparently it's quite common with someone with ED. The more cogent point is that his interest in sex, along with a hard dick, seems to disappear when he's around me. I'm beginning to think that he doesn't find me attractive anymore and is using this post-injury impotence thing as an excuse."

"Cousin, I don't think that's the case at all. I think that he's still dealing with his war wounds."

"His legs are fine now."

"I do believe that she's talking about the scars you can't see," Lena added gently.

"I get that and I'm trying to meet him in the middle but he's not giving up any ground. We can't even hug or cuddle because if I touch him the wrong way, he thinks it's going to lead to sex, and then he blows up. And then everything becomes my fault."

"Sounds like the typical husband," Lena commented.

"But Walter was never typical. He's always been heads and shoulders above typical. That's why his 'best defense is a good offense' crap is befuddling. I'd expect that from Bill, not Walt."

"Lees, we've talked about this before," Livia said. "I think Walter wants to, but isn't able to live up to his old superman image anymore. Things change. He's changed, but you're expecting everything to be the same."

"Yeah, I've thought about that. But what if he doesn't love me anymore? What if in the two years he's been away, he's fallen out of love with me?"

"You didn't feel that way when he surprised you in Puerto Rico," Lena said. "And that was less than nine months ago. So, you can cross Walter *not* loving you off your worries list."

"Okay, so if he loves me, why doesn't he want to have sex with me?"

"I'd bet my bakery that's not the case at all. I'd say it's more that he loves you and needs to work through some demons so he can have sex with you again," Livia said.

"I'm with Liv on this one. Walt has never struck me as anything but a one-woman man, and you—Mrs. Davis—are that one woman," Lena interjected.

"And what do I do in the meantime? I want to feel sexy and hot again. But, now I feel old and undesirable."

"You might have to DIY for a while longer. Maybe it's time to get Buzz Lightyear a playmate, a pet rabbit maybe," Lena suggested, only half-joking.

"When's the last time you felt like that—you know, sexy and hot?" Livia asked. "Go back to that time and hold on to it for dear life until it becomes your reality again."

"Josiah and the photo shoot," she said quietly into the wind so the others wouldn't hear.

"What?" Livia said, turning down the music.

"I said attraction is not action," Aleesa told them.

"No, not unless you make it so," Lena replied, blasting the music again, leaving Aleesa wondering if she was suggesting what she thought she was, or was it simply her own mind floating the unthinkable to the forefront?

While the others tried unsuccessfully to sing harmony on "Sunshine and Rain," Aleesa leaned back into the soft leather seats. Her head was spinning. She had so much on her mind, so many questions that she wanted immediate answers to. She needed to speak with Walter while it was all fresh on her mind, but now wasn't an option. So she did the next best thing; pulled out her phone and sent him an email.

THE PICTURES MADE HIM LAUGH. NOT BECAUSE THEY WERE funny, but because they were hell of clever. Aleesa looked like the perfect snack, sitting naked in a bathtub full of all that popcorn with a licorice whip in her mouth. His wife was sexy and funny, and he loved the hell out of her.

Looking closer at the picture, he had to give big props to this photographer. While friendly and outgoing, Walt had never known his wife to be an exhibitionist. This camera man had managed to pull from her a side that, even after all of these years of marriage, he had never seen.

A sharp stab of jealousy pierced his psyche. Who the fuck was this guy? And how had this stranger managed to reach his wife in a place that he, even when times were great between them, had not? What had he said to her? Done to her? Where had he touched her, emotionally, spiritually and God forbid physically to evoke such a natural state of eroticism within her? How well did this photographer get to know his wife? Did Aleesa fuck him?

Walter closed his eyes tight, trying to squeeze out the ridiculously jealous thoughts overtaking his mind. His own guilt was turning him into a jealous lunatic. If there was one thing he could bet his life on, it was the fact that his wife would never cheat on him. Aleesa loved him. This fact he knew. This fact he need not ever question.

This true knowledge about his wife calmed him. For this reason, Walter pushed away thoughts that his intense love for Aleesa had not kept him from putting his dick in another woman.

"Extenuating circumstances, extenuating circumstances," Walt repeated to himself, trying to justify his wrong with the wrongs of war.

Pushing all thoughts from his brain, he opened his eyes again and turned the page to *Aqua Boink*. Hopefully, it would be the perfect story to get his morning started.

Dear Walt,

Today I am in Phoenix for that broadcasters' conference I emailed you about. Everybody is out at some cocktail party, but I wanted to come back to my room, think about you, and share the thoughts that occupy my downtime while I am here without you.

Sweetie, you would absolutely love this hotel. It's nestled into Camelback Mountain, and is absolutely spectacular. The desert really has an austere beauty that is unmatchable and just as beautiful as any garden, once you take the time to really look at it. There's a reason they call it Paradise Valley. We are so coming back here together when you are stateside again. I really want to share this with you.

My sexy thoughts are influenced not just by all of the natural beauty surrounding me, but my casita as well, which is laid out a lot like a New York apartment. Darling, believe me when I say this suite was built for some seriously sensuous lovemaking! It has a living area with a fireplace and wet bar, and a patio that looks out into the Arizona mountains. The bedroom shares the patio on one end and then you walk back through a huge dressing room and bathroom out into a walled terrace, complete with a chaise and soaking tub for two. Very private. Very sexy. Perfect for some very hot outdoor lovin'!

Reading those words made his jaw tense. Walt exhaled loudly through his clenched teeth, filling the room with a bittersweet hiss, as he continued reading.

You know how whenever there's a full moon, I'm always asking you to dance naked with me in the moonlight? Well, right now, I'm outside, moon-bathing naked under the stars, missing you and thinking about all of the lovely, nasty things I could be doing to you under that full moon!

Hmm...Okay, I'm closing my eyes to bring you here with me...

"Dancing naked in the moonlight," he said to himself, smiling at the memory. Every month, they'd strip down and dance in the light of the full moon dripping through their bedroom window. It was silly, but was another reason why he loved that woman so.

Walt stopped reading for a moment, once again touched by how Aleesa had included all of her thoughts about him with her fantasies. She had been absolutely right. This was indeed the perfect gift and let him know how deeply she missed and loved him. It was a loving, thoughtful, sexy gesture and he was a total ass for ruining it for her. "Add that to the guilt list, you stupid motherfucker," he told himself before continuing.

Aqua Boink

The October night is absolutely perfection. The Arizona air is warm and dry. I decide to take a soak in the tub outside while you are at the gym working out that fine and sexy body of yours. I grab the bottle of champagne and two glasses from the bar and place them tubside. I run back into the suite for my iPod and speakers. In the mood for some seductive Spanish guitar music, I turn on that album you bought me. I light the candles out on the terrace and pour bath oil into the running water. As the heat hits the oil, the scent of lavender rises from the water and permeates the air. I take in a deep breath, convinced that I am in heaven.

I feel like I am in a movie as I untie my robe, let it slip off my shoulders, fall to the floor and pool on the tile in a puddle of white terry cloth. I don't know why, but that simple move makes me feel sexy as hell. Of course, you come to mind. Teeth capture my lower lip as my hands do what yours would, slide across my breasts, pushing them together and tweaking my nipples before drifting down my stomach, combing through my newly trimmed kit cat, and finger kissing my tender inner thighs. A sigh escapes my lips as I telepathically will you back to me so you can do your husbandly duty and fuck me 'til the stars in the sky become one with those in my eyes.

I dip my toe into the tub and a liquid flame shimmies up my leg. I slowly submerge myself, letting the combination of hot, silky water and lavender smells seduce the fret from my frame, and allow calm to seep in. I quickly down a glass of champagne and pour another. I am so in the mood for some sexy languishing tonight.

I lean back against the porcelain curve of the tub as the steamy water relaxes every inch of my body except its sex center. Heat envelops my lower lips, and the oh, so pleasurable burn intensifies as I spread my legs and let the warmth tickle my coochie.

I look up into the night sky, drinking champagne, wishing on a star that you will immediately walk through the door. My desire is intense, but tonight I am not interested in fast, furious passion. I want to love you lazily. I want slow and romantic lovemaking that pays homage to the beauty of this gorgeous fall night. Love pulls at my heart and a surge of want forces my eyes shut and my hands to reach out and fill themselves with oil. My right hand starts tracing slow, sexy circles around my breasts, and now hard and protruding nipples, as the left replicates the slick moves across my belly and down my thighs. My hips rise to meet sneaky fingers that slip past the prickly hedge and into the soft, warm folds of my pussy.

I rub for a moment, tracing the same circles, now tinier in scope, across the inner folds of my labia and up towards the hooded nib. Like a deejay's scratching, tiny circles turn into back and forth gyrations, as I attempt to make my clit sing. She begins to hum, but the water blocks my natural lube, detrimentally affecting my ability to stroke myself from a pleasant R & B hook to the serious, off the chart jazz riff I am craving.

Frustrated but determined, I open my eyes in search of a solution. My eyes skim past the bottle of lavender oil and come to rest on the handheld shower massager. A huge smile traipses across my face as the solution to my problem becomes clear.

I pull myself from the water and sit on the side of the tube. I finish another glass of the bubbly and my head is pleasantly dizzy. I turn on the faucet, adjusting the flow so it becomes one firm, solid column of water. After applying a dab of bath oil, I tease my clit with a slippery rub and thoughts of you licking me. My free hand reaches up to pinch my nipples hard, releasing a spasm of painful pleasure. As the pressure begins to build, I stand and pick up the handheld, holding the strong surging water over my kit cat. My hips move forward to greet the warm hard snake of water, trying to drink up the pleasure as the vibrations from the rushing water stimulate my vag lips. I momentarily freeze, enjoying the quivering kiss of vibrating delight. Lifting my torso ever so slightly allows the heat to sneak in between my lips and the heat hits my clit. It feels like the lick of a candle flame. The burn is searing, but satisfying. I move my hips up and around, toward and away from the hard jet of strong current teasing my pussy, before directing the strong surging water to the space above my wanting clit. It pounds the nerves connected to my nip, producing the most exquisite pressure. I will my body perfectly still, close my eyes, breathe deep and slow and allow myself to simply enjoy the ride. I hold myself there as long as I can stand it.

From the other side of the wall, I hear the sound of footsteps approaching and the key in the door. The thought of you catching me in mid-masturbation, and knowing how much you love to watch me, sets off a series of micro-orgasms. The pops and twitches, combine with the champagne, causing me to slip from my tubside perch. Not wanting to hurt myself, and knowing you are near, I decide to move my party for one to the oversized chaise, and wait for you to finish me off.

I lay back, marveling at the stars shooting across the blackness of my closed eyelids, while witnessing the dueling regions of my lust filled body. Up north, my head feels fabulously fuzzy, drained of inhibition but left heavy with alcohol and a horde of deliciously whorish thoughts. My southern extremities, however, feel light and effervescent, sizzling with electric cravings.

I hear the doors close and footsteps pad across the carpet. My inner muscles clutch, well aware of the pleasurable pounding they are about to receive. But I have a more urgent need.

"Baby, back here," I call out. "I need you to come eat my pussy."

"Oh shit," I hear a female voice call from the other side of the wall.

I forget that I am outside and other guests can hear me. Rather than embarrass, it excites me and the subsequent tug on my clit demands action.

"Please, baby, please come suck my clit."

I say it louder, loving the thrill of my outrageousness, as I lift my arms over my head, grab the frame of the chaise, and spread my legs. My eyelids, like Clitina, are heavy with pleasure. They refuse to open, enjoying the anticipation of your northern mouth meeting my southern lips.

I hear the surprise catch in your throat as you step onto the terrace and pause.

"Come get this," I say, spreading my legs further, in order to entice you with my glistening pink pussy.

The first lap of tongue is slow and delicious. I swear I can hear that kit cat purr! You follow up with a succession of fast and slow licks before switching to a gentle nibble. I can't remember you ever feasting on my vagina with such feverish technique, but I'm drunk. Who knows, and frankly, who gives a fuck at this point? Your clever dining habits are driving me to the edge and I'm loving every moment of it.

Already primed by the water pump, my clit is hard as a rod and ready to bust a nut, as you would say. I release the chaise and grab my stiff nipples. I tug at my nips, each twist causing a twitch in my vagina. Your nibble changes to a strong, rhythmic suckle and I can feel waves of sexual release begin to roll through my body. I lift my hips to meet your mouth as I pump your face. The exquisite rush of impending orgasm begins. My thighs clench and I grind against you. I reach down to push your head closer to my pussy and my hands come in contact not with the close shaven waves lying against your skull, but with locks of silken strands. Surprise pushes a scream from my mouth but I am too far gone to push the stranger away. Instead, I allow this talented and unfamiliar mouth to continue ravishing my throbbing pussy.

The water toy, the champagne, the absurd pleasure from a stranger eating my vag creates a scandalous determination within me. I can feel the suction from his mouth taking me higher and higher until I feel my cunt squeeze so hard that I think I might faint. I grab the side of the chaise for leverage, as I buck hard against his face while he sucks every last bit of pussy juice from my body.

As the most tremendous, vagina clutching, titty engorging, orgasm sweeps me up and over the terrace wall, I hear, "WHAT THE FUCK?"

My eyes fly open, first landing on the pussy slicked face of our butler, and then turning my head and resting on the bulge of your cock straining against your pants. In a split second decision, I choose not to say a word. Besides, I don't quite know what happened. The butler will be of no help. With cowardly satisfaction, he dashes off, announcing his departure with the slam of the door. Explanations can wait, my greedy pussy decides.

Apparently, we are on the same page as you say nothing as I reach over and unzip your pants, freeing my treasure and pulling it to my lips.

Jealous arousal burns in your eyes as I lean over and take your dick in my hand and then start kissing the head. Your groans announce your full-fledged participation. Loving you, I take you in my mouth, making sure my tongue is tickling the underneath portion of your rod while its head is rubbing up on the roof of my mouth. Your moans tell me that years of sucking your cock have perfected my technique. I go deeper, alternating the strength of my suction before gently running my teeth up the length of your shaft.*

Walter felt his dick get hard. He quickly removed it from his pants, closed the book and started jacking off to the Aleesa's image on the cover. "Baby, I want to fuck you, too," he told her, begging her photo to believe him. Her words beckoned him, and stroking his cock, he opened the book to continue reading.

You stand there watching me work on your cock, enjoying the show and how good I am making you feel. "Fuck yeah, baby. Fuck yeah, baby," you repeat over and over.

Your repetitiveness tells me that you are fast reaching your peak. Knowing that you are locked and loaded, I continue to suck you, changing my technique in order to get you off. I suck up and down your dick, going up just far enough to keep the purple plum in my mouth and suck really hard while grabbing your balls and giving them a squeeze.

"Oh, you're gonna make me cum. I'm about to give you some cum, baby," the gentleman in you warns, giving me time to remove you from my mouth.

I have no intention of doing any such thing. I am craving the salty taste of your jism on my tongue. To illustrate my point, I reach for your magic button, the space between your ass and your balls, and apply a little pressure.

"Oh God, girl. Right there, you know the spot," Walter called out, imagining Aleesa's fingers pressing him over the edge.

Like I knew it would, it releases you of all control and you buck up against my face, shooting warm cum into the back of my throat. Your satiated sighs jostle the stars as you collapse on top of me.

Goodnight love. I'm going to sleep tonight, tasting you in my dreams.

Walter sprayed cum all over his stomach in a wicked release of both pent-up sperm and frustration. How unfair was it that he could remain rock-hard while alone with a picture of his wife, but not in the company of the real thing? Something had to give, and give fucking soon.

He lay back against the pillows, enjoying the warmth on his stomach, commiserating over the fact that he felt closer to his wife at this moment, though she was three thousand miles away, than he had these past few months living in the same house. He missed the intimacy they shared, both in and out of the bed. Goddamn it, he missed his wife.

Chapter Fourteen

Lena, Livia and Aleesa sat on the beach in Carmel, watching the waves roll. Their picnic lunch was spread out in front of them, but the majesty before them had captured their attention and was currently satisfying their sensual appetites.

"Keep an eye on the time," Lena requested. "I don't want to miss the show at the art gallery."

"What's with you and this show?" Aleesa asked. "This is the third time you've mentioned it."

"I wanna buy some art. I have a lot of empty wall space."

"Lena, you're rich," Livia said. "I propose that you buy a condo out here for all of us to use. Kind of a girls' beach house. Better yet, buy it for me for my next birthday, and I'll move out here."

"I thought you were afraid of earthquakes," Aleesa said.

"For this, I could get over my fear."

"You should have talked to me sooner. I bought a place in Miami, thus the empty walls," she said, making a face at Aleesa.

"I don't see what that has to do with my birthday present, but okay, I can do Miami!"

"You know you're both welcome to use it anytime."

"I'm surprised that you'd choose Miami to have a second home," Aleesa said. "I mean, after the Jason misadventure, I thought that the last place you'd want to escape to on the regular would be the place you met."

"I've moved on, plus I like Miami. No point in me not enjoying it because of one blip on my romantic scale. And besides, those memories weren't the worst in the world."

"Let's toast to good memories with good men," Livia said, cracking open the wine and pouring everyone a glass. "You have to admit, even though each one of us has been divorced, we've been pretty lucky. All and all, the men in our lives have been pretty good guys."

"Between his adulterous ways, the fact that he had a baby with another woman while we were married, and did three years in jail for embezzlement, you can't possibly be including Bill in that toast," Aleesa said.

"True dat," Lena said, laughing.

"Okay, maybe not Bill. But Walt has more than made up for him," Liv pointed out.

"Yep," Aleesa said, leaving it at that. She didn't want to ruin this lovely moment by bringing up the latest snag in her marital saga. Walter basically refusing to get couples counseling had thrown her for a huge loop and frankly, she didn't know what to think anymore.

"And photo man was quite a hot memory," Lena said, redirecting the current topic. She could tell from Aleesa's face that the subject of Walter, at least for now, was off the table.

"Yes, you speak the truth. Omigod, those locks, that body, that boy was fine." Aleesa's tone and face brightened at the memory.

"Hey, watch it. You're drooling in the lobster salad," Livia said, passing on the container.

"Yeah, but look at her face. If you are still wondering how to feel hot and sexy again, I think Josiah might be the answer," Lena remarked. "Come on, 'fess up. You wouldn't mind seeing him again, would you?"

"I don't know. Some fantasies are better left unfulfilled. I think Josiah might be one of them," Aleesa declared.

"Maybe, but some are too tempting to ignore," Lena countered, before pushing the conversation on to a different topic. "So Livia, how's the online dating thing going? You never reported back on your date with the young'in."

"I was way too embarrassed to tell anyone," Livia admitted.

"Well, drink up and spill it now, sister," Aleesa told her.

"Okay, but let me begin by saying that I don't think I'm cut out for this online dating stuff. That said, I had my date with Jeremy."

"This was Mr. I Think You're So Gorgeous?" Aleesa asked.

"Yes."

"So what did he look like?"

"Cute. White. Tall, about six-foot-two, athletic build. Short, sandy hair. Kind of preppy. We were supposed to have drinks, and then after we saw how that went, go to dinner. So I met him in the city. When I got there, he was already waiting for me, and had already started on the cocktails."

"Those young'ins do like to drink."

"Well, it was more about nerves. He told me that he *was* nervous because he thought I was so, and I quote 'fucking hot.' He kept telling me how beautiful and exotic I was, which is great to hear a few times, but when it becomes the main topic of conversation, it's a bit much."

"Oh, there's that word—exotic. Sounds like Jeremy had a bad case of jungle fever," Lena offered.

"Tiresome," Aleesa commented.

"Anyway, it was a little awkward at first, but then we found some common ground with cooking. He thought it was cool that I was a pastry chef because he's a foodie, too. He also likes to watch a lot of the same Food Network shows that I like. So we got to talking and I was having a good time. I wasn't really physically attracted to him, but the company was nice."

"So no jungle fever of your own? No desire to break off a little piece?" Lena teased.

"NO! I just met him. I wasn't going to have sex with him."

"Did you go to dinner?" Aleesa asked, amused by her cousin's conservative ways.

"Well, we started to. We got in a cab and he leaned over and kissed me. I was shocked but went with it. The whole time I was trying to figure out how to let him know that that kiss was all he was getting."

"Could he kiss?" Lena queried.

"Not really. It was kind of wet and sloppy. Anyway, I didn't realize how much he'd drunk until, all of a sudden, the booze kicked in and he passed out on me in the backseat of the damn cab!"

"So basically you're telling us that you had a teenager passed out and drooling on your chest?" Lena said, giving a comical visual to Livia's description.

"Omigod, what did you do?" Aleesa asked, cracking up.

"I didn't know what to do. I didn't know this kid. I kept trying to wake him up to ask him where he lived but all I could get out of him was Jersey City. Well, I wasn't about to pay for a cab all the way to New Jersey, so I did the only thing I could do. I told the cab driver to take us to the Holiday Inn on 57th Street. When we got there, I took his wallet and checked him into the hotel with all of his damn cash. Then I woke his drunk ass up and the cab driver helped me put his ass in the bed. He was out cold in minutes. I left him there and went home."

"I have to say, cousin, you've got some serious problem-solving skills."

"Hopefully he didn't die of alcohol poisoning or anything," Lena teased.

"Yeah, well, I wouldn't know. I closed down my eHarmony account. I was too afraid he'd try to contact me again. I am officially retired from online dating. If I can't meet a man the old-fashioned way, I'll have to stay single."

"Well, you gave it the yeoman try," Aleesa said, lying back into the sand and watching the clouds roll by, "which is more than I can say for your cousin-in-law." She'd tried to avoid the subject, but found it to be an impossible task.

"What happened?" Lena asked, lying back to join her in the sand.

"Walter basically refuses to go to couples counseling. He keeps insisting that it is his problem, and that he'll deal with it on his own. Our sixteenth anniversary is in a few weeks, our marriage is falling apart, and he doesn't see this as a couple's problem. I don't understand. Why won't he let me in?"

"Men are weird about counseling," Livia told her. "Dale wouldn't go with me either. Said we didn't need a stranger meddling in the middle of our marriage. I think it makes them feel guilty."

"Michael and I went, but it didn't help. He was too afraid of looking like the bad guy to be really honest."

"So, you two agree with Walt? That it's his problem to solve?"

"No, I'm saying that counseling doesn't always make things better. Sometimes it brings up more crap for you to deal with," Lena said.

"So what will work?"

"For you and Walt? Communication, patience and love on both parts," Livia, ever the optimist, offered.

"At the very least, you've got a 50-50 shot," Lena said.

"And if I don't like my odds?"

"Then you redefine what winning means to you," her friend offered with her cousin's agreement. "The best advice I ever got when my marriage was in crisis was from my mother," Lena continued. "Tina told me to communicate and work hard to straighten things out with my husband, but at the same time, keep on doing me. I found it to be good advice when dealing with both Michael and Jason."

"Lees, you should take Tina's advice, too. Because if you do, whether your relationship survives or not, you'll be stronger and ready to deal with whatever comes your way."

Aleesa began packing up their picnic without saying a word. The idea of her relationship with Walter not surviving hit Aleesa hard in the gut, and robbed her of any response.

"It's two o'clock," Livia informed them, breaking up the serious air that had descended on their conversation. She gently caressed her cousin's back in a show of support before standing up and brushing the sand from her pants.

"Let's boogie over to the gallery before all the good stuff is gone," Lena said.

While walking to the car and on the drive back into the beautiful coastal village, Aleesa thought about everything that had been said by her husband and her friends. Working on herself while she worked on her marriage sounded, at least in theory, like a reasonable and wise thing to do. However, taking real life action was an entirely different proposition. For the past two years, ever since Walter left for the Middle East, Aleesa had been laser-focused on only one thing—keeping her husband close to her by any means possible until he returned home safely so they could get on with their marriage. The year she'd spent writing his damn freak book had kept her focused on that task. In all honesty, she had no idea what 'working on herself' even meant, let alone entailed. Nearly sixteen years ago they'd said, "I do" and exchanged vows for better or worse. Adamant not to put herself in the same lonely position she was in during her first marriage, Aleesa worked damn hard to ensure that she and Walter were truly one. Her life had totally, and happily, revolved around their family and him. Now that things had changed, Aleesa didn't know how to do anything different.

"So, what do we know about this artist?" Livia asked as they parked the car and walked around the corner past all of the quaint artisan shops.

"He's from New York and his specializes in portraits," Lena revealed with a grin.

"Why do you want to fill your walls up with portraits of strangers?" Aleesa inquired as they reached the gallery. "It seems like it would be kinda creepy to…OMIGOD! I can't believe you did this," she hissed, stopping in her tracks. "Damn it, Lena. I'm not going in there."

"What's wrong?" Livia asked, confused by Aleesa's quick shift in mood.

Aleesa stepped aside so her cousin could view the window display announcing "Nude Visions" by Josiah Newman. "She set me up."

"Don't be so dramatic. I only set you up a little bit," Lena said, laughing. "When I was online looking for things to do here, I stumbled across an event calendar and low and behold, there was your hottie camera boy. Josiah Newman's reputation in the art world is growing fast and I wanted to see his work, and maybe buy a piece or two. Plus, I figured it would be a fun reminder of your illicit photo shoot. A nice pick-me-up, if you will. Don't panic. It's the last day, not the opening. I seriously doubt that he'll be here. In fact, I can guarantee it."

"How can you do that?" Livia asked for her cousin.

"Because I called and asked the gallery."

Aleesa felt her stomach drop back into place. If her heart was honest with her head, she'd have to admit that wrapped up in her relief knowing that Josiah was not on the other side of those doors was the tiniest nugget of disappointment. She couldn't pinpoint why she felt that way, and frankly didn't want to.

The three stepped inside and into the cool air of the Gallery Noire. They walked further into the main space, all eyes on the waves of form and color adorning the stark white walls. Josiah's work splashed across the walls, and illuminated by tracks of lights hanging from the ceiling, beckoned their eyes from every direction. Several other visitors milled around the perimeter of the room, lured in by the seductive trilogy of female form, composition and light.

The three women stepped over to witness the series "Naked Nudes," photos of the female form taken without props or the propaganda of sexual objectification. Both the models and their poses were natural, unadorned and subtly sensuous. Aleesa studied the series in total awe. The endless variety of textures, tones and forms of the female body were creatively presented through the eyes of a craftsman.

"This is truly art," Lena declared with a hushed reverence.

"I agree," Livia said, the artist in her recognizing a kindred spirit. "His use of light and form almost make the nudity obsolete."

While Livia and Lena moved quickly down the wall, quickly eyeballing each photograph, Aleesa hung back, wanting to study each of the models and their moods. She looked into the eyes of each subject, wondering if they could boast of the same sexy experience with Josiah as she could. Had he flirted with them, too, using his powerful good looks and considerable charm to bewitch and bewilder them as he'd done her? Had the sexual energy crackled between them as it had when she was on the other side of his lens?

"Lees, get over here. I'm pretty sure that your face is hanging on the wall," Livia beckoned.

"More than your face," Lena piped up.

"Is this you?"

Aleesa crossed the room to join them, and took a closer look at the photograph. Under the group heading, "Candidly Nude" was hers and several other photographs of women naked in their relaxed and natural state. But with her head thrown back like that, it took a second look to determine that it was indeed her.

"Omigod. Apparently so."

"It's called "Naked Laughter," Livia said, reading the card below. "You're a muse hanging in an art gallery! How amazing is that?"

"I think extreme embarrassment would be a more accurate description."

"I think it's hot," Lena said. "You look beautiful."

Of all of the pictures he'd taken of her during their shoot, Josiah had chosen to display a shot where she hadn't posed at all, but where he'd caught her off-guard, laughing. She was curled up on the studio bed, with one breast exposed, and her hands clutching the sheet around her waist. Her back was arched to support her head, which was thrown back in a fit of giggles. She had to admit, it was a very sexy image. She looked like a woman who'd just experienced the most exquisite, blissful orgasm. Though at the time, she remembered feeling nervous and unsure of herself, this photo revealed an outward joy and an innate, honest beauty that she'd never seen revealed before. How had Josiah not only seen that side of her, but pulled it out and captured it on camera?

Aleesa stood alone, smiling at her image. Suddenly she felt flush, and not of the hot flash variety. Her hand traveled to her collarbone and lightly stroked her neck. She felt exactly as she'd expressed wanting to feel in the car coming down—hot and sexy. The disturbing thing was that once again, it was Josiah, not Walter, who was causing her mind and priming her body to respond in this way.

"Attraction is not action," she whispered to her snapshot self. Still, Aleesa could not help wondering if her resolve to keep action at bay would be so strong if Josiah Newman were to walk into the room.

Damn you, Walter! Aleesa's emotions clicked over from desire to ire. Because of his physical and mental states, coupled with his reluctance to get help to deal with them, Walter had put her in the uncomfortable position of lusting after another man. A position, she never, ever thought or wanted to find herself in.

War was hell, and thanks to it, so now was her life.

His phone vibrated but he ignored it. He was sure it was Monica, and as much as he felt obliged to be there for her, he couldn't be bothered. In so many ways, Monica had breathed life back into his soul that night, but at the same time, their tryst had killed the fairytale quality of his marriage for both he and Aleesa. The time of the princess and her white knight dancing naked in the moonlight was over. Suddenly, real-life drama had moved into their marriage, and living happily ever after seemed like a distant dream.

The thought depressed him, and in an effort to hold onto his connection with Aleesa, he dismissed the thoughts of Monica and picked up Aleesa's book. He needed to feel and bask in his wife's love again, if only words on paper.

Hey Sweetheart,

Do I have a good one for you today. I went shopping for new bed linens today. I redecorated the bedroom in anticipation of your return, and wanted you to have some super soft Egyptian cotton sheets to fall asleep and make love on (not necessarily in that order!). Anyway, I was in Bed Bath & Beyond. The gentleman helping me suggested that I lay back on the sheets to see for myself how soft they were and I did. Of course, I couldn't help thinking about you wrapped up in the sheets with me, and well, one thought led to another and before you know it, we were...

BETWEEN THE SHEETS

"Baby, what do you think about this," I ask, pointing out a taupe and burgundy raw silk duvet set.

"Nice."

"But do you like these sheets? Enough to sleep on them for the next five years?" I press, appreciating your being such a good sport as I drag you around on all these mundane errands.

"Baby, as long as this is in the bed with me, I can sleep on dishrags," you say, slipping your nasty boy hands between my legs and squeezing my kit cat.

"Don't start nothin' you can't finish, Colonel."

"And you, wifey, don't write a check your pretty ass can't cash."

"Are you daring me?" I ask, as my eyes light up with passion and audacity. Your look says yes, so I grab your hand and lead you through the aisles. I am obviously on a mission. We make a quick stop at the shower section and after I covertly grab a tester bottle of lotion and a hand towel from the shelf, we make haste to the back of the store to the clearance section and into the storage area.

"What are you doing, Aleesa? We're not supposed to be back here."

"Then you better shut up so we don't get caught."

By now I have your pants undone and your dick in my hand. I wrap my slick hand around your pole and begin to jerk you off, slowly at first, sliding my hand up and down your shaft.

"You...you are crazy," you manage to eke out. Your words catch the wind of your heavy breathing and they have a sexy, breathless quality about them. "And I am....oohh...crazy about your...mmph...ass."

Your exquisite agitation excites me and I treat you to that quick, hand-over-the-top move you like. "Uhh...uhhh...uhhhh," you moan into my neck. I speed up and get a good rhythm going. I feel your delectable, black dick swell in my hand, and it is really making me juicy. But this wicked moment is all about your pleasure, so I shift gears and sheath your cock with my two palms. I rub back and forth, using your growing stiffy like one would a stick trying to spark a campfire.

"Talk to me," I request, knowing you understand that I am not interested in casual conversation.

"You are such an insatiable freak, Mrs. Davis. You like being my nasty girl, don't you? Don't you?" you hiss in my ear.

"Yes, baby. I like being nasty. You make me that way. I think about your dick all the time. Inside me, fucking me like only you can. I can't get enough of your sweet, black dick. I want it all the time. Like now, so give it to me," I say, squeezing your cock with one hand and your balls with the other.

It works because the log in my hand is getting hotter and hotter as you bite your lip to muffle the sound of a happy motherfucker about to get the fuck off. I hear voices approaching, but try to stay calm. I'm not going to stop until you get yours.

"Let it go. Come for me, baby," I whisper. "Pour all that sweet juice in my hands." I change techniques again, back to the hand-over-top, while using the other to reach down to squeeze and play with your balls some more. After years of experience, I know this will hasten your orgasm, and while I usually love for you to take your sweet time and enjoy every nanosecond of pleasure you can at my hands, the voices are getting closer.

Your body begins the telling tense and quiver as your jism appears at the tip. I give your nuts one more squeeze and you erupt in my hand, muffling the sounds of your satisfaction with a soldier's determination. I quickly take the lifted hand towel and tidy you and my hands up, before stuffing it into my purse.

We slip out of the storage area and pretend to check out the bargains before making a quick beeline out of the store and out into the June sunshine.

"You do realize that you shoplifted that towel from the store," you turn and tell me.

"Consider it stolen pleasure," I reply with a twisted smile on my lips, "and me a thief of the heart."

Chapter Fifteen

"The key to grilling steak is the rub," Walter schooled Soup as they stood in his backyard over the barbeque grill. "Aleesa usually gets it all together for me, but I think I did a fine job on my own."

"I guess we'll know in few. Another brew?"

"Yeah," Walter said as he pulled his buzzing phone from his pocket, took a quick look and put it away.

"Monica?" Soup asked, handing his friend a Heineken.

"Yeah. I saw her a couple of days ago."

"You what?"

"She was in a bad way so I told her to come by the office to talk."

"Talk?"

"*Talk*. She's definitely suffering from PTSD."

"Post-traumatic stress?"

"Disorder. Suggesting to meet at the office was a big mistake. I knew she hadn't been back to work, but I didn't realize that seeing the dental set-up would set her off, and now she's been blowing my phone up more than ever."

"So how does this PTS shit work?"

"Basically, you suffer from flashbacks that make you relive whatever traumatic event you experienced. Different things can set you off, so people who have PTS tend to avoid places, people, or other things that might remind them of the event. It makes them super sensitive to normal life experiences. So you can imagine what a pain in the ass it can be and what a toll it takes on their lives."

"Thus the dental office, but why don't you set her off? You were there with her," Soup queried.

"I guess because I went through it with her. But, she did do something that I found disturbing. Before she flipped out, she started coming on to me. She kissed me and started grabbing me. She wants us to be together again. She said she can't get her life back together, and it only makes sense when she is with me. She said the memory of our one night together is the only beautiful thing left in her life. But I think it's just the stress talking."

"Whatever it is doing the chit-chatting, it's not good. Don't mess with that, man. I know you want to be a good friend, but girlfriend is crossing the line. So when is your wife coming back?"

"Monday. But she seems twice as pissed as when she left, so shit should be interesting two days from now."

"What did you do? I thought you and she haven't talked much since she's been away. Or is this a case of her girlfriends talking shit in her ear?"

"Nah. This was all me. She sent me an email the other night. I was checking out her book and thought it was a text from Monica again, so I ignored it. Bad move. It was basically Aleesa's version of an ultimatum. She is expecting things to be different when she gets back. Bottom line: She says if I'm not willing to face our issues head on, and work proactively on getting our marriage and sex life back on track, then she doesn't see a future for us."

"Doesn't sound unreasonable."

"No, it doesn't," Walt said, flipping the steaks onto plates.

"So?"

"I called her to discuss it. I agreed to get counseling, at first. But she wants to go together. She said this all affects us both, so we should both be there. She said to go with her as an anniversary gift. I can't do it."

"I feel you, man; I hated doing that shit with Jasmine. But you gotta suck it up and go, if it makes her happy."

"You don't get it. I can't go with her because the crux of our problems is the fact that I fucked another woman. If that comes out, my marriage is definitely over right there on the couch."

"Man, tell her the truth."

"I told you before; I can't."

"She'll eventually understand. She'll forgive you."

"I am not taking the chance that she won't."

"Well, like I've said before, you've got to do something."

"I know. And based on this book of hers, she's horny as shit, and now mad as hell. That's not a good combination. I have to tell you, Charlie, I'm reading some shit in this book that I never would have thought even crossed Aleesa's mind. If I don't get it together soon, and seriously give her some, somebody else will."

"Well, if you think it's going to happen anyway, give her a free pass. Let her fuck somebody else. Then maybe the mutual guilt will cancel each other out," Soup said, laughing at the absurdity of his own suggestion before filling his mouth with beef. "Hey, drastic times call for drastic measures."

Walter looked at his partner with disbelief. Was Soup honestly suggesting that he give Aleesa his blessing to screw someone else, just to assuage his guilt? His mind pondered the idea. If he allowed her to fulfill one of her fantasies, would they then be even? With each of them having tipped out on the other, could they start over with a clean slate? Would Aleesa even go for it? And if she did, could he handle it, knowing that her satisfaction was coming from another dude's dick at the expense of his ego and pride? Would it work?

"What the fuck am I doing, even considering such nonsense?" Walter mumbled to himself.

"What was that?"

"I said, you're fucking crazy for even suggesting something so stupid."

"Yeah, I'm crazy. Like a fox, baby. Like a fox."

ALEESA SAT AT HER DESK IN THE PROMOTION AND MARKETING department of the Sports Fan Network, trying to compose an email. She'd been working on it for the past hour and still couldn't get it right. Since returning from San Francisco, and despite the ever-expanding 'To Do' list sitting unattended on her desk, contacting Josiah Newman was the only order of business occupying her mind.

Seeing her photograph included in his California show felt like a signal from the Universe to get in contact and let him know that she'd been thinking of him. But relaying that information without saying it outright, was proving to be much more of a challenge than she'd anticipated. She wanted her communiqué to be clever and funny without sounding too forward or flirtatious. Perturbed with her ineffective writing, Aleesa pressed the backspace button until all of the letters on her screen disappeared, and then began again.

Hi there.

I was in California recently and stumbled on your show at the Gallery Noire in Carmel. The good news is that the gallery was full of admiring fans. The bad news is that I believe I may have to sue you for displaying my photograph without my consent! Now, granted, it was a beautiful photo (if I do say so myself), and exhibited within a tasteful display of obvious beauty and artistry. And true, your photograph made me feel beautiful, and while I was proud to have been placed among your master-

pieces, I am contemplating my legal options. That said, I do hope that my warning finds you in good health and happy spirits, and immensely proud of yourself for a wonderful job.

Best,

Aleesa

She read over her email, satisfied that she'd finally accomplished a suitable balance of coyness and cordiality. Aleesa quickly pressed "send" before she could change her mind. She knew that contacting Josiah could result in two distinct possibilities: Being ignored or even worse, providing an opening for them to further explore the energy between them. In her heart and mind, Aleesa didn't want to start an affair with him, only a flirtation. But she was also well aware that she was teetering on dangerous ground. Interacting up close and personal with Josiah Newman was definitely a temptation that could have disastrous consequences if not managed properly. But at this point, the reward outweighed the risk. Aleesa was so parched for attention that the sexual tension between Josiah and her was too compelling to ignore.

Aleesa craved the heightened level of sexual consciousness she'd maintained over the past year or so, while waiting for Walter's return. Regularly fantasizing, writing, and self-pleasuring in his absence had kept sex squarely on her brain, giving her a sense of sexual liberation, and a proud ownership of her juicy, sexual persona. Aleesa really understood what Lena had been saying about how Jason had changed the way she looked at herself.

Though pleasing her husband had been the impetus, the result was that she'd gotten to really know, and adore, the sexual side of Aleesa Davis while he was away. It was a side of herself that excited and empowered her with a newfound feeling of confidence. Before Walter left, sex, as much as she enjoyed it, was really more about keeping him satisfied to ensure he didn't stray. Now, some switch inside of her had clicked to the "on" position. Aleesa felt the confidence and desire to really explore her sexual side for her own sense of gratification, not just her husband's. And despite the fact that at age fifty-two, society deemed her a sexual relic and past her prime, Aleesa felt the exact opposite. In her mind, she'd only just begun to bloom.

The unfortunate truth was that her desire had remained steadfast since Walter had come home from Afghanistan, but her frustrations had multiplied one hundred fold. She and Walt were now living like roommates, full of polite chatter and surface conversation while their marriage was spiraling into the abyss of angry discontent. Due to his failure to communicate, along with his refusal to seek counseling, nothing was getting better between them. Aleesa's initial fears that she was not attractive to him or that he no longer loved her, had now been heightened and complicated by depression, anger and deep frustration. Walter no longer made her feel sexy and desirable. The last man to do that had been Josiah Newman.

The phone rang. Aleesa checked her watch. It was 10:24 a.m. Her scheduled 10:30 call with the advertising agency was apparently a few minutes early, but she was grateful for the interruption. She needed to get her mind back on work and off her sorry love life.

"There must be a way to work this out without lawyers getting involved," Josiah commented, in his low and alluring voice.

"How did you get my number?" Aleesa's surprise was evident. It had been less than five minutes since she'd sent the email, and yet Josiah Newman was on the other end of her phone.

"It's in your file along with the standard release that all of my clients sign, giving me the right to display their images."

"Surely, there must be a legal loophole for me to wiggle through," she replied, feeling her inner flirt come alive.

Josiah paused a split second as he imagined Aleesa wiggling beneath him. "Perhaps we should get together and discuss it."

"Interesting idea. When?"

"You know what they say; no time like the present."

"Can you hold for a minute while I check my schedule?" she asked. Aleesa pushed the mute button on her phone and took a deep breath. She exhaled into the room, trying to expel the mishmash of thoughts running through her head so she could make a coherent decision. On one hand, she hadn't expected to see Josiah so soon. On the other, in the back of her mind, she'd wished for it and had moved toward making it happen, so she might as well go for it.

"No time like the present," she said to herself before pushing the button and letting Josiah in on her thoughts. "I have a phone appointment in a few minutes that should last about half an hour. So, shall we meet for lunch? Say around noon?"

"Sounds like a plan. I know a great little coffee shop in the East Village. A coffee-bar-cum-tapas-bar-cum-pastry-shop with a Bay Area pedigree. You know, to keep our California connection alive. I'm sure you'll find something there to tempt you."

"I'm sure I will," Aleesa responded, knowing that no matter how extensive, the only tempting thing on the menu would be him. "My other call is coming in. Can you email me the address and I'll see you there at noon."

Aleesa hung up on Josiah and took a beat to settle down before picking up her next call. Anticipation was bubbling up inside her. She felt giddy with excitement like a kid on Christmas Eve. And after these past months of dragging around a heart that felt as heavy as lead, the lightness in her chest delighted her.

JOSIAH WAS ALREADY SITTING AT A TABLE IN THE MIDDLE OF THE coffee shop when she arrived. His attention was captured by some article in the *New York Times* open in front of him, so Aleesa took the opportunity to study the man who had her willingly walking through temptation's door. Ever the photographer, his trusty camera sat on the table by his side. She hadn't seen him in months, but dressed in all black, his trademark locks and casual good looks were duly showcased. She sighed. Josiah still held the power to take her breath away.

As she started to step toward him, her phone rang.

"Hey, Liv."

"Hey, I'm on my way to the doctor for my annual physical and thought we could hook up for lunch when I'm done. Are you free?"

Aleesa paused before replying. Part of her was dying to tell Liv what she was up to, but she knew her cousin would have a fit if she knew. Aleesa stood staring at Josiah drinking his coffee and reading the paper, captivated by the sheer sensuality of his every movement.

"Lees, are you there?"

"No, sorry. I have a lunch meeting," she told her cousin, not lying, but not actually telling the truth either. "Rain check?"

"Of course. I'll catch you later."

Aleesa hung up and pocketed her phone, unexpectedly enjoying the delicious thrill of her secret behavior.

"Hi, stranger," Aleesa said lightly, approaching the table. She hoped she sounded and looked more laid-back than she felt. Josiah smiled with glowing approval. Gratefully, she'd worn a decent outfit to work this morning. The simple turquoise blue sheath, belted at the waist, played well against her dark skin and hugged her body in all the right places. On the outside, she looked work appropriate. Inside, she was bursting with the unabashed thrill of mutual attraction.

The sound of metal scraping tile sounded throughout the café as Josiah stood up and looked at her with appreciative eyes. They drank her in from head to toe, starting a chain reaction in his face and pulling the corners of his mouth toward the edges of his face. He took another quick look around the room before speaking. "Well, you were definitely right," he said, pulling her chair out so she could sit.

"Of course I was. About what this time?" she joshed through a smile. Josiah's gentlemanly behavior still impressed her.

"That the sexiest place in the world is wherever you are."

"You remembered that? I didn't mean it like…you know…that I was what made a place…uh…sexy. What I trying to say is that whereever you are, you can find sexy all around you," Aleesa replied, gesturing around the room as she tried to explain.

"Well, either way, it's a true statement."

"Oh, I see what you're doing. You're trying to get on my good side so I don't sue you," Aleesa joked, trying to lighten the air so she could breathe again. Damn; the effect this man had on her was downright life-threatening.

"I don't know. I kind of like the idea of you suing the pants off of me," Josiah remarked, upping the banter to judge where her head was. He'd done the gentlemanly thing and left her alone. Now she'd made the move toward him. The question now was, where did she intend for this to go?

He'd been uncharacteristically intrigued and excited to receive her email. Aleesa had crossed his mind often since they'd last seen each other, and the fact that without any engineering on either of their parts, she'd seen the show and they'd reconnected. Surely this was a sign that the Universe intended for them to meet again and explore the sexual energy that had existed between them from the get-go.

Aleesa smiled at Josiah, letting his comment slide, determined not to let her high levels of desire and discontent get her into trouble.

"So lawsuits aside, how did you end up at the show in Carmel?" he asked, slowing his roll. Opportunity was still knocking, albeit soft and tentative.

"My girlfriends and I went out to San Francisco for a vacation. We decided to drive down to Carmel and were wandering around town, and there you were in the window of the Gallery Noire."

"And you decided to take a peek."

"It was like an irresistible force pulling me inside," she told him, only half-kidding. "So, when did you decide to include me in the show?"

"You're not really going to sue me, are you?" Josiah asked with a crooked grin.

"No, I'm not. I was surprised to see myself, but once I realized that I wasn't readily identifiable, I was actually quite flattered."

"I'm glad you were pleased. And to answer your question, I included you at the very last minute, because I found that I really needed you in the show. Not only was it a beautiful photograph, but the way your skin tone played within the grouping made that particular collection pop off the wall," he revealed, staring at her face. "So you were actually the superstar of the group."

Aleesa felt herself blush with embarrassed delight. "I didn't see that one when we picked the photos for Walter's book."

"And how did he like the book? Was he blown away?" Josiah asked, buying a little decision time. Should he admit to her that he'd saved this favorite photograph for his own album of models who had somehow touched him beyond their shared photo session.

"He loved it," Aleesa lied. There was no way she was going to admit that Walter had no interest in her project.

"How could he not? Well, I'm not sure how I missed sending 'Naked Laughter' to you," he said with a sincerity that made his little white lie ring true. "But I'm kind of glad that I didn't."

"Why?"

"Because now I have a very small piece of you that belongs to me."

His admission left them both silent for a beat. In the absence of talk, the magnetic pull that had existed between them during the photo shoot returned full force to fill the empty space between words. They smiled at each other, each wondering what to say next. Josiah didn't want to push too hard, but he surely wanted to make his intentions known. His attraction to Aleesa was still alive and well, and he was game to explore it if she was. Aleesa lowered her eyes and played with her wedding ring. She chose to remain quiet, afraid that the next words out of her mouth might lead her down a wild and wicked path, a road she wasn't sure she was ready to travel.

Their silence was broken by the click of Josiah's camera.

"What are you doing?" she asked, lifting her eyes and giggling nervously as the silly teen feeling returned.

"Ah, the infamous giggle. You know, it's very sexy."

"How so?" she asked, genuinely curious.

"Because it tells me that you still feel *it*, too, which is why you're nervous."

"It could be that," Aleesa said, playing coy, "or it could be because you're taking my picture...in *public*."

"At least you're not naked this time," he said, biting his lip in the most distracting manner.

"This is true."

"Anyway, I can't help it. The light is hitting your face in such a phenomenal way. I had to capture it."

"Because that's what you do."

"Exactly. I capture the beauty around me, and right now it's staring me in the face."

Aleesa felt herself smile from the inside. God bless this handsome man. In less time than it took to bake a cake, he had her feeling sexed up and desirable again. At this moment, all she wanted to do was lean across the table and put her mouth on top of his. Instead, she shut up and let Josiah kiss her with his camera. He, too, said nothing, but the intensity in his eyes was as seductive as any foreplay she could imagine...and God knows, she surely had imagined it!

"Tilt your head slightly to the left. There it is. God, you're beautiful!" Josiah announced with a reverence that rang true in her ears. He got up from his chair and crouched down at her feet, tilting his head to catch the light at the angle he desired. When his locks fell into his face, Josiah casually flung them back over his shoulder, causing Aleesa's vagina to spontaneously contract. For the first time, she understood the seductive pull of long hair from the male point of view. Josiah looked so incredibly sexy right now, and to keep the moan poised at the tip of her tongue from escaping, she bit her lip.

"Oh, baby. That's a good one. These are definitely going into my private collection...yeah, baby, give it me."

Aleesa sat, trying to relax and simply take in the experience as it happened around her. She made no attempt to pose, only tried to be herself. To give herself something to do, she began to speak to Josiah through her eyes. She told him of how often he'd crossed her mind. How whenever she felt the most defeated and undesired in her marriage, she'd relive the fantasy she'd written about him, and pleasure herself. Aleesa told him all of that without saying one word, but the look on his face let her know that Josiah had heard everything.

As Josiah continued his impromptu photo session, the café got increasingly quiet. The chatter around them stopped and Aleesa could feel all eyes in the room on the two of them. The current between them was electric and palatable and it was obvious that the other customers felt the energy between them as well. The way they were gawking at the two of them, you'd think she and Josiah were in the middle of the place having sex.

The heat between them caused Aleesa to feel flush and unsettled. She needed to break this connection or she was going to embarrass herself, right here in public. "Um…I'm sorry but I'll be right back," she told him. Without waiting for his reply, she broke loose of his powerful force field and headed for the safety of the ladies' room.

"Omigod, omigod, OMIGOD," she said as she burst through the door and headed over to the mirror. "What happened out there?" she queried her image. One minute, they were talking hypothetical lawsuits and the next minute, Josiah was fucking her with his camera. At least that's what it felt like, and she had the drenched panties to prove it!

Aleesa turned on the faucet and ran cold water on her wrists. It was her remedy for the hot flashes she occasionally experienced, and this was one of epic proportions. Yes, this hot flash was brought on by a rush of hormones; and yes, it produced the urge to take off her clothes. But unlike the age-related kind, this blaze of heat left her wanting to get naked so she could get down and dirty.

"Attraction is not action. Attraction is not action," Aleesa repeated her mantra until she calmed down and felt together enough to go out, look into Josiah's face, and tell him goodbye. As she retouched her lipstick, Aleesa realized that she'd achieved what she'd come for, an innocent flirtation and hit of desire to pump up her deflated ego. She'd also learned an important lesson that she was sure would serve her well in the future. Unless she planned to wrap herself up in those gorgeous dreads and fuck the fine off of Josiah Newman, she was never going to see him again.

She took a deep breath, walked out of the door and smack dab into a waiting Josiah. At that moment, Aleesa did the only thing a woman in her position could do. She grabbed him by the collar and pulled him to her. Their mouths came together in a kiss that sizzled with an overwhelming passion demanding to be satisfied. Aleesa's tongue penetrated his lips, checking out the territory before taking possession of his lower lip and sucking it with seductive intent. If this was their first and only kiss, her ego demanded that she leave him wondering and wanting more.

The slightest groan slunk from Josiah's mouth, letting Aleesa know her intent had become his reality. He pulled his lip from her grasp and with a head full of his own intentions, used his tongue to give Aleesa's closed mouth a few long and luxurious licks. Immediately, her pussy clutched as she pictured him tonguing her clit. And then to add delicious discomfort, Josiah parted her lips with a stiff and hard tongue, thrusting in and out in a sexy demonstration of things to come.

Oh, shit! Attraction had definitely crossed over and morphed into action.

"Uh, sorry about that," she said, pulling away.

"Are you? Really?" Josiah asked, his interest piqued and his dick hard.

"Well, honestly, no, because now I won't have to wonder all of my life," Aleesa admitted.

"Now see, that's where we part ways. That was one hell of a kiss. And now, all I'm going to do is wonder what might have come next."

"You will never know what a gift you have been to me," Aleesa said, reaching up and kissing him lightly on the cheek. "Goodbye, Josiah."

"Or not." He refused to give up so easily, not when the chase seemed destined to end somewhere spectacular. "If you ever want to know what comes next, you know where to find me."

Aleesa laughed before she turned and walked through the café and out into the sunshine. She was beaming, mainly because feeling sexy always made her feel good, but also because there was a man nearly twenty years her junior who found her irresistible. And that was such a novel feeling for her these days.

That really was a goodbye kiss, she told herself. Aleesa would not put herself in this position with Josiah again. Her resistance was low, and lust had become the monkey on her back. She had neither the desire nor the willpower to tangle with such a powerful and dangerous bitch. Her life was complicated enough as it was.

Chapter Sixteen

"I don't understand how you can watch this show," Walter commented. He walked into the family room and joined Aleesa on the couch as the bickering between NeNe Leakes and Kim Zolciak had reached a fever pitch.

"Hmmm?" Aleesa said, Walt's voice pulling her out of her daydream.

"I said, I don't see how you can watch this trash."

"*The Housewives of Atlanta* is my guilty pleasure. What's yours?" Aleesa asked, not recognizing the sexual innuendo until it had escaped her lips.

"What does that that mean?" he replied, his tone suddenly doused with irritation.

"Just what it sounds like it means. What inane television program are you ashamed to admit that you can't get enough of?" Aleesa's voice reflected her annoyance. Now what had him acting so pissy?

"I don't know, Lees. It's been a long time since I watched any television other than the news and sports." Not wanting to argue, Walt tried to check his exasperation. And truth be told, she hadn't actually done anything this evening to warrant his anger.

"Well, sit down and turn the channel to CNN if you'd like. This is a rerun anyway."

Walter moved down on the couch, increasing the distance between them, and gratefully flipped the channel. Aleesa marveled for a moment over how little they talked about anything of substance anymore. It used to be they'd run out of time before conversation, but that was B.A., Before Afghanistan. And he'd been particularly snarky since she'd returned from San Francisco. Because he wouldn't talk about anything, Aleesa could only assume it was because she'd gone out of town so soon after his return, but what did he expect her to do? Sit around the house longing for sex and affection while he slipped into the other room and secretly masturbated?

Tonight, however, Aleesa was grateful for the opportunity to be alone with her thoughts. Her mind was consumed with Josiah and their café kiss earlier in the day. She kept turning the events around and around in her head, trying to observe them from every angle so she could tuck them into her memory for retrieval when her bruised ego required fluffing.

Bad idea. Get this man off your mind and keep him off, the loving wife in her advised. *You're a married woman; you have no business thinking about some young boy in such an inappropriate manner.*

Aleesa had to agree with her wifely conscience; she should not be thinking about Josiah in such unacceptable ways. But as much as she wanted to feel guilty about her thoughts and actions, she couldn't.

That's because you finally get the whole sexual energy thing, the sexy Diva inside of her spoke up. Your coochie will shrivel up like an old prune if you don't stay feeling hot and passionate. And then where will you be? And it's okay to feel; you don't have to do anything about it.

But you did cross that line, Wifey reminded her.

It was true. The line had been crossed and she was the one who had jumped it. She had kissed another man. Not only had she and Josiah kissed, she'd been the one who had grabbed him by the collar and sucked his face like she was trying to revive herself.

But weren't you? Diva asked. *You've been suffocating in this marriage. You wrote about Josiah giving you his special brand of CPR in your story. Words beg reality. Don't get down on yourself. You believe in fairytales. Look at it like the prince kissing and bringing back to life the sleeping princess.*

But Walter is your prince, Wifey argued.

Or at least he used to be. But no matter what role he was playing in her life these days, Walt was still her husband and she had no right to cheat on him like that. Had she technically cheated? Lena would say no, not with the circumstances she'd been dealing with. Livia, with her more conservative views, would say yes. Aleesa didn't know what to say, but in her heart of hearts she was definitely feeling like she had tiptoed, however briefly, into the fields of infidelity.

"Can I get you anything from the kitchen?" Walt asked, pulling Aleesa out of her stream of consciousness.

"Some tea would be great," she requested. She watched Walt depart again, happy that other than a barely detectible limp, he was walking normally again. Feeling a twinge of remorse ride up her spine, Aleesa quickly turned her attention to CNN and the latest news about the international space station.

The old-fashioned sound of a ringing phone filled the room. It was Walter's cell phone. Answering each other's phones had always been their practice through the years, so Aleesa picked it up.

"Omigod! Monica, hello. How are you? Are you okay?" Aleesa asked, genuinely happy to hear from her husband's colleague. "Yes, it's been quite an adjustment for us, too. It's good to surround yourself with friends who really understand."

Who's that? Walter silently mouthed as he handed Aleesa her cup of tea.

"Okay, Monica," she said answering his question. "Well, here's

Walt. You take care of yourself. We have to get you over here for dinner real soon."

"I think she's crying," Aleesa whispered, handing him the phone.

"Monica," Walt said, unconsciously shifting his body position away from his wife. "How are you?" Walter kept his voice low and the conversation short and somewhat cryptic.

"That was quick," Aleesa commented after he hung up.

"It was Buddy's birthday today; one of the guys we lost. She was calling to see how I was doing," Walt told her, avoiding her eyes. "I told her I'd call her back. I don't feel like talking now."

"Maybe you should talk to her more. Maybe it would help you," Aleesa suggested, treading lightly. If Monica could help him work through all of these demons he couldn't talk to her about, than Aleesa was all for it. "I think it's nice that she checks in on you, and I hope you do the same for her. She said she's been having some serious issues adjusting to normal life again. She needs you. You two should do whatever you can to help each other get through this."

"Hey, well...you know...we do what we can," he said, confident that what he'd already done was far outside the Good Samaritan role than she was suggesting.

"She's single now and alone. We should really have her over."

"Sure," he said as his guilt rose through the roof. It was just like Aleesa to be thoughtful when it came to other people. Her sense of empathy and compassion was one of the things he loved most about her. But would she be so kind toward Monica if she knew the truth?

Maybe he should tell her and confess everything while Aleesa was feeling so charitable and empathetic. Maybe, after talking to Monica and hearing how messed up she was because of what they'd been through together, Aleesa would understand and be able to forgive and forget.

"Lees, I need to tell you something," Walter began, feeling nervous. "I hope you'll understand and not get too upset, but…"

He looked over at his wife's beautiful face, and the thought of disfiguring it, even temporarily, with the swollen eyes and gruesome contortions that accompany heartbreak, kept him from speaking the truth.

"Upset about what?" Aleesa asked, her antennae rising.

"About next week," he said, deftly changing the subject.

"What about it?" she asked, knowing full well he was referring to their anniversary. It struck her as sad that, for the first time in sixteen years, she'd made no plans to celebrate. But considering the present state of their marriage, and after Walter's homecoming fiasco, she was afraid to prepare anything.

"Our anniversary. I know how you can be, but I'd like to take care of everything this year," he told Aleesa. "Like I said, I hope you won't be upset."

"Oh. No, not at all. That's very sweet of you," she said, with cocktail of mixed emotions. A few minutes ago, he was sounding all put out and irritated, and now he was all warm and fuzzy, talking about anniversary plans. These mood swings of his were killing her.

Guilt swiftly inserted itself into the mix. Aleesa really did find his desire to plan a surprise celebration, all on his own, a sweet gesture, which only made her feel all the more remorseful about kissing Josiah.

"Sweetheart, I know things have been rough since I've been back, and I really want to do this for you," Walter said, putting his arms around her. "So save Saturday for us."

Aleesa gave her husband a hug. Appreciation, confusion and guilt were now being supplemented by trepidation. "Us" didn't feel like it used to and the pressure of an evening traditionally centered around romance, could easily ruin their evening and topple their fragile relationship. Aleesa was hoping like hell that Walt was planning to give her the one gift that she'd requested, couple's counseling. If he didn't, Aleesa was even more fearful that after her actions today, her marriage was in serious trouble.

ALEESA WALKED INTO A QUIET HOUSE AS THE CLOCK ON THE FIREplace mantle chimed. It was seven o'clock on the dot. After part one of her anniversary surprise, a massage and facial at her favorite spa, she was home right on time as Walter's instructions had requested. She wasn't sure what she'd expected to find when she returned, but a dark and quiet house had not been on the list.

As she walked further into the house, a single candle sitting on the dining room table caught her eye and beckoned her over. There she found a note, in Walt's handwriting, instructing her to look in the hallway closet. She felt her excitement grow as she crossed the living room and opened the closet to find a Saks Fifth Avenue garment bag bearing a red rose and another note pinned to it. She smiled. Thoughtful, playful, and full of surprises. This was the Walter she remembered, and was beginning to think she'd lost.

Aleesa pulled the flower from the bag and brought it to her nose. She loved the sensual scent of roses. Sexy, but pure. Immediately, her mind shot back to Walt's freak book and her last fantasy, *Photo Finish*, starring her and Josiah. Aleesa allowed herself to savor the saucy scene of Josiah caressing her body with a white rose before quickly shutting it down. This was her wedding anniversary. It was not good etiquette to think about having sex with another man, particularly when your husband is trying very hard to make this a special night.

She tried, but her thoughts insisted on lingering on the freak book. Was Walter ever going to read it and enjoy the fruits of her labor? She'd poured so much into that tome, and had been so excited about giving it to him and sharing her creativity with him. But after hearing just one story, Walter could only see it as a reminder of his sexual failure as a husband instead of the expression of love it was meant to be. The entire exercise had turned out to be such a sad disappointment.

"Moving on," she told herself as she opened the accompanying note and read Walter's endearing chicken scratch.

Happy Anniversary!
I chose this dress for you because it reminded me of the dress you wore on our honeymoon. It's a different style, but the same shades of blue. As I called you then, you remain to me now, my Blue Angel. So, Angel, once you are dressed, please float on out to the terrace. I know you'll look beautiful.
All my love,
Walt

Aleesa felt her heart glow, warmed by her husband's thoughtfulness. The fog of disappointment and anger that had clouded their life these past few months was lifting. How could she feel anything but love and appreciation for Walter's romantic gesture? The evening was starting off so wonderfully. She said a quick prayer that tonight would mark a new start for the two of them.

She gathered up the Saks bag and rushed back to the bedroom to make a quick change. As soon as Aleesa unzipped the bag, the brilliant colors of their wedding trip escaped into the room. Aleesa smiled broadly as she quickly shed her slacks and sweater and slipped on the flirty floral sundress Walter had chosen for her. She admired the flattering sweetheart neck and then took a twirl in the gathered full skirt. It was perfect. Exactly the kind of dress she would have, and did wear on their honeymoon. And he was absolutely correct about the color. The mix of aqua and royal blue flowers against the white were reminiscent of colorful and picturesque Santorini, Greece.

Aleesa strapped on a pair of sky high sandals, and feeling dressed to thrill, tucked the rose into her hair, adding a pop of color to her ensemble, and headed out to the terrace to find her groom. By the time she got to the family room, she could hear the soft strains of Spanish guitar, her favorite, playing. Aleesa walked through the sliding doors and out onto the terrace, which had been transformed into a romantic dinner party for two. The pool lights were on, giving the backyard a beautiful blue glow, and candles were everywhere. Walter sat on the double chaise lounge, champagne flutes in his hands, waiting. He stood and watched her enter the space, struck by how exquisitely gracefully his wife was aging. She was even sexier now than when they married. At thirty-six, Aleesa had been gorgeous, but at fifty-two, she was stunning.

"This is absolutely beautiful," she told him, gesturing to include everything from her dress to the environment.

"Not as beautiful as you," Walter responded, bending down to greet her mouth with his. Though tentative at first, their lips melted into a gentle and loving kiss. Aleesa closed her eyes and savored the contact as Walter wrapped his arms around her. It felt so wonderful to be in his arms again.

Walter was nervous, but tried hard not to let it show. He knew he was running a huge risk, setting up such a romantic scenario, one that would surely lead to sex, but he had to take the chance. His wife needed a champion, not only in the house, but in her bed, and he was going to try his damnedest to be her hero again.

"Thank you for all of this," Aleesa said, once their kiss came to a sweet end. "All the planning, the dress, this amazing space. This doesn't even look like our backyard!"

"You are very welcome," Walter replied, handing her a glass of champagne. "Happy anniversary, Lees."

"Happy anniversary, Walt." They bumped glasses and drank, each grateful for a loving past and hoping for solid future.

"So for dinner, lovely lady, we have surf and turf and a Caesar salad," he informed her. "And for dessert, well, uh you'll get that later."

"Before we eat, do you know what I'd really like to do?" she asked.

"No, what?" Walt inquired, his stomach tensing.

"Dance with you…"

"In the moonlight," he said, smiling as he finished her sentence. "As you wish." Walter extended his hand to escort her to their makeshift dance floor.

The couple stepped out into the middle of the terrace and embraced in the night. The August air, usually hot and humid this time of year, was an ideal combination of warmth and dryness, perfect for a night spent dancing under the stars. With her arms wrapped around his waist, they slow danced to the sweet guitar sounds and vocals of one of her favorite songs, "Perdido de Amor" by Luiz Bonfá, piped in through the speaker rocks situated around the yard. Aleesa found the musical selection to be particularly thoughtful, as Walter's musical tastes were markedly different from hers. His choice would have been more along the lines of Marvin Gaye or Luther Vandross. No, this he did for her. Aleesa closed her eyes and breathed in Walt's citrusy scent and let herself be intoxicated by the night, the man, and the romance of the occasion.

Aleesa lifted her arms and placed them around Walter's neck. She smiled into his eyes, thanking him for his efforts. She felt happy. The happiest since he'd returned from the Middle East.

She lifted her face to his. "Happy anniversary, baby," she said again before her lips took possession of his.

Aleesa let her tongue do the talking. Lip to lip, she spoke to him of love, of how much he and their marriage meant to her. She apologized for kissing Josiah, explaining that it was only out of frustration and her love and desire for him, that she allowed herself to be tempted. As Aleesa reacquainted her tongue to the warm nooks and crannies of her husband's mouth, her hand caressed his cheek and played with his earlobe as she told him how much she missed him and wanted to make love to him. She pressed her body against his, emphasizing her point.

Eureka! Walt's erection pressed back. She opened her eyes and stared into her husband's face. The hard edges of a soldier's face had been replaced by the soft folds of a lover's. His forehead was slightly furrowed as he concentrated on holding on to his wife, and his hard-on. Feeling her eyes on him, Walter opened his and they locked gazes.

Reminiscent of her blue lights in the basement days, she began to grind his pelvis with hers. Dancing eye-to-eye, Aleesa could feel her body become flushed with arousal. Not wanting to panic him into deflation, she kissed him again, taking his bottom lip between hers and sucking it in soft seduction. A moan dripped from her mouth into his, letting him know the effect this dance was having on her.

Walter loosened his embrace and took hold of her hand, leading her over to the double chaise by the pool. They'd bought the chair years back so they could snuggle together by the pool and his intention, by incorporating the guitar music and outdoor setting, was to make her Phoenix fantasy, the one where she'd written about them making love on the chaise outdoors in the moonlight, become a reality. He prayed he could hold up his part of the performance.

They settled belly to belly onto the chaise, and Aleesa happily began to unbutton his shirt, and strip his upper torso bare. She ran her fingers through the hair on his chest, pausing at his nipples to give them some extra loving attention. Walt's kiss intensified as his hands unzipped her dress before sliding the straps of her dress down her shoulders. Braless, her naked breasts greeted him, their delight revealed by the way her nipples stood at attention.

"You still have the best breasts on the planet," he told her, dipping his head down to devour her tits. He suckled her breasts, feeling them grow in his mouth, knowing they were communicating with his beloved kit cat. The sensitivity of her breasts and the way her body reacted to being stimulated, always turned him on, and happily, tonight was no different.

At this very moment, life was perfect. His wife was in his arms, the mood was loving and kind like it was in the old days, and his dick was feeling strong and responsive. Walter felt the need, to coin a well-worn cliché, to strike while the iron was hot. He did not want to take the chance that his erection would abandon him. He pushed his pants and drawers down around his knees, pushed his wife's dress to her waist and wrangled her panties down her legs. Within seconds, he had pushed past the prickly pubes covering her vagina and was inside her.

Aleesa understood his urgency and went with it. She brushed off her desire for prolonged foreplay, making his frantic attempt to enter her part of the "gotta have it" romance. He bucked against her, concentrating on keeping Monica out of his thoughts and his head and dick in his wife.

"Aleesa, I love you."

"Oh, baby," she said, "I love you, too. Right now, I feel like you and I are the only people left on this earth."

Walter felt his dick begin to soften and wither. There were over a million words in the English language. What were the odds that his wife would string together the same ten or so uttered by Monica during their mutually administered bout of sexual healing?

"Baby, what? What did I say?" Aleesa asked, as she felt his limp penis slip from her vagina. "What did I do wrong?"

"I'm so sorry, Lees. My head's just… It's not you. It's me. It's me," he kept repeating.

"Shh. It's okay. It's okay," she whispered, pulling him to her. "If it got hard once, it can do it again. Relax. We'll do this together."

Aleesa punctuated her statement with a long, reassuring kiss. Taking the lead, she switched positions with him, letting him lay on his back while she straddled his hips. She bent over and kissed him again, this time rubbing her naked breasts against his furry chest. Sitting up again, Aleesa leaned back and placed her hand between his legs, tickling his balls and playing with the sensitive skin along his perineum. She reached over to grab his dick, which was semi-hard at best.

And then it hit her. Walter had no issues staying hard when he masturbated. If you can't fight 'em, join 'em, she told herself as she climbed off of him and laid next to him. Her eyes met his and she smiled before lubing up the fingers of her right hand and reaching down to rub her clit. Her left hand traveled in the opposite direction, massaging her tits before latching on to one nipple and pinching it.

Walter grunted, revealing his enjoyment. She took his hand and put it on his dick, encouraging him to stroke himself into a hard-on with which to please her. He watched his wife, fondling his dick back into service.

Aleesa continued to caress herself, enjoying not only the bodily sensations her touch was stirring up, but the power she felt knowing Walter was watching her. Masturbating in front of him was new, and she liked it. And the way his dick was rising, Walt obviously did, too.

"You're getting hard for me, baby?" she asked, not wanting to say anything to annoy his temperamental dick, but still wanting to coax him along to success.

"Yes." Walt's reply was short and breathless. Aleesa took it as a good sign.

Emboldened by his appreciative eyes on her, Aleesa closed her eyes, pulled the red rose from her hair, and used it to retrace the invisible trail her fingers had left. The velvety soft petals tickled her aroused skin, causing her to laugh out loud with pleasure.

The next sound she heard was Walter sitting up and putting his feet on the ground.

"Now what?" she asked, getting more confused and frustrated, and less able to hide it.

"Why did you start laughing?" he asked. Somebody was really fucking with him this evening. First, Aleesa had repeated, nearly verbatim, Monica's words, reminding him that no matter how hard he tried to push it away and love his wife, he was still a lying cheat. And now here Aleesa was feeling herself up with that damn flower, giggling like a fucking teenager. What was so fucking funny about the fact that he couldn't keep his dick hard enough to make love to his wife? Walter felt like he was stuck in a goddamn nightmare that he couldn't wake up from.

"I laughed because I was making myself feel good. Something I've had to learn to do all on my own since you left for Afghanistan and unfortunately, since you've returned." Aleesa was angry that their anniversary celebration, which had started out so promising, had disintegrated into this. She'd hoped for a reprieve in the awkwardness between them, and had gotten it, up until sex. The very thing that was supposed to bring them closer as husband and wife was once again tearing them apart.

"I'm sorry. I don't know what to do."

"You keep apologizing, and it's quite apparent that you don't know what to do, but you still refuse to go see someone who might give us some answers."

"I can't."

"You won't. There is a huge and defining difference. Going to counseling together was the only gift I asked for. It's the only gift I need. That and sex. You know what, Walter? I have changed since you've been gone. Not having you and not having sex for so long made me really come to appreciate it. And if you'd taken the time to read that book I so painstakingly wrote for you, you'd realize what I finally did. I am a sexual woman. I like sex. I crave it, and want it regularly. Is there something wrong with that?"

"No, nothing at all," he replied softly, not wanting to make things worse by revealing that he'd secretly begun reading the book.

"Well, I can't go on like this. I won't."

Walt didn't know what to do. He wanted to clear the air between them and tell her about Monica, sure it would be the end of them; but did it matter? He was screwing things up anyway. He looked into his wife's angry face and saw the truth in her eyes. She was serious. But about what? Was she making some kind of veiled threat? Was she threatening to leave him or fuck someone else? Walter wasn't sure, and frankly, he was afraid to ask.

Drastic times call for drastic measures. Soup's words ran through his head, helping him to make up his mind. Aleesa seemed to have this new sexual air about her. Reading the book and watching her in action, she appeared more adventurous and spontaneous. Even though she'd always said "yes" to sex and enjoyed making love together, there was a hunger in her that he'd never witnessed before. It could very well be that this new Aleesa would welcome the opportunity and appreciate him for giving it to her. Maybe it would work and then everything would be even between them and they could get on with their marriage without her ever finding out about Monica. It was time to go for broke.

"Wait here," he said, as he pulled up his pants and walked into the house. He returned moments later, carrying a small gift bag. "Happy anniversary," he said, handing it to her.

Was he kidding her? Was he trying to push everything aside by giving her some fucking trinket. "I told you what I wanted."

"I understand, but I want to give you this," he said in a firm voice. "Inside is a gift certificate for a romantic weekend getaway at the Mandarin Oriental hotel in New York. I've booked for you the romance package, which has a lot of perks like champagne and an in-room massage."

"For *me*?" she asked, confused as to why he'd book a romantic weekend getaway for one.

"I'm also giving you a free pass…"

"A free pass? What are you talking about?"

"I started reading your book…"

"Why didn't tell me?"

"I started reading it while you were in San Francisco. It's beautiful and very sexy. It's like you discovered your sexual self through those stories. I can see that you're ready to soar and experiment and let loose. I don't want to stand in your way.

"Lees, I don't know what's wrong with me," he lied convincingly, "but you're right. You need sex, and it's become increasingly obvious that I can't give it to you. I love you so much, Aleesa. Only you. You deserve better. You deserve more," he said, still not able to let the words loose from his lips. Once they were out, there was no taking them back.

"Walter, what are you talking about?"

"I don't want you to be deprived of something you really want, something you say you really need, and I don't want to risk losing you. So, I'm fighting to keep you. I'm giving you forty-eight hours to make one of your fantasies come true. No harm. No foul. No questions asked. Whatever happens will never be spoken about."

"Walter, what are you telling me?" she asked, not believing what her ears were hearing.

"I'm telling you that for your anniversary gift, I want you to go do you. I want you to have what you want and need, and what I can't give you. Sex."

Chapter Seventeen

"Of course you can stay with me as long as you want," Livia said, handing her cousin a mug of steaming Chai tea. "And Lena called. She's five minutes away and said to tell you not to start talking until she gets here."

Aleesa gave her a lifeless smile and nodded. Livia sat next to her, in silent solidarity, sipping her tea and watching Aleesa's eyes fill with tears as her emotions ping ponged across her face.

Not talking for a while longer was not going to be a problem. Aleesa had so many perplexing thoughts pouring through her mind that there was no way she could organize them in any coherent fashion yet. Before Walter's gift-giving bombshell, confusion and hurt had been her constant companions. But those emotions paled by comparison to the chaos and devastation she now felt. The wish for a new beginning between them had been granted. The problem was it looked like they'd be starting over apart, instead of together.

The thought set Aleesa off on another crying jag. Livia moved in closer and wrapped her arms around Aleesa's shoulders, giving her a sideways hug.

"I don't know what to do," she sobbed.

"We'll figure it out," Livia said, sliding the box of Kleenex over toward her as the doorbell sounded. "Be right back," she said, jumping up to answer the door.

"I brought chocolate," Lena announced as she swooped into the room with a bag of groceries swinging from her arm. "Ice cream, potato chips, and of course, vodka. Let me get unpacked, and then you can tell us what the hell happened!"

It took Lena and Livia minutes to get the comfort food on the table.

Aleesa looked up at her friends, and with teary eyes, announced, "I think my marriage is over."

Each of the women let the seriousness of her declaration sink in. "This is not a conversation for tea," Aleesa announced, and placed a glass of vodka in front of each of them.

"I know things have been rough, but over? Are you sure about that?" Livia probed gently.

"Why else would he give me forty-eight hours to fuck anybody I want for my anniversary? Men who love their wives and love being married to them, don't hand them a fucking key to the Mandarin hotel and tell them to make their sexual fantasies come true, no questions asked."

Lena and Livia sat in disbelief as Aleesa described how the evening unfolded, ending in the presentation of Walter's unbelievable gift.

"Why would he want to share me with somebody else?" she asked in a very small and obviously hurt voice.

"You said that he tried to have sex again with you and couldn't. I'm sure he's feeling guilty and ineffective as a husband and lover. He didn't mean it," Livia commented.

"Yes, he did mean it. There was no wavering in his presentation. He said he knew I wanted sex and that he couldn't give it to me, and didn't know when he could, so I had his blessing to go out and make my sexual fantasies come true. Said he didn't want to *deprive* me of something I really wanted.

"This doesn't make sense. I wrote that book to show Walter how much I love him," Aleesa said. "Instead, it's coming back to haunt me."

"If I may play devil's advocate for a moment, you do realize that Walter has given you a prize that many married people around the world would covet? How many women in this world, married as long as you have been, would kill for the chance to receive a husband-sanctioned tryst? Millions, I tell you. I wouldn't be so quick to blow it off if I were you."

"You can't mean that, Lena," Livia jumped in. "Going to bed with some other guy, even if Walter gives her permission, is not going to solve their problems. It's only going to complicate them."

"Or maybe make things clearer."

"Did you see that movie with Demi Moore? The one where Robert Redford offers to pay one million dollars to spend one night with her?"

"*Indecent Proposal*," Lena replied.

"Yes, that's the one. The husband says it's okay, and she sleeps with him and it wrecks everything between her and her husband. Men say it's okay, but it really isn't."

"But didn't they end up together in the end?" Lena pointed out. "Lees, you and I are kindred spirits in so many ways. We both grew up happily toeing the line and following all the rules in the good girl guidebook. I know that I've lived my life making decisions that would not disappoint Douglas, and if I was lucky, I could live with too. I know you did the same. We both got married around what, twenty-three? How many lovers had you been with before you married Bill?" Lena asked.

"One."

"And between Bill and Walt?"

"One."

"So after nearly thirty-five years of having sex, you've spent roughly thirty of them boinking a husband," Lena calculated. "That's three decades of boring, marital sex."

"It wasn't always boring. I liked my sex life with Walter," Aleesa countered. It hurt that she was discussing her sex life in the past tense.

"Yes, you *liked* it," Lena continued. "But did you *love* it? Was it really as hot as you remember it? I know you've never complained about your sex life over the years, but you never really bragged about it either. Since you and Walt have been married, I think I could count on one hand the number of times you told me you were horny. Your constant sex on the brain didn't start until you two were forced to be apart. My question is: Have you built up this great sex life in your mind since you've been unlocking all of the fantasies in your head?"

Aleesa wasn't sure how to respond. On some level, Lena was correct. While she definitely has been satisfied with her sex life B.A., the new Aleesa had to admit that her motives for maintaining such an active sex life had more to do with her fear of Walt being unfaithful than a true "she's gotta have it" desire for sex.

"What's your point, and what does it have to do with what's going on now?" Livia inquired, asking the questions that Aleesa was not. Lena's words were hitting very close to her own past marital relations, and she was curious to hear more.

"My point is, you've spent your adult life playing by the rules. Walter is giving you the chance to break a few. You've had wife sex all your life, except for when you were creating fantasies. I think that you should seriously consider this a chance to explore yourself like you never have had the opportunity to do before.

"It could be that the Universe is sending you a message that it's time to stop writing about mind-blowing sex and experience it, at least once in your life. Would it be optimum if it were with your husband? Yes. But in your case, it looks like it will be because of him. I say don't look a gift horse in the mouth," Lena advised her. "Go for it."

"So you honestly think that Walt's offer is a message to Aleesa from the Universe to cheat?" Livia asked, talking about Aleesa while ignoring the fact that she was sitting right next to her.

Aleesa sipped her cocktail and listened to her friends as they argued the pros and cons of this baffling situation. In so many ways, it felt like both of them were reading her mind. Lena was spot-on about how she felt about herself these days. She wanted to explore and stretch the limits of her passion. She'd assumed she'd be doing it with Walter, but how interesting would it be to bring her nasty girl out to play for a weekend with a fresh lover who came without baggage or pretense of a future? Josiah fit the bill perfectly.

But Livia's assessment was bull's-eye accurate as well. Acting out, even with Walter's permission, could cook up a whole new batch of troubles that their fragile relationship definitely did not need and could not handle. The risks were so high and the consequences so dire, she felt numb and absolutely clueless as to what to do, and therefore had little to add to their discussion. Maybe they could come up with an answer.

"First, let's be clear. She wouldn't be cheating on him. He gave her permission. Secondly, yes, between Walter's anniversary gift and meeting Josiah Newman, I think this is one of those times in her life where outside forces are helping to push her into a new direction."

"Sounds like she's got the devil at her back."

Aleesa continued to let her attention ping pong back and forth between her two friends and their insights without comment. It was only hearing Josiah's name that caught Aleesa's attention and pulled her back into the conversation.

"I kissed him," she admitted softly.

"You what?" Livia asked, not believing her cousin's confession. "When did you see him?"

"And why are you just now telling us about it?" Lena probed.

"After we got back from California, I sent him an email, congratulating him on the show. He invited me to meet for coffee," Aleesa informed them. She went on to tell them how he'd charmed and bewitched her by taking photographs in the middle of the café. Aleesa revealed how everyone looked at them like they were having sex, and how the tension was so thick between them that it felt that way. How she had to excuse herself and escape to the ladies' room, but how when she came out, there he was.

"I reached up and kissed him," Aleesa informed them. "After it was over, I said goodbye and left."

"How was it?" Lena had to ask, surprised that her friend had been so bold.

"He's an amazing kisser. The truth is, I've always been attracted to him, but I think I've just been feeling so lonely and unwanted at home that I let it go further than I should have."

"Do you think that's why you got so upset with Walt? Because you feel guilty about being attracted to Josiah, and kissing him?" Livia asked.

"Maybe. It's crazy; a part of me feels guilty as hell, and another part of me feels kind of giddy and excited."

"So, then maybe you should go for it and take your husband up on his offer. If the itch needs scratching, and he's handing you a backscratcher, you might as well use it," Lena suggested. "Explore your attraction to Josiah, and then get on with your marriage, if that's what you decide you want to do."

"Of course, she wants to get on with her marriage," Livia argued on her cousin's behalf. "Lees, this is just a rough patch you're going through. You know your husband. This doesn't even sound like him. He loves you, has always loved you, and has never given you cause to worry about that fact. If Walter has done something this stupid, it's because he's so lost and so upset that he can't be the man you've always needed him to be. He's desperate, so don't make things worse by sleeping with Josiah."

"Josiah says it's simply sexual energy to feel and enjoy, knowing you don't have to do anything with it," Aleesa shared with them.

"So you felt it, even enjoyed a little taste of it. Now let it go and move on with your husband," Livia counseled.

"I think that's the whole point of this," Lena said. "Nothing is moving at home. Aleesa knows it, and Walter knows it, too."

"I don't know how things got to this point. I mean, think about it. For my sixteenth anniversary gift, my husband gave me permission to go have sex with somebody else. It makes no damn sense."

"I think Walter feels guilty. Guilty that he can't be the man he knows you need and deserve, and your book makes it worse because it puts down in black and white the things you want from him, i.e. great sex that he can't give you, at least for the moment," Livia suggested.

"So what am I supposed to do?"

"The basic question is what do you WANT to do?" Lena said, giving up her point of view so she could help her friend find her own.

Aleesa took a deep breath before speaking her truth. "What I *don't* want to do is make things any worse than they already are. Like I said in California, some things are best left a fantasy, so no more tempting myself with Josiah. I will not be accepting my husband's gift, but I don't know what I want after that. The fact that Walt would pawn me off like this," she said, feeling the tears begin to well up again, "tells me that I don't know my husband anymore, and he doesn't know me. Really, what kind of man makes an offer like that? And what kind of woman says yes?"

Aleesa's cell phone rang, interrupting their conversation. She picked it up, saw Walter's image on the screen, and handed it to her cousin. "He has no idea where I am. Please tell him I'm okay, but that I can't talk to him right now."

"I'm going to bed," she announced on her way out of the room. All she wanted was this day marking her sixteen years of marriage to be over, and for tomorrow to bring her the answers that were evading her tonight.

THE WEE HOURS OF THE MORNING FOUND ALEESA STILL AWAKE. Sitting in the darkness of Livia's spare bedroom, she tried to clear her mind of all the advice she'd received from her friends, and listen to her gut. She knew that her girls meant well, but neither woman was in the position to fully determine what was best for her. Lena and her cousin stood on disparate ends of the sexual spectrum. Ever since her wild and wanton affair with Jason Armstrong had provided Lena with her explosive sexual awakening, she'd become a tireless advocate for women unleashing and owning their inner freak. Livia was the exact opposite. Sexually repressed and morally conservative, her views were often so narrow that there was little wiggle room for the many nuances of human relationships.

As she sat deliberating her situation, the familiar adage, "If you love something, let it go free. If it returns, it's yours forever," kept cycling through her head. Aleesa took its unsolicited appearance as a clue offered by the powers that be, to be broken down and studied so she could better understand her current predicament.

She began with the notion of loving someone. In her heart of hearts, Aleesa believed that, despite his recent aloof behavior and sexual difficulties, Walter truly loved her. His eyes didn't lie.

There were times when she could feel them on her, pleading for her to understand and give him time to work through his troubles.

And despite the rough patch they were experiencing, she still loved him so much. Their evening had started out so wonderfully, so vintage Walter. The grouch in him had receded, and all of his Prince Charming qualities had been on display. Aleesa knew if he'd agree to get counseling, they could talk their way out of this state of misery their marriage had fallen into since his return.

"Let them go..." Just saying the words out loud made her heart sink. She certainly did not want Walter to let her go; she wanted to save their relationship. But did he want the same thing? Or was he feeling so guilty, as Liv had suggested, that he was willing to push her into the arms of someone else? Was he telling the truth when he said that he loved her so much that he was ready to sacrifice his manhood and let her experience in someone else's bed what he could not give her in their own? In her mind, that was crazy talk, but had the ravages of war altered Walter's way of thinking and feeling in ways that she could not fathom?

"If it returns, it's yours forever," she recited into the darkness. Perhaps his unusual gift was actually meant to be an experiment of sorts. His obscure way of testing her loyalty and devotion to him and their marriage? Was Walter playing her like a boomerang, throwing her to the wind with hopes of her returning?

The further she traveled down this line of thought, the clearer her course of action became. She would 'return' his gift and exchange it for a homecoming *redux*, a fresh start for their marriage and a chance for the two of them to finally begin to address the very real issues—Walt's impotence and his refusal to seek help—that confronted them. Because as confused and distant as things might feel between them right now, Aleesa loved her husband, and had no true desire to find intimacy with anyone else. Yes, she had given into temptation and slipped up by kissing Josiah, but was ashamed of herself for being so selfish. Aleesa was truly sorry for being disloyal to Walter. He was a good man, and a true war hero. He'd been hurt serving his country. He deserved nothing less than a loyal wife who, forsaking all others, loved and stood by him for better or for worse, in sickness and in health.

Chapter Eighteen

Hung over and exhausted from a night of tossing and turning with very little sleep, Walter was gratefully surprised to find his wife in the kitchen cooking breakfast. He was ecstatic to see her, but as he approached, he felt like he was walking on the eggshells she'd cracked to make scrambled eggs.

"Good morning," Walter greeted her, the tentativeness clear in his voice. "I'm surprised to see you here." As was his habit, he headed straight for the table. "I thought you were at Liv's."

"Good morning," Aleesa responded while plating up their breakfast and bringing it to the table. "I spent the night there, but got up early to come home."

"I'm glad you came home," Walter said, taking her hand and kissing it.

"Coffee?" she asked, ignoring his overture. She might be home. She might be eager to talk, but she was still angry.

"Yes, please."

Aleesa put the coffee mugs down on the table and sat down. "I thought we needed to talk sooner rather than later."

"I know it's all I seem to be saying lately, but I'm sorry. Truly sorry," Walt said, jumping right in. "I don't know what I was thinking by giving you that stupid free pass. I didn't mean to upset you; I just thought…"

"I'm honestly not sure what you were thinking, either," Aleesa said, jumping in and not letting him finish. "But I need you to know that your gift wasn't only confusing, it was hurtful," she told him, keeping her voice calm. "I don't understand how you could feel right about yourself or this relationship, and let me be with another man for forty-eight hours. Not if you love me. Just the thought of you being with someone else kills me."

Walter felt his stomach flip as remorse stole the oxygen from his lungs and replaced it with the shame for his multitude of sins.

"I do love you, Lees." Walter stopped talking, taking the less is more course of action.

"I stayed up all night turning this thing over in my head and it wasn't until Livia suggested something that it all began to make sense to me."

"And what was that?"

"She thinks you feel guilty, and you're trying to make yourself feel better by giving me the chance to, well, you know…be with someone else." Not wanting to cause him any embarrassment by thinking that she told all their business, Aleesa did not mention his impotence by name.

The series of looks that Aleesa watched traipse across Walter's face were both telling and baffling. By the panic-stricken gleam in his eye, it was clear that her comment had hit a very raw nerve. But, at the same time, there was an obvious look of resigned relief softening his face. It was his eyes beginning to brim with tears; however, that totally threw her for a loop.

"Honey, what's wrong?"

Walter wasn't sure what the women had figured out on their own, but he didn't care. Aleesa walking out on him last night had brought him to the breaking point. Nothing was going to change between them for the better if he didn't come clean. Livia's assessment had cracked the seal on the window of opportunity. It was now or never. Hopefully, in time, Aleesa would learn to forgive and forget. And even if she didn't, he couldn't live this way anymore. The guilt was eating him alive.

"Livia is right. I feel incredibly guilty about so many things, but mostly for betraying you. I never meant to hurt you, Aleesa. Never. It just happened."

The sound of Aleesa's fork dropping on to her plate resounded throughout the kitchen.

"Never meant to hurt you." "Betray you." "I feel guilty." As Walter sat spewing out the key words, which had historically been used to announce an oncoming personal disaster, Aleesa felt the all too familiar clutch of dread grab her body. She knew exactly what 'it' meant. The words, the tears, the pained look contorting Walt's features. She'd heard and seen them all before on Bill's face, when he finally found the need to confess all of his wrongdoings.

Aleesa tried to force feed her lungs air as the panic began to rise up and threaten to take over. Walter, seeing her obvious distress, grabbed her hands to keep them from shaking. "Omigod. Omigod, not again," Aleesa whispered under her breath, pulling her hands away.

"I promise you. It meant nothing, certainly not in any sexual way," Walt clumsily tried to explain.

Aleesa felt herself go still as another part of her heart died a quiet death. She could not possibly be sitting at another kitchen table, with yet another husband confessing his infidelity. With Bill, it had taken them two years to have this conversation, which sadly became a recurring discussion throughout their ten-year marriage. Aleesa guessed she'd made progress, as it had taken Walt sixteen years. As it had been with Bill, Walter's betrayal came out of the blue without Aleesa suspecting a thing. Obviously, she still had "gullible wife," tattooed on her forehead with invisible ink, because here she was again. But this time, she was armed with all of the right questions that, unfortunately, experience had taught her to ask.

"When?"

"While I was away in Afghanistan."

"Who was she?"

Walter paused, knowing this answer was going to hurt.

"Who was it? Do I know her?" Aleesa repeated.

"Yes. It was Monica."

Walter could see Aleesa's jaw tighten at the mention of Monica's name. He braced himself to get hit or have something thrown at him, as he was sure Aleesa must have felt like a fool. It was only a week ago that she was insisting they not only invite Monica over for dinner, but that he spend more time with her. But if she felt stupid or betrayed, he couldn't tell because Aleesa remained perfectly composed. This lack of emotion concerned him. He'd expected an outburst of some kind; instead she faced him calmly while he imagined she was raging inside.

"Well, doesn't that give a whole new meaning to soldiers-in-arms," Aleesa commented with a sarcastic bite. "So she's the reason you won't have sex with me," Aleesa said, her voice remaining low, but possessing a shrillness associated with rising anger.

"Yes, but…"

"So, let me make sure that I have this right. While I was at home, putting all of my sexual frustrations down on paper, for your enjoyment, I might add, you were satisfying yours with Monica."

"It wasn't like that. It's not what you think."

"It never is," Aleesa said, while starting to laugh. It was an eerie, ironic chuckle that sent a chill through him. "Omigod, it is true. You all do have the same manual. All you men use the same stupid, insulting lines to explain your bad behavior."

"Aleesa, let me explain. It was only…"

"STOP!" Aleesa shouted, holding her hand up in his face. She did not want to hear any of the details. Walter stopped talking, shocked by her icy tone. "Did you or did you not have sex with Monica while you were in Afghanistan?"

"Yes," he answered sheepishly.

"I know you two speak, but have you seen her since you've been home?"

"Well, yes, but…"

Again, she raised her hand, cutting off all explanation.

"WHO ARE YOU?" she screamed in his face. "I don't know you anymore! You are a liar, whether outright or by omission. You let me believe things that are not true. Like you being healthy and well in Afghanistan, when you were actually four hours away in Washington. Was she there with you? Nursing you back to health? Kissing your war wounds?"

"She visited on…"

That news sent a knife stab through Aleesa's heart, but did not let the air out of her tirade. "Then you led me to believe that you can't get your dick hard so we can have sex, but I find you masturbating after leaving my bed. Were you thinking of her when you had your dick in your hand, instead of inside of me?"

"Lees…"

"You refused to get counseling with me, and then drop not one but TWO ultimate betrayals. First, you had an affair, and then you wanted to pawn me off to another man.

"You don't think I didn't think about sleeping with someone else in the two years you were away? What, you don't think your old wife still can turn heads and get offers? Well, I was tempted while you were gone, more than you know. But you know what? Whenever those opportunities came up, I'd ask myself, 'Is this worth losing Walter and everything I have?' And the answer was always, 'no.' Stupid me. Apparently, once again I was fooling myself."

"Aleesa, you have to let me explain. You have to listen to me," Walter pleaded.

"I DON'T HAVE TO DO ANYTHING," she said with a wicked clip to her tone. "I listened to you when you said you loved me. I listened to you when you promised that you would never cheat on me. I listened to you when you told me that you and Monica were friends trying to help each other through a tough time. I listened to you when you gift-wrapped a hotel room key and told me to go fuck another man. I'm done listening to you."

To make her point, Aleesa stood up and walked out of the kitchen. Walter, feeling like his head was about to explode, followed her into the bedroom. How was he ever going to make things right between them again? He watched as Aleesa began to pack with fierce determination. He felt the slightest bit of relief in the knowledge that she'd pulled out an overnight bag.

"Where are you going?" he asked.

"Tonight to Livia's," she told him, before dropping her bomb. "And then tomorrow, after I make a few phone calls, I'm checking into the Mandarin Hotel." To make her intentions perfectly clear, she made sure Walt saw her pull out the cherry-red lingerie she'd purchased for the photo shoot, and drop it into her suitcase. "I've decided to accept your gift after all."

"But I only gave you that gift because I felt guilty for not telling you the truth," he said, feeling the sweat drip down his back. "I had this stupid idea that if you had a free pass, we'd be…"

"What? Even? That's why you were all, 'no harm. No foul.' It would have been a lot smarter to have gone to counseling, don't you think? But I guess we're both dumb asses, because last night, I had convinced myself that you were doing this out of love, so I came running home. Now I find it was guilt that was driving all of this."

"It is out of love. I swear to you. Aleesa, please don't do this. I'll go to counseling. I'll do whatever you want me to do."

Aleesa grabbed her overnight bag and brushed Walter's body as she pushed past him to leave the room. He grabbed her around the waist, looking straight into her eyes, pleading with her not to leave. Her steely stare delivered her return message loud and clear. Walter dropped his arms, stepped aside and watched as his wife walked out of their bedroom.

"I'm begging you. Please do not go to that hotel."

"Walter, you're already a liar and a cheat. Don't be an Indian-giver as well."

Walt heard the garage door open and close. He was alone again, this time drowning in regret. First and foremost, he regretted sleeping with Monica. If only he'd had the strength in that defining moment to just say "no." But despite the superman accolades his wife had given him in the past, that day he had learned what a sad, mere mortal he was. His night with Monica was closely followed by allowing Soup to convince him to try and wipe away his guilt by force-feeding Aleesa a huge dose of her own. He'd let fear determine his strategy, and as any soldier worth a damn knew that was a sure way to lose the battle. Those two errors in judgment would haunt him for the rest of his life.

ALEESA PULLED OUT OF THE GARAGE AND WAITED UNTIL SHE GOT to the stop sign at the end of their block to call. If fate was in play, she decided, Josiah would answer before the fifth ring. If he didn't, she'd let it go forever. The phone rang four times, each ring taking forever. One more and she was hanging up. Right before the fifth ended, she heard his sexy hello.

"Hi. It's Aleesa Davis."

"Hello. I've been waiting for you to call," he said, the buttery timbre of his voice melting away her surface anger. "So you're ready to find out what comes next?"

Aleesa didn't know if she found his swagger egotistical or just plain sexy. It must have been the latter because she didn't hesitate to confirm her desire.

"I was wondering if you were busy tomorrow night? If not, I was hoping that maybe we could have a drink."

"I think that a drink is a perfect place to start."

"Okay, then. MObar in the Mandarin Hotel. 7 p.m. And, Josiah…" She paused.

"Yes?"

"Leave your camera at home," Aleesa said, making him laugh.

"Okay. But thank God, I have a photographic memory. See you tomorrow."

"Fuck you, Walter," Aleesa swore after hanging up. She pulled off into the street, both amazed and proud of herself. Josiah was the perfect man for this rather imperfect situation. The physical attraction between them was smoking hot and there was a feeling of friendship bubbling underneath. Who could ask for anything more when it came to her first affair? Yes, making this date with Josiah felt very right. In the back of her mind, Aleesa only hoped she hadn't made it for all the wrong reasons.

At the next stop light, she dialed Livia's number. She'd left her cousin's house so early this morning, and her return was unexpected, so the least Aleesa could do was give her a heads-up. The phone continued ringing until Liv's voice came on explaining she wasn't available. Aleesa let her know that she was on her way over, and she'd use her key if nobody was home.

Aleesa drove through the streets of Montclair to Livia's on automatic pilot. Her mind was churning with the words, thoughts and feelings surrounding Walter's confession. Years ago, she'd heard a quote from somebody who said, 'all husbands are alike, but have different faces so you can tell them apart.' Before this morning, she would have thought that to be a crock of bullshit, at least in her home. Before this morning, she had thought Walter to be unique unto himself, a perfect blend of provider, confidante, playmate, lover, husband, and friend. Before this morning, she never would have put Bill and Walt in the same category. But, oh, how quickly the times had changed. Now they both belonged on the stupid, fucking, cheating husband list, and she was once again, one scorned and angry wife.

Interestingly enough, twenty years ago, she'd been absolutely devastated when she learned about Bill's shenanigans. Bill had left her with such a mess to clean up, that there had been no time to weep and wallow. Back then, anger only got in the way of her survival. But finding out about Walter and Monica had left Aleesa feeling like the kid who'd been bullied all through school and was now walking back into class with a black belt wrapped around her waist. She felt a fury like she'd never experienced before. Aleesa was tired of feeling like the victim. She was done feeling sorry for herself and wondering what she did wrong or didn't have that caused her man to stray. That's why she didn't bother to let Walt explain. The details didn't matter. He'd lied. He'd cheated. Case closed. But this time, she was taking it like a man. It was time for the hubby to find out how it felt to be at home, waiting and wondering while wifey was out spreading her love around.

Within twenty minutes, Aleesa was opening the front door to Livia's dark and empty house. Calling out, but getting no response, she assumed Liv must be out delivering a cake or grocery shopping, so Aleesa let herself in and headed straight for the freezer. Aleesa actually was glad that Livia was out. She had a big adventure planned for tomorrow and she didn't want anybody trying to talk her out of it. Aleesa's strategy was to be in a drunken sleep by the time her cousin returned. Ice cold vodka would take away her ability to think, to feel, and to dream. Eight hours in the black hole of sleep was what she craved, and she knew just the Grey Goose to fly her there.

Chapter Nineteen

"Liv, where are you?" Aleesa asked into her cell phone. "I've been calling you all day. You never came home last night. Where are you? It's not like I am expecting to be privy to your every whereabouts; who knows, you and Jeremy might have hooked up again. But since I did sleep at your house without your knowledge, I thought I should at least check on you.

"I do want to make sure you are okay, but I wanted to talk, too. So much has happened. Sorry to be hunting you down like a jealous wife, though that would be entirely apropos, considering my life right now, but Lena is in Hong Kong, and you're still around, but where?

"I'm at the hotel relaxing and waiting for Josiah. I decided to theme this forty-eight hours, 'Guilty Pleasures.' Walter has been so generous, and he'll find out just how much when he gets his credit cards statements! I've been shopping all afternoon, and just got back from the spa. My body is baby butt soft; so much so that I can't keep my hands off my damn self! I bought this amazing dress at the shop downstairs. It's one shoulder, kind of an '80's vibe. Remember those blouson minis we used to wear? Like that, but sleeker. It's short and makes my legs look amazing, and it's red. Show-stopping, heart-dropping red. I look scrumptious if I do say so myself!

"I'm scheduled to meet Josiah at the bar in an hour. Okay, shut up, Liv. I can hear you saying, 'Aleesa, I can't believe you're doing this', and frankly, I can't believe I'm doing this either. But you know what? Walter deserves it. What's good for the goose, right? I figure if every man I marry is going to cheat on me, I might as well join the ranks of the unfaithful. Apparently, the list is long and very distinguished.

"Oh, but wait, I'm not being unfaithful. This was a gift from my dear, loving, cheating husband. I'm simply the lucky recipient of a rather unique anniversary present. So if he wants to even things up by 'allowing' me one weekend of uninhibited bliss, who am I to say 'no'?

"That's right; you don't know. When I got home after the night I spent with you and Lena, Walter dropped another 'gift' on me. When I told him you thought he was acting out of guilt, he must have thought I knew something, because broke down and confessed to me that he had an affair with his hygienist, Monica, over in Afghanistan. I actually talked to the bitch. She's been calling my husband for months, and apparently visited him in the hospital when I didn't even know he was in the damn country. So I guess we now know why he couldn't keep it up.

"So there, now you're caught up. I'm about to partake in my forty-eight hours of guilt-free pleasure with one very hot and sexy photographer, and then, while wallowing in the afterglow, I will figure out the rest of my life.

"Text me and le—" Aleesa heard the beep, signaling her that she'd used all of the time on Livia's answering machine. She hung up, happy to have vented, even if it was to herself, but still concerned about her cousin.

Freshly showered from the spa, Aleesa slipped into her photo shoot red lingerie and new dress, before moving on to her next guilty pleasure purchase. Aleesa pulled the Jimmy Choo shoes from their box and held them up to admire. They were four inches of walking sex. Nude in color, they made her legs look ten miles long. Aleesa strapped them around her feet and stood, instantly knowing the $775 Walter had paid for them was well worth the money. She also now understood why Lena loved shoes like this so much. There was no way you could say "no" to a woman wearing such sexy footwear. Aleesa did a final touch on her make-up and added a spritz of Princess, grabbed her new evening clutch and was out the door.

She intentionally arrived at the MObar half an hour early, so she could secure the perfect table—away from the door and hopefully by the window so they could enjoy the seductive silhouette of the best city on earth. She walked inside and was immediately struck by its spicy appeal. It was early, so there were a few thirty- and forty-something customers, relaxing in posh, brown leather chairs or against tall, carved stone-back seats. The cinnabar-painted walls, gauzy gold curtains and bulbs with electric-orange filaments gave the ambience a sexy spark. Aleesa was disappointed to see that there wasn't really much of a view, but still, this was the perfect spot—intimate and out of the way.

Aleesa decided on one of the low lounge tables in the back. Almost immediately, she was greeted by a lovely young woman wearing a silk, Chinese-inspired top, eager to take her order. "A MO-politan, perhaps? Rum with blood orange juice?" the waitress suggested.

"Sounds good," Aleesa said, figuring that a little something to take the edge of her nerves couldn't be a bad thing. Suddenly she felt a bit more dubious about the adventure she was about to embark on.

At seven-fifteen, Aleesa was well into sipping her way into courageousness. She'd already finished two delicious MO-politans, and was feeling light and flirty and a tad tipsy. She had decided to slow her roll and sip on water while waiting for her date before ordering anything else.

She didn't have to wait long. Josiah arrived fashionably late and looking utterly edible. Replacing his jeans and T-shirt was a navy suit worn with a blue, open collar shirt. The suit was cut to perfection and with his locks tied back into a low ponytail, he looked like a frickin' supermodel walking through the place. His smile broadened as he approached and Aleesa took girlish joy in the fact that both the men and women he left in his wake were staring with eyes full of admiration.

"Good evening, pretty lady," he spoke before leaning over and kissing her on the cheek, while his hand lightly brushed against her exposed shoulder. His lips lingered on the side of her face while his caress let her know that there was nothing chaste about this kiss, despite its public appearance. "You look stunning."

"Hi," was all that she could manage to respond.

Instead of sitting on the opposite side of the table, Josiah pulled his chair next to her. His close proximity allowed her to breathe in the "come get me" scent of musk he was wearing. He smiled, flashing those beautiful teeth at her, and making her curious to find out exactly what flavor toothpaste he used.

"Would you like a drink?" she asked, leaning toward him while running her index finger around the rim of her glass. He smiled, liking what her body language was telling him.

"Dewar's neat, please," he requested from their waitress. "And one more for the lady."

"My husband orders..." Aleesa said, pushing her nails into her palm for being so stupid. In what world does one try to seduce someone by mentioning her husband? *Great move, dumb ass*, she chastised herself.

"Like I said before, the man has good taste," Josiah said, coolly slipping past the awkwardness. It was so incredibly obvious that Aleesa was a newbie at all of this. It amused as well as honored him. "Looks like you got started without me," he said, noticing her near empty martini glass.

"I did. I had to. Honestly, this is the first, you know, date...I've had in a long time. I'm kind of nervous," she admitted.

"Are you going to start giggling again? You know what that does to me," he said, lacing his fingers through hers.

"I'm going try to refrain from all inappropriate laughter," Aleesa said, slightly slurring and mispronouncing her words.

Josiah let loose an amused chuckle. "You are so cute."

"Cute, is not what I had in mind," Aleesa said, getting very serious, very fast. She didn't come here to be cute. Cute was for kittens and puppies and babies, none of which interested her this evening.

To make her point, she leaned over and kissed him, giving Josiah part two of the kiss she'd begun at the café. Aleesa loved the feel of his soft lips against hers. She could taste the cherry chapstick he used to keep them that way. Her tongue, made lazy by the liquor, explored the violet-tasting recesses of his mouth. "Omigod, your mouth tastes good," she commented, pulling away from him.

"Thank you. Please feel free to taste away." Josiah pulled the violet mints from his pocket to offer her one.

"Were you surprised to hear from me so soon?" Aleesa asked, turning to talk as her mouth savored the mint and her body the aftermath of his kiss. Their conversation momentarily ceased as their waitress sat down their drinks.

"Not really. I knew from our first meeting that we'd end up in this place. The pull between us is too strong not to be explored. I felt it and I knew you felt it, too."

"I do," she said, before laughing softly. The laughs ended as she looked him in the eye. "I like the way it feels." Aleesa smiled at him again as she reached for the rose at the center of the table. As was her habit, she picked it up and carried it to her nose, inhaling the scent. "Ah, real roses, not some hybrid they grew all the fragrance out of. Here, smell."

Aleesa placed the flower under his nose, allowing him to sniff. Without concern or consent, she looked him in the eyes while gently wiping the rose across his lips, stroking his cheeks and neck, down into the vee of his unbuttoned shirt, before bringing it back under her nose. Josiah felt his skin react, first with goosebumps and then shooting tingles down his leg and to his testicles. She dropped her eyes into the bloom and then lifted them back up to his.

"I, uh, wrote a fantasy about you taking a flower and massaging me with it," she revealed.

"I'm in your book?"

"Yes, the very last story."

"So are you going to tell me about it?"

"Maybe, if you're a very good boy," Aleesa said, beginning to feel the full effect of her cocktails.

Josiah smiled broadly, his ego as happy as his dick right now. "So, tonight we're going to make this a fantasy real, as Maxwell would say?"

"That appears to be the case." Aleesa leaned over again and captured his face between her two hands, pulling him toward her. She liked feeling aggressive and demanding, and the twinkle in Josiah's eye let her know that he liked it, too. She gently sucked on his lower lip before transferred the mint in her mouth to his. "Or at least most of it," she added, remembering his twin brother also had a featured role.

"Shouldn't we take this to a room?" he asked, totally aware that he was sitting in public sucking face with a married woman. "We'd have much more privacy. I wouldn't want this to cause any problems for you…you know if someone saw you here with me. We certainly couldn't pass this off as a business meeting. Not with you looking so hot."

"It's okay," Aleesa told him, helping herself to a long, healthy swig of her drink. "My husband approves."

"Oh. You two have an open marriage?"

"Affairrently," she slurred and started laughing. "I said affairently! How funny is that?

"Besides, I like being here with preople watching us. It turns me on. And who cares, if someone tells him."

I care, Josiah wanted to tell her. He knew full well that she was a married woman, and frankly, that was a non-issue in his world, but coming face to face with her husband was another story. Yes, he was there with another man's wife, by his own volition, but there was no reason to be stupid about things.

"Aleesa, baby, I really think that we should move this party to the room. The things I want to do with you are not for public consumption."

"Okay," she agreed, finishing her drink. "Here's your key. I'm going to go up; you wait ten minutes and come up after me."

"Cool. I'll take care of the bill here."

"No, just sign it to the room. This is a gift. *Everything* is included." Aleesa stood up and steadied herself on the back of her chair before leaning her body into Josiah's. She ran her tongue across his lips. "I'll see you in ten."

Josiah watched her tight ass as it walked away. Hmpf! Aleesa was fine and he was so ready to dive in and see what was under all of that girlish charm and drunk bravado. That said, he was beginning to get a whole different vibe from this booty call. He didn't know what had happened in her life these past few weeks, but based on the snide remarks and drunken clues she was sending out, hubby had been a bad boy and his Mrs. was out for revenge.

Suddenly, Josiah was feeling less like a boy toy and more like a pawn in a messy game of marital chess. But, hey, if she was willing, he was entirely able.

He sipped on his drink and people watched while he waited out the requested ten minutes. Even at fifty plus, the young girls in the room had nothing on Aleesa Davis. She had more style and sex appeal than eighty percent of the women half her age, and he couldn't wait to put all of that good wisdom and experience to work. Josiah stood up, grabbed the rose from the vase, and headed out to see, after all of these months of wondering, exactly what Aleesa Davis was working with.

Upstairs, Aleesa found herself in a quandary. As she'd told Josiah, it had been a long time since she'd had a date like this and she'd made a crucial wardrobe error. The dress she'd chosen was fantastic on, but with no zippers and only one arm, it wasn't built for a quick and easy exit. They'd have to pull it over head and risk messing her hair and getting makeup over it, or try to pull it down over her hips and risk it getting stuck or torn.

"Add dress without a zipper to your list of seduction DON"Ts," Aleesa told herself in the mirror. "Right after, don't bring up your husband's drink preferences.

"Okay, focus. You either need to take off the dress, and greet him in your undies, which will make you look all too eager, or completely change, which will have him thinking you're fricking Diana Ross."

With time ticking away and Josiah's arrival imminent, she decided on a middle-ground approach. Bra and panties under the hotel robe. Aleesa had just enough time to change, hang up her dress, and brush her teeth before Josiah's subtle knock heralded his arrival.

"Here we go. Don't think; go with the flow.

"Walt, this one is for you."

Aleesa answered the door, moving aside so Josiah could enter. Once inside, he presented her with the flower from behind his back, making her laugh. "You said a fantasy real," he reminded her, as he pulled Aleesa to him, and swallowed her smile in his kiss.

Still lip-to-lip, they pushed back into the room, happily landing on the king-sized bed with an equally large view of the upper west side. "Great view of the city, isn't it?" Aleesa whispered in his mouth.

"Hadn't noticed. Too busy gazing at the amazing view below me," Josiah answered before beginning a trail of butterfly kisses down her chin, neck and over the narrow crevice of skin peeking out from underneath her still tied robe. "You know, the good news," Josiah said, stopping to reach down and untie the knot in her belt, "is that we don't have to go through that awkward, 'what will he think of me naked' stage." He punctuated his statement by pulling the terry cloth belt from under her and flinging open her robe to unveil her goodies. "Now that, pretty lady, is a *view*."

Aleesa said nothing, as she felt a nervous niggling in her toes. Josiah noticed nothing, as he kicked off his shoes and pulled off his jacket before continuing his trail of kisses across her lovely collarbone. He lifted his head up to admire her lingerie, recognizing it from the shoot. "How did you know that these were my favorite?"

Aleesa simply shrugged her shoulders and smiled with a 'lucky guess' look on her face. Her head couldn't possibly be concerned with coming up with an answer to such an inane question when a much more important one was knocking hard and loud against her head, *WHAT THE FUCK ARE YOU DOING?*

Josiah sucked her nipples through the lace of her brassiere, feeling them swell in his mouth. His hand joined the activity, squeezing them both together so he could give them a simultaneous tongue bath.

He reached behind her back and unhooked the bra before lifting his head and sliding the straps from her shoulders. "I wish I had my camera now because you look absolutely breathtaking," he told her as he removed her bra and cupped her breasts in his hands.

Aleesa closed her eyes as his hands began to explore the landscape of her body. His caress was soft and endearing, yet masterful. She tried to give into the temptation of his touch, but her mind refused to let her relax and kept badgering her with questions. *Why didn't she feel breathtaking? Why didn't she feel sexy and in control like she had when they were at MObar? And why did all of this feel like it was turning her inside out, instead of turning her on?*

"Tell me about the fantasy you wrote about us," he requested, turning his mouth away from her belly button. "Tell me what you dreamed about me doing to you?"

It was a simple question, and yet Aleesa found it incredibly difficult to answer. The tears were too busy forming and drowning the words in her throat before they could sputter from her mouth. She lay there on the bed, tears quietly flowing down her cheeks, as he ravished her. Josiah was trying hard to give her the pleasure she had requested, but in a split second, everything had changed. Shame had replaced lust. Desire had given away to doubt. She should not be here.

Josiah felt the change in her response. Aleesa had gone from a straight up seductress to a scared virgin. As much as he wanted her, this was not the way. No matter how angry she might be, no matter what dreams of revenge she might harbor, Aleesa was not ready to give herself to a man who was not her husband. He would not try push or cajole her into doing anything she was not one hundred percent willing to do. He might be a hound, but he was not a dog. His mama had raised a gentleman, and Josiah had no desire to play any part in ruining Aleesa's life.

'It's okay, baby," he said, sitting up, scooping Aleesa into his arms and holding her close.

"I'm so…so…sorry," she sobbed into his shoulder. "I can't do this."

"I know, and it's okay. Really."

"He told me I could do it, and I wanted to…with you…but I can't."

"Baby, take it from me. A man may say he's okay with it, but if it happens, he will never be able to get over it. He'll hate himself for suggesting it, and you for taking him up on it."

"Josiah, I didn't mean to lead you on…or tease…"

"I know. You aren't that kind of woman. I believe that in your head you wanted this. And you're not the kind of woman who can get even with her husband by sleeping with someone else, either. I told you before, he's a lucky man, but this isn't the way to remind him, not if you want things to work out. If that's what you want, you both need to talk and listen to each other."

"My cousin said the same thing."

Josiah kissed her on her forehead before standing and putting his jacket on. Aleesa pulled on her robe and walked over to give him a big hug.

"Thank you so much for being the man you are," she told him and she reached up and kissed him lightly on the lips. "You have no idea what an impact you've had on my life."

"And you, my beauty, will remain my reoccurring fantasy. I'll always be wondering what happens next," he said, smiling down on her.

"I'll tell you what. I'll send you a copy of my story, and then we'll both know."

Aleesa stood in the threshold of her room and watched Josiah walk all the way down the length of the hall and turn the corner to the elevator. She stepped back inside and closed the door, overwhelmed by the feeling that Josiah Newman had just saved her life. For his gallantry, she would be forever grateful.

Aleesa turned out the lights and crawled into bed. She lay there going over the events of the evening, happy she hadn't gone too far, frustrated that nothing else had changed. Walter had still cheated on her and she had no idea what to do. She closed her eyes, hoping that between the three MO-politans and all the stress, sleep would come soon. Just as she'd became accustomed to the sounds of her hotel rooms, the chime of her phone intruded. She had a text message.

She reached over to the nightstand and pulled her phone out of her evening bag. It was Livia, sending a powerful, one-word text: *DON'T*.

Aleesa laughed, happy to text back that she hadn't.

GOOD, again all in capital letters came back, followed by, @ *the beach must tlk asap cll me.*

"Well apparently, you learned something from those young'ins after all," Aleesa said out loud, making herself chuckle. *Ok*, she texted back.

Aleesa closed her phone and then her eyes. She'd call Livia in the morning. They opened up again as a thought dawned on her. She had never asked the question about Josiah. Was he worth losing what she already had? Again, as it always had been in the past, the answer was no. Once that question had been asked and answered, more queries came rushing at her in a huge ball, pushing one after another out in front of her to reflect upon and resolve.

So if it wasn't worth losing Walter over, what drove you here?

I guess that would have to be revenge. And anger. And hurt. How could Walter betray me, just like Bill?

Why didn't you let him explain to you what happened? Do you really think he's another Bill?

No, not even close. But aren't all men programmed to cheat? If temptation is put in front of them, they'll lap it up.

Didn't Josiah just prove that wrong?

True. He did. I guess there are some good men out there.

Your husband included. Walt deserves the opportunity to explain, and apologize, and tell you how he's going to fix this.

"We'll discuss this later," a drowsy Aleesa informed the voices in her head. As things quieted down and sleep settled in, Aleesa thought she saw the tiniest ray of light beaming ahead at the end of the tunnel.

Chapter Twenty

It was after four o'clock in the early hours of Friday morning when Walter turned the page to the last story in Aleesa's freak book. He'd stayed up all night reading each story and trying to find clues to tell him where and with whom Aleesa might be spending the weekend.

Starting with the first sentence of *Photo Finish*, he noticed a difference. From the beginning, this last story seemed out of step with the others. There was no introduction or set-up accompanying it like there had been with the others. There was no revealing note to him with insight on Aleesa's thoughts as she slipped from reality into her sexual fantasies. An intrusive red flag went up in Walter's mind, as he read on.

Photo Finish

"So are you volunteering for the job?" I ask this incredibly sexy man holding the camera.

"Which? Fluffer or stud?"

"I see the way you're looking at me. You'd love for me to give you all this good pussy, wouldn't you, picture boy? You want to be the stud, don't you, baby?"

"Absolutely. I want to get all up in that hot, wet pink of yours and tear it up."

I shift in the bed. The idea of Josiah inside me sends an electric volt down my spine. "So who can be my fluffer?" I ask, though I know exactly whose tongue and dick I want between my legs.

"My crew is full service. Cheri? Milo? Jesse"

"How about we bring your look-alike brother in here and he fluffs my pussy while you take pictures? That would really turn me on."

"And then?" he asks, with a wink in his voice.

"And then I'd like both fluffer and stud to service me. Double the pleasure. Double the fun."

"Jesse!" he calls out.

Walter looked up from the book. His stomach was churning with the jealous bile of the green-eyed monster. This was the first, and only story he'd read, that Aleesa had written about someone she actually knew. The rest had featured figments of her imagination. But the star of this escapade was none other than her, how had she put it, "young and attentive" photographer. All of Walter's previous thoughts about Aleesa and this photographer came flooding back, submerging his common sense and allowing his jealous insecurities to bob to the top. He went back to reading, but this time with a detective's eyes, looking for clues.

I lay in bed listening. Maxwell sounds so damn sexy, and downright sensible, singing about saying nothing and proving things in the nude. His suggestion is pouring into my ears, through my brain and landing straight between my legs. When Josiah's look-alike brother enters, my eyes are forced to take a second and third look at both of them. Their likeness is eerie, but the idea of identical faces kissing, licking and servicing me, is truly a sexy turn-on.

I watch from the bed as Jesse proceeds to remove his shirt, revealing a lean and chiseled torso. I stare at both of them as they stare at me. We exchange currents of lusty electricity. They wait for my invitation for one or both of them to join me. Just debating where and with whom to start, brings a tingle to my breasts, and my hand reaches up to stimulate them further.

"That's my job," Jesse tells me, taking my action as his summons. As he steps, bare-chested, to the bed, his hands reach for my tits and begin an aggressive massage. His rough handling excites me and causes a sharp gasp to escape my lips. He smiles with devilish intent as his face comes close to my ear, close enough for his goatee to tickle. "Baby, it might hurt just a little, but I'm going to make your hot box cream," he whispers.

I don't say a word as Jesse begins his fluff job by giving me a tongue massage. He sticks his index finger in my mouth as a pacifier as he begins at the nape of my neck. His tongue and lips work in tandem creating a symphony of soft, wet licks and quick, hard bites across my shoulders and down my chest. I suck hungrily on his finger, treating it like a dick, while he uses his other hand to pinch and roll my nipples, getting ready for his oral assault.

"Yeah, you suck like you're used to having a big, black dick in your mouth," he says before teething on my now hard and stiff nips. The bite is quick, and a delicious pain flashes through my breast and radiates across my body. My raspy ouch, hisses past his finger and out into the room. "It hurts good, doesn't it?" he asks.

My legs spread in an affirmative response. I hear the clicking of Josiah's camera and look up to see that he's placed it on a tripod so that one hand is free to stroke his dick. The sight of him working while masturbating strikes me as insanely seductive. My legs reach further for the edges of the bed.

"Yeah. You're a bad girl, aren't you? Your pussy is dripping like ice cream, you want it so bad. Girl, you're making my dick hard," he says, removing his finger from my mouth. Jesse takes off his jeans, revealing himself to be a briefs man. Size large.

The touch of cotton, complete with protruding dick, presses against my side as my fluffer returns to work. His nails follow his mouth down my torso and toward my belly button. Jesse slips his free hand between my legs and pushes one, then two fingers inside my snatch. He fingers me, stirring up my pussy pudding and, in my head, getting me ready for twin brother. His fingers, slick with desire, cease working on my inner sex and begin to concentrate their magic on my clit.

"Ooh, ooh. Feels sooo good," my mouth moans. I can feel my clit get hard and like a sunflower, lift itself toward the lusty light shining in Jesse's eyes. My hips rise in search of satisfaction. "Lick it," I request.

Expecting to feel the spongy touch of a soft, wet tongue, I am shocked when Jesse gently slaps my pussy with his open hand. It stings, but again, his rough handling excites me. "Don't be such a greedy girl." He slaps me between the legs again and I writhe in exquisite pain. My twat is tingling and I feel bad and nasty and oh-so-fucking sexy.

"Yeah, spank me, damn it. Spank me for being a greedy, bad girl."

"Oh, you like that, huh?" Jesse asks. His hard dick straining against his shorts, telling me that he likes it, too.

"Yes," I say as he flips me over and directs me to get on my hands and knees. I do as I am told. As Jesse primes my ass cheek by rubbing circles over it with his palm, my eyes search out Josiah's. He steps away from the camera and locks his gaze onto mine. I watch him unbuckle his belt and drop his jeans to the floor. The outstanding bulge through Josiah's tighty-whiteys makes me smile. My stud is gifted.

Jesse pulls back his hand and pops me on the ass. I hear the smack and feel the sting as shocked nerve endings spread an intense heat through my butt cheeks. Jesse bends down and treats the residual handprint with wet kisses and soothing licks, while reaching around to play with my clit. My hips move toward the bed, meeting his hands with a hungry pussy.

Josiah watches me, lifting his penis out of his drawers to better stroke his dick. He swallows hard, pleasure pulling his head back and then forward. This causes several of his locks to fly forward, partially covering his face. From my vantage point, he makes one sexy-as-fuck living photograph, and I feel my clit twitch in Jesse's hand.

Jesse's hand comes down hard on my ass again. My cheek, wet with his saliva, stings more this time, so much that I scream and buck forward, collapsing on my elbows. My ass remains high in the air, and Jesse tries to calm my throbbing skin by drawing my attention elsewhere. With the grace of a gymnast, he deftly turns and slips between my legs. His tongue replaces his hand and he begins to lick my ravenous snatch, giving plenty of attention to my clitoris. Like the rest of his foreplay, his pussy eating is rough and frenzied. Surprisingly, it turns me on more and I hump his face and wiggle my nib in his mouth.

Josiah, unable to remain an inactive spectator, rushes toward the bed. He covers my mouth with his own, gently nibbling and sucking on my lips. The juxtaposition of soft angel kisses above my waist and aggressive devil kisses below, becomes a struggle between my good girl desires and my bad girl demands.

I rise up onto my hands again, raising my upper body high enough for Josiah to slip underneath. He and his twin are head-to-head as he plays with my breasts, suckling each nipple, while Jesse works on my clit. Every nerve ending in my body is alert and alive and I feel a huge orgasm building in strength. I don't know how much longer I can go without detonating.

"Omigod. Omigod. You're going to make me cum," I announce.

"Don't make her cum," Josiah says. "That's my job."

"What the fuck!" That statement, fantasy or not, incensed Walter. Josiah's job to satisfy his wife? Why did this man think it was his job to make Aleesa scream with passion and delight? "That's MY job, motherfucker," Walter informed the pages as he pounded his chest, reminding himself. It was his job, but one he had basically taken leave from without notice. Was he getting pink slipped? Judging from what was going on in the recesses of Aleesa's mind, she appeared to be interviewing.

Not one, but two men? A threesome? And twins at that! Was he such a fucking eunuch at this point that it took two men to please his wife? Come to think of it, in most of these fantasies, there was someone else servicing Aleesa before he took over. There was the woman at the birthday party, the butler in Arizona, now these fucking twins. And while Soup or somebody else might take that as a compliment to his manhood, his wife fantasizing about having two men meeting her needs solidified Walter's angst.

Walter drained his glass and picked up the book again. Unlike the earlier fantasies, he found little to tempt and tantalize him. His intrigue now went deeper. He was looking for clearer insight into his wife's thoughts and actions toward a man who clearly had captured her interest and now had Walter questioning her intentions. Like Josiah being the one to kiss her. He knew how much kissing meant to his wife. She loved kissing, and believed a kiss was more personal than a blow job. The twin she kissed was the twin she really wanted. Josiah.

Jesse moves away and Josiah slides down under me to take his place. His mouth covers my vagina and replaces his brother's rough tongue slaps, with long, luscious laps. The change in technique is slowing up my orgasm, but making it grow in intensity. I push aside his drawers and try to reciprocate, but cannot concentrate on both my impending orgasm and giving him head. I opt for my own gratification.

Josiah licks and sucks and coaxes the pleasure out of me until I can't hold back anymore. My hips rise and I burst all over his head. Josiah grabs my ass and holds me to his face, his tongue tasting every contraction of my grateful pussy.

When my body becomes still, Josiah gently lays me down and slips out from under me to remove his Calvin Kleins. His dick springs from its confinement. His cock is hard and long. His large balls rest close by in a hairy thatch. The combination is a beautiful work of chocolate brown, erotic art. I am pleased.

"Can I watch?" Jesse asks, disengaging from the scene. Clearly, I am primed and ready for his brother. His job is complete.

"It's entirely up to Aleesa," Josiah says, nibbling my ear from behind. I am kneeling like a geisha, on the bed. I feel his lean and muscular chest press against my back.

"Only if he is quiet and I don't know he's here," I respond. Like a practiced voyeur, Jesse slips into the shadows of the bedroom, and within seconds of feeling Josiah's tongue running down my spine, I forget he is there.

Josiah reaches over to the nightstand and plucks one of the white roses from the prop vase. He holds the bloom to my nose and I inhale the soft, sexy scent.

"Lie back," he requests.

Again, I obey, as Josiah brushes my hair away, clearing the way for a rosy assault. He runs the bloom down my neck and across my shoulders, before cupping my breast in the fullness of the flower. The coolness of the petals makes my already excited nipples smile, as he drags the rose across my belly and down between my legs. Josiah tickles my inner thighs and tender pussy lips before plucking a petal from the blossom and rubbing my bud, causing it to open.

His flower massage feels incredible and every nerve in my body is begging for release.

A fucking rose massage? Just like the one Aleesa had given herself on the chaise the other night. Was she thinking about this bastard the entire time? Walt thought she was laughing at him, but she was reliving in her head their "way more than a fucking photo shoot" together while sharing intimate time with him.

"Fuck me," I beg. I am done with foreplay. My body wants him so badly I actually am in pain. It feels as if I have been waiting forever to

have him between my legs, making love to me. I've been craving his unique brand of CPR (Cock in Pussy Resuscitation) to bring me back to life and make me feel alive again.

"Make love?" Walter growled. "Bring her fucking back to life?" His ire was growing quickly, adding a layer of outrage to his jealousy. His hands clutched the book as he forced himself to finish.

The difference between brothers becomes immediately clear. While Jesse excelled at the art of hardcore fucking, Josiah was clearly a connoisseur of making love. He rears up on his knees above me, showing me the tool he will use to enhance my delight before honoring my request. Josiah enters me slowly, making sure his dick makes contact with every nerve ending inside my wet and waiting vagina. Once inside, he continues to move in a winning pattern of tiny circles and back and forth movements. He works slowly at first, drawing out the juices from the walls of my pussy, and then, when he sees how crazy he is making me, he increases the speed with every stroke.

I can see him beginning to sweat as pleasure eats away his control and begins to take over. His hard work has set free his hair and his locks drape across his face with winning appeal. I find the sight alluring as hell and clutch my inner muscles to hug his rod.

"Oh, baby, you feel good. Your pussy is so tight and so fucking juicy."

Unlike his twin, Josiah's curses are soft like a song. Jesse's curses did much to excite me, but Josiah's delight me. I lift my pelvis up to meet his, once again clenching to grab his dick on the down stroke. I can hear Jesse's soft, but frenetic, breathing off in the distance. Now the idea of being watched seems to add wood to an already scorching fire.

"Give it to me, baby. Yes. Oh, yes," Josiah called out. Our bodies dance together in perfect rhythm, with each bump and grind, and dip of the hip producing erotic shocks of pleasure. After fifteen minutes of

strong fucking, Josiah lets loose, bucks up against me and busts his nut. He pulls out, kisses my shoulder, and collapses onto the bed next to me.
  All I can think is, OMIGOD!

Walter finished the story and slammed the book shut. It occurred to him that despite this being a threesome, it was clearly Josiah whom Aleesa favored. Based on her words, Josiah was the one she wanted inside her making love to her, giving her an orgasm and bringing her back to life.

And where was he? In all of her other stories, Walter was the one who watched. His dick was the only one that Aleesa rode. She'd written him into every other fantasy, but in this one, he was nowhere to be found. The realization infuriated him, inciting Walter to tear the pages of *Photo Finish* out of the book and toss the entire thing across the room.

He left the freak book on the floor where it landed as he took his glass out to the bar for a much needed bottle of water. Enough of the brown juice. Walter needed to get his head straight so he could think. He plopped down on the sofa, and sat in the dark silence brooding. This fantasy scenario hit Walter hard in the gut. It didn't matter to him that Aleesa had obviously written this story before his return, and before his dick problems had come between them; they felt too much like her solution to their current issues. Nor did it matter that these were fantasies from her head, not her experiences. Or were they? Aleesa may try to pass them off as the lustful musing of a lonely wife, but for the first time in their marriage, he felt like he had competition for her affections. This last story changed the game. And for the first time in their marriage, he questioned her fidelity. Had Aleesa actually fucked this man?

Walter downed his bottle of water with fear and loathing. He was losing his wife, and because of his supreme stupidity, it looked like things between them were literally coming down to a "photo finish."

"Hell, fucking no!" he said, slamming his bottle down on the coffee table. He was not going to lose his wife over his stupid lapses in judgment. His marriage was not going down without a fight. If she was going to choose between him and some random cameraman, she was going to do it based on the whole truth. He had over a decade of memories, and most of them damn good, in his corner. Seemed to Walt that if it came down to sixteen years of marriage, versus forty-eight hours of monkey business, he was in pretty good shape to emerge the victor.

Walter walked back into the study. He had some of his own writing to do. Aleesa wasn't the only one in the family who could put her feelings down on paper in a way that could reach out and touch someone.

Chapter Twenty-One

By 6:00 a.m., Walter was showered, shaved and was ready to leave the house. He tucked the business-sized envelope, along with the name and telephone number he'd jotted down on a yellow Post-It, into his inner jacket pocket, grabbed his keys and headed out of the house on his way to New York City.

Saturday morning traffic out of New Jersey and through the Lincoln Tunnel and down the West Side Highway was light, allowing him to make great time. As he zeroed in on the Upper West Side and Columbus Circle, the thought occurred to him that he should check to make sure that Aleesa was still a guest at the Mandarin Oriental.

"Good morning. Can you please ring Mrs. Aleesa Davis?" he requested once 4-1-1 had connected him to the hotel.

"I'm sorry, sir, but Mrs. Davis has asked that all her calls be held. Would you like to leave a message?"

"No, I'll try back later," Walter replied, trying to keep the jealous rage out of his voice.

Sonofabitch! She'd actually gone through with it. Aleesa had actually checked into the hotel, with Josiah what's-his-name, with the expressed wish not to be disturbed. Walter was crushed. In the back of his mind, he never thought she'd go through with it. He pounded his hand against the steering wheel of his BMW. Things had suddenly gotten a hundred times more complicated because of him and his ridiculous offer. He had only himself to blame. If only he'd kept his stupid mouth shut, Aleesa might have felt the need to sleep away from home for a few days, but probably with her cousin, Livia, and not some other feel-good man.

It was after 6:45 a.m. when he pulled into valet parking and hopped out of the car. Walter pulled a fifty-dollar bill from his pocket and immediately headed for the bell captain's station. Minutes later, he was camped out in one of the comfortable lobby chairs, in full sight of the elevators, while his letter was being delivered to his wife. If her dick-wad photographer had any shred of decency about him, he'd get to stepping as soon as he realized that Aleesa's husband was down in the lobby waiting. And he'd wait...all day if necessary.

ALEESA WAS AWAKENING WHEN SHE HEARD SOMETHING SLIDE UNDER her door. At first, she thought it was the bill, but she was booked for two nights, so it was way too early to receive that. Whatever it was, it could wait, Aleesa decided as she fluffed her pillow and turned over. Two straight nights of drinking, coupled with the stress of realizing herself to be both a scorned *and* cheating wife had taken its toll. Sleeping in for another couple hours, followed by room service and a little self-reflection seemed like the perfect plan for her morning. She'd tackle dinner plans and other minor details, like where she was going to go once she checked out of the hotel, sometime later this afternoon.

It was a few minutes after ten o'clock when a sliver of sun peeking through the blackout drapes caught her eye and coaxed her awake again. Aleesa climbed out of bed, drew open the curtains, and took in her beautiful surroundings. The view of Central Park outside her floor-to-ceiling windows was breathtaking, as was the beautifully appointed room around her. It was a shame to be experiencing all of this loveliness alone.

She called room service to order coffee and her usual breakfast of yogurt and fresh fruit, before padding into the bathroom to freshen up. If only Walt were here with her. Funny, that thought had crossed her mind a thousand times while he was in the Middle East. Every time she saw something beautiful or heard something funny, she'd wished that her husband was there to share it with her. It didn't matter if it was the appearance of the first snowfall or spring daffodil; anything that she found interesting, she knew that he would, too. That had been the beauty of their marriage all these years—experiencing life through each other's eyes. Theirs had been a partnership based on mutual interests and individual tastes. It was a winning combination that kept them unified and engrossed both in each other and the world around them. So why had Walter felt the need to stray?

The pain associated with the question caused Aleesa to shut down that particular train of thought and concentrate instead on drowning her sorrows in the huge sunken marble tub that took up most of the bathroom. She ran the water, steaming hot like she liked it, squeezing the entire contents of the Aromatherapy Associates bath gel in for good measure.

Aleesa sunk down into the tub and lay back, willing the water to do its magic and soak away her problems. Within minutes, the bath therapy was doing its job, melting away the layers of tension and allowing her to relax. The only issue was that once the cobwebs cleared, the thought first and foremost on her mind, was the very one she'd been trying to run from.

Why had Walter stepped out on her? Lena, Livia, and even Josiah had counseled her to sit down and listen to her husband. And, they were right. There was no way she could move forward on any decisions about her life with Walter until she knew everything. But even then, knowing everything would not change the fact that he'd slept with Monica. And though she might be able to eventually forgive, forgetting would be an entirely different undertaking.

Her cell phone rang. She dried her hands and pulled the phone from her robe's pocket, sitting on the tub's ledge. It was Livia. Damn! She'd promised to call her and had totally forgotten.

"Hey, Liv," Aleesa greeted her cousin. "You can stop worrying. I told you, nothing happened with Josiah."

Livia's response took the form of hysterical sobs coming through the phone.

"What's wrong? Calm down and tell me what's wrong," Aleesa said, sitting up and feeling scared as hell. She stayed on the line for several more minutes, listening to her cousin's woeful attempts to regulate both her breath and her sobs so she could talk.

"Where are you?"

"I'm in Miami. I flew down a few days ago. I needed to be in the sun and by the ocean," Livia sputtered out through her tears.

"Why? What happened?" Aleesa asked again, climbing out of the tub and pulling on the thick terry cloth robe without bothering to dry off.

"Lees, I have breast cancer!" she cried.

"Omigod, Liv. I'm so sorry. How did you find out?"

"At my doctor's appointment, she thought she felt a lump, so she sent me for a mammogram. It's stage one."

"Well that's good, right? That means they caught it early. And that's a really good thing, right?" Aleesa asked.

"Yes. That's what they tell me."

"When are you coming home?"

"Tomorrow. Lees, I'm scared," Livia admitted, sounding like a very tiny child.

"I know, baby, but don't you worry; we'll get through this together. And you're going to be fine, do you hear me?" she said, forcing herself to sound upbeat and cheery even though her heart was breaking. "Stage one is great news, and you do realize that there's even better news," Aleesa told her.

"If there is, give it to me now, 'cause I sure can use it."

"There's a good chance you could get some great looking tits out of this, cuz."

For the first time since she'd picked up the phone, Aleesa heard Livia let go of the slightest giggle.

"Leave it to you to find even the slightest silver lining," Liv said. "I know your life is crazy right now, but I'm going to need you. You're all the family I've got."

"Don't even think about it. I'm there. Like white on rice. I love you, Liv. I'll talk with you tomorrow. Call me as soon as you get home."

Aleesa hung up the phone and immediately burst into tears. Here she was dealing with stupid, who-fucked-who issues, while her cousin was just dealt a life-threatening blow. Just like that, Livia's sad news had put her own situation into perspective. Life was too short for such nonsense.

Aleesa sat up after hearing the knock on the door. "Ms. Davis, room service. May I come in?" a voice called out.

Omigod! She'd completely forgotten about her breakfast. "Just leave it on the table, please," Aleesa replied, as he stepped inside.

"And this was under the door, ma'am," the server said, handing Aleesa an envelope addressed in Walter's handwriting. Aleesa took the letter and tucked in the pocket of her robe, the same robe that she'd worn for Josiah last night. This morning she took great comfort in the fact that, thanks to his gallantry, she had not gone too far past the point of no return. She signed the bill and walked the waiter to the door.

As soon as she was alone, she retrieved the envelope from her pocket. Remembering the noise under her door early this morning, Aleesa's eyes immediately went to the floor in front of the entry. Nothing. Room service must have been the one to pick it up and put it on the tray. Walter must have been the one who delivered it.

But when? He had obviously come to the hotel looking for her, but when? Last night? Had Walter seen her together with Josiah? If so, why hadn't he come up to the room and put a halt to things? How early had he dropped this letter off? And what was in that envelope that her gut told her was going to change her life forever. Was it an apology, perhaps? Or maybe an ultimatum? She had no idea.

"Why don't you open the damn thing and find out?" Aleesa questioned herself out loud. She ripped open the envelope and there was a menu of their favorite take out restaurant. Aleesa smiled. Chinese food had always been their favorite after-sex meal. Was Walter being satirical or clever?

Aleesa looked in the envelope, but there was nothing else. It wasn't until she flipped the menu over that she found his note.

My Dearest Aleesa,
I am downstairs in the hotel lobby waiting for you. I love you, and I'm not giving up on us. I will wait for you here or anywhere else you say, for as long as you say. Forever if I have to, because that's what husbands who can't possibly live without their wives do.
I love you. Only you.
Walter

Aleesa finished the letter through tearful eyes. She glanced at the clock. It was nearly noon. Walter had been sitting downstairs for hours. Rather than go downstairs and risk having an emotional scene in front of the hotel staff and their patrons, Aleesa decided to call and have him paged.

After talking to the front desk and asking them to find and send her husband upstairs, Aleesa got straight to the business of tidying up the room and making herself presentable. Her eyes were still red and slightly puffy from her crying jag about Livia, but her makeup and a drop or two of Visine, provided the perfect camouflage. Aleesa pulled on a simple white dress, a show of innocence after her devil red of last night, and flat sandals. She pulled her hair back into a ponytail, and inspected herself closely. She looked cool and chic and ready to face whatever the next few hours had to bring.

In less than ten minutes, Walter was at her door. As she opened it to let him in, she felt a mix of trepidation and excitement melding into a counterbalance of wait-and-see anxiety.

"He's not here?" Walter asked stiffly, not really interested in a confrontation, while at the same time ready to kick some ass if need be.

Aleesa simply shook her head.

"He didn't stay?"

"What happened to 'no harm, no foul.' No questions asked?" Aleesa couldn't help inquiring. The look of extreme pain that crossed Walter's face made her immediately regret her snide remark.

"No, he didn't stay. Once he got up here, we both realized that he didn't belong here."

"So nothing...?"

"No. Nothing happened. We had a couple of drinks and he left shortly thereafter." Aleesa didn't think it was necessary to go into any further details.

"Thank God," he said, rushing toward her and grabbing her up in his arms. "I went crazy last night after I read the story you wrote about you and him. I ripped it out of the book. I was so jealous that I was afraid that if I came here last night, I would hurt somebody. And let me be clear, there is no fucking way I want anyone else touching you.

"I've been sitting down in that lobby since seven a.m. staring down every guy who fit the description of the photographer from your book. There are at least a few men who must think I am absolutely crazy," he told her as he felt his spirits lifting.

"Lees, I was such a fucking ass for even putting the thought in your head, and for hurting you like I have. Baby, I am so incredibly sorry."

The two stood in the entry hanging on to each other for dear life. At this moment, words were inadequate and utterly useless. The confessions were too recent, the hurts too deep for anything but love and kindness in its most base form to step in and comfort the two of them.

Aleesa broke away first. She poured coffee for the both of them and carried it over to the sofa near the window. Walter joined her there, sitting close enough for Aleesa to feel the shame and remorse that seeped from his every pore.

"I know things have been rough since I got back, but I do love you. Our marriage has brought me the best sixteen years of my life and I continue to thank God for the day that you and the boys became my family."

"Then why?" They both knew what she was talking about. There was no need to clarify.

"I promise you, if you let me explain, you'll see that what happened is not what you think. I'm not saying it wasn't wrong. But it's not what you think."

Aleesa felt the hairs on the back of her neck begin to rise. Why didn't they eliminate that phrase from the English vocabulary? Right up there with "fuck you" and "kiss my ass," it was an ultimate insult. She took a deep breath, and forced herself to listen.

He explained to her the circumstances in which he and Monica had found themselves that night. The sights and smells of death happening so up close and personal had left them feeling both scared and vulnerable.

As Walter began to clarify the situation, Aleesa could feel her levels of understanding rise, though she still felt bruised and battered by his admission. At least, his dalliance had not been about some long, forbidden attraction or even, like hers with Josiah, a sexual energy that pushed and pulled them close to the brink until free will took over.

"We were holding each other, scared out of our minds and totally numbed by it all. She reached up and kissed me and from there, it just happened. You have to understand, Lees, that when there is so much violence and death milling around, anything that makes you feel safe and alive is welcome.

"I promise you, there was no getting lost in any great throes of passion, no loving words exchanged. Nothing but the most base sexual act by two people trying to remind themselves that they were still alive in the midst of unbelievable carnage.

"The whole truth is that I needed you that night, but only had her. Please believe me that I was in no way trying to fulfill a sexual need nor was I seeking pleasure. I am so sorry that I betrayed you and our marriage, and I will do anything I must to win your trust again."

"But you said you've seen her since you've been back."

"I have and we've talked a lot. You said it yourself, she's suffering. I've been trying to help her, and she's been a help to me. I felt like I had to sneak around because of what had happened in Asmar. And I won't lie to you ever again. The truth is, she tried to make it more between us, but I'm not interested. I only love you. I only want you."

"I love you, too, Walter. And I have realized that so much of what

I expected from you all these years was because of what Bill did to the boys and me. And that wasn't fair. You saved my life and you have always been there for the kids and me. I know you said that you didn't want to be up on a pedestal anymore…"

"I didn't mean that I didn't want you to…"

"Shh," she said, putting her index finger up to his lips. "I don't want you standing up there alone anymore. I'm sorry if I made you feel imprisoned in any way, but you are my superman and white knight and my Good Samaritan all rolled into one.

"Now, I'm going to be the same for you. Equal partners. I'm no longer the damsel in distress. You don't have to worry about me like that anymore."

"We still have some things to work out, but I want us to start again fresh and on the right footing."

"Perfect, because I have another gift for you," he said.

"I think you've been going overboard on the gift thing. Maybe we both have. That book seems to have created nothing but problems."

"Oh, no, dear. That gift of yours was a true work of art, and it will be our blueprint for years to come. I can't wait to hit a Bed, Bath and Beyond with you," he said, smiling broadly.

"Look, I agree that we still have a lot to work out. But I have faith in us. We'll talk things out until we're blue in the face, if that's what it takes. I want us to get back to being us. And that's why I got you what you said you said you really wanted," Walt told her, pulling out the yellow Post-It.

"Darling, you shouldn't have," Aleesa said, smiling.

"Yeah, I should have, months ago."

"What, or should I say, who is it?"

"A therapist who comes highly recommended."

Aleesa stood up and sat across her husband's lap. She gently caressed the side of his face with her hand as she brought her face down on his and kissed away the remains of his salty tears. Their lips found each other, their tongues said hello and danced a slow, sweet waltz. It was both a kiss of forgiveness, and a long-awaited hello. Their kiss quickly morphed from sweet and tender, into an intense reawakening of pushed aside passions. Aleesa felt Walter's hands reach up and pull down her zipper. At that moment, there was no sexier sound than that of a zipper splitting open for the express purpose of having sex with the man she loved.

Aleesa smiled in his mouth, knowing she'd worn the perfect seduction dress, for the absolutely right occasion.

"You are so damn sexy," Walter whispered, nibbling on her earlobe first, then her neck, then her shoulders.

Their kisses grew more and more passionate, each of them getting caught up in the pleasure of rediscovery without the constraints of guilt and anger holding them back. With no lies left between them, their damaged emotions surrendered to their bodies, and the sounds of low simmering passion filled the room. Aleesa could feel Walt's hardness press against her. She tensed for a split second, wondering if this time, his erection would stand the test of time.

Walt grew bolder as his dick grew stronger. He pulled Aleesa's dress up over her head and threw it to the floor. She shifted her weight to her knees, lifting her ass from his lap long enough for Walter to push his trousers and briefs to his ankles. A collective sigh of pleasure, tinged with relief, escaped her lips as she lowered her body, enjoying the slow, aching pleasure of impaling herself on Walt's beautiful, hard-as-a-rod, black dick.

The tears began to flow as the feeling of being home again penetrated their love making. As she slid up and down and all around, Walt's cock remained stalwart and firm. The two searched out each other's eyes and smiled broadly, cementing their joy over the fact that what had been broken between them had healed, and husband and wife were back in business.

Eyes opened to each other and their future, Aleesa and Walt's ride to ecstasy took a fast and furious turn. Unlike other times they'd attempted to make love since his return, this time was different because they were no longer afraid of failure. Neither could stop the flow of want, love, and need that had been bottled up in each of them for the last two-and-a-half years. Slow and steady simply wasn't an option this time around.

"I love you, Lees," Walter declared, as he clenched his buttocks and pushed deeper into her.

His mouth devoured hers again, his tongue mimicking his dick's actions. Their hips found a mutually satisfying rhythm, rocking back and forth, while their mouths loudly expressed their pleasure. Aleesa found herself letting go and focusing on the delicious friction the rejoining of their bodies was creating. She shifted her position slightly so his dick hit her clit with a new directness. It wasn't long before her insides detonated.

"I love you, too," Aleesa moaned. "Welcome home." As the words left her mouth, Walter's body went taut. He came inside his wife with a powerful orgasm that seemed to go on forever. They fell happily against each other, their mutual afterglow mixing with the luscious agitation of cravings yet to be satisfied.

"A delicious appetizer, Mrs. Davis, but I think it's time we move to the bed. What do you say?"

Aleesa's reply was to reach over and push the "do not disturb" button. It was finally time for Walter's big, albeit belated, sexfest of a homecoming to begin.

THE END

About the Author

Eden Davis is the erotic alter ego of one grown and sexy *Essence* best-selling author. An accomplished writer of both fiction and nonfiction, she created the Eden Davis Series featuring women of a certain age, to be enjoyed by lusty women of all ages. Eden lives in the New York area and is currently working on her next series.

EDEN'S TICKET TO PARADISE:
Write Your Own Freak Book

Aleesa had a lot of fun stretching the limits of her imagination and turning herself, and her husband on with her fantasies. Why not treat your loved one to a tempting tome of some of your sexiest secret fantasies? Or better yet, write them together. If you're currently single and sexy, try recording your fantasies as a homage to the beautiful, sexy diva inside or as a surprise to your future lover when the time is right. You're going to be surprised how sexually liberating this exercise can be.

What you need:
A beautiful journal and an open mind.

What you do:
Create a special date night—light some candles, put on some sexy music, open a bottle of your favorite libation and grab a pen and paper. Together, mine your sexual fantasies and come up with a theme you'd both like to write about; then take turns filling out the story, putting in all of the very sexy details. Copy your final draft into the journal.

Eden's advice:
Here are a couple of ideas to get the ball rolling. First, go back to some of your favorite sexy scenarios in the pages of this book. Use the situation presented to get your story started and continue the scene with your own ideas and fantasies. You can also pull

out your favorite movies, watch how they set up the sex scenes and then let your own desires take over.

Build a vocabulary of dirty words that feel naturally sexy to you. Include the private words you and your lover use to refer to each other's privates. Walter called Aleesa's vagina, "kit cat" and "Clitina." Create and use your own pet names to make your story personal.

Don't let embarrassment or expectations curb your imagination. This private playground is where you get to explore your secret desires and play out in words what you can't or won't do with action.

Lastly, don't be intimidated by the act of writing. You're not worried about getting published. Your only quest is to make this a fun and sexy project where the goal is to turn yourselves on—and create an inspired "happy ending" of your own.

IF YOU ENJOYED "DARE TO BE TEMPTED,"
BE SURE TO READ

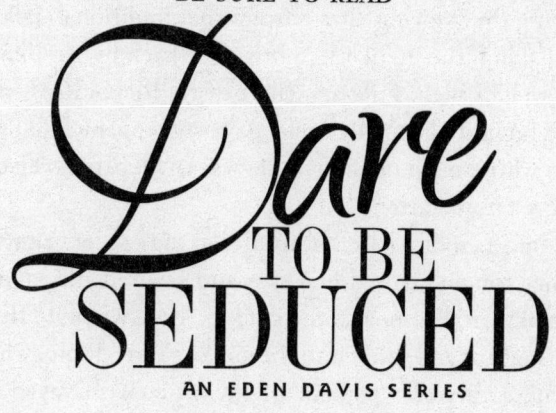

AN EDEN DAVIS SERIES

BY EDEN DAVIS
AVAILABLE THIS FALL FROM STREBOR BOOKS

Lena Macy rummaged through her Super Bowl party swag bag in search of the only thing she could think of that would satisfy her urge for sex—chocolate. On any given day, Miami was a hotbed of testosterone, estrogen, alcohol, drugs and hot and horny beautiful people, there to party and have sex. But on a Super Bowl weekend, the place was like an orgy on steroids. The Miami heat was definitely getting to her, in more ways, and in more body parts, than one.

She'd been down in Magic City for two days, losing much needed sleep and reluctantly partaking in the pre-game festivities—all in an attempt to land her man—Rickie Ross. Lena wanted Rickie. She needed him. And she wasn't leaving town without him knowing how much.

She'd been damn near stalking him for months—calling, emailing, showing up wherever and whenever, trying to make a good impression. But getting next to a famous and hugely popular football hero, a man surrounded by groupies and hangers-on, all trying to get him or give him some, was no simple task. It would be a lot easier if she merely wanted to fuck him, but she didn't. Lena wanted to hire him.

Since being put in charge of Sports Fan Network a year ago, her job was to turn the struggling SFN around and make it a must-see experience for sports-loving viewers. Lena's plan was to shake up the programming by moving away from the traditional talking head analysis, making the network more user-friendly and inviting to women as well as men. Fine-ass, charismatic Rickie Ross was central to that task, but until he finally decided on a new agent, talking business with a man whose main mission in life was to fuck, fraternize and play football, was a non-starter.

Lena bit into a Godiva hazelnut truffle, let the sweet creamy goodness settle on her tongue, closed her eyes and savored the moment. She heard several wordless moans, the kind let loose when THE spot gets hit, escape her lips and settle into the air. She'd read somewhere about a study where fifty-two percent of the women surveyed said they preferred eating chocolate to having sex. Lena couldn't rightly say where she stood in that poll, but at this moment she understood it. Between her demanding work schedule, her last break-up nearly a year ago, and her crazy family issues, the only thing rushing her endorphins these days was chocolate. Usually all she had the energy and desire for was Godiva and Big, her trusty, always on the ready, never argumentative vibrator. But at this moment, after two days spent immersed in the closest thing to a modern-day Sodom and Gomorrah, she wanted more than chocolate. More than Big. She wanted dick. Real. Live. Hard as a rod. All up in her fuzzy stuff, penetrating dick.

Lena moaned again, this time out of frustration, and popped another truffle into her mouth. It was halftime and being upstairs in her suite watching this gridiron face-off alone was depressing. She decided to head down to the bar, grab a bite, down a drink or three, and watch the rest of the game in the company of strangers. Changing into a slim, white, shirt dress with a long string of gray, gold, and white pearls, Lena slipped on her strappy Jimmy Choos, added a spritz of Bellissima by Blumarine, and headed downstairs.

"ONE GRAN PATRON PLATINUM COMING UP," THE BARTENDER SAID, removing her empty glass and smiling over the anticipated size of his tip. This pretty lady not only had looks, but class, and a wallet to match. He removed the sterling silver stopper from the lead crystal decanter and poured the thirty-dollar-a-shot, premium tequila into a shaker, gently chilling the liquor before pouring it into a shot glass with a twist of orange.

Lena sat, sipped her drink and people watched, uninterested, like most in the room, in the half-time show currently in progress. His cologne, a heady shot of Creed, hit her nostrils and commanded her attention seconds before his words. He smelled delicious. Downright edible.

"Well, it ain't nipplegate, that's for sure," a low voice painted with wit and audacity, spoke to her as the celebratory crowd milled around them.

"Where's Janet when you need her?" Lena responded, making friendly bar talk but keeping her eyes purposely glued to the row of flat-screen televisions lining the lounge walls. "But in the big picture, does it really matter who plays during halftime?"

"Absolutely! Everyone knows that if you wanna hold someone's attention, a little sex, or even the idea of a little sex, will always do the job." He finished his statement and let a devilish grin loose on her.

She heard his tongue-in-cheek delivery, and it made her laugh. *Do I have* horny bitch *flashing across my forehead*, she wondered. Usually, such an obnoxious opening would have been ignored, but the shot of tequila that preceded his arrival was too smooth, and she was too bored to brush his comment aside.

"So you're saying that a two-second glimpse of a naked breast—fake at that—trumps a world-renowned, internationally revered rock band?"

"Fake but with a pierced nipple. There is a difference," he schooled her, the flirtatious smile in his tone enticing Lena to turn his way.

Not sure if it was the talk of erotic piercings or the chocolate brown face sporting a dazzling combination of pleading brown eyes and a can't-say-no smile that made her nipples stiffen, but he'd proven his theory. He definitely had her attention.

STOP IT, her brain shouted, demanding that the girls ignore his Djimon Hounsou look-alike qualities and simmer down.

"So you're saying all men like body piercings on a woman?" his prize questioned, surprised to find herself willing and wanting to engage in the conversation.

"Nooo. Not all men. And not all body piercings. Take belly button or nipple rings. What men are drawn to is *the idea* that a woman who would do such a thing is sexually free and adventurous. The piercings suggest that she's daring and willing to experiment."

"And down there?" Lena inquired, too polite to say the word *clit*, even though hers was warming up, without permission mind you, to the conversation.

"A clit ring? That's like crazy sexy, and not in a good way. Little too hard-core S & M for my tastes."

"And tongue piercings?"

"Nah. That just screams slut. Too visible. Too obvious. Unless, you know, you're simply looking to get your knob slobbed."

Witnessing the widening smile of this bodacious charmer, one who had the nerve to be talking blowjobs to a perfect stranger, for some odd reason, only made the girls tingle all the more.

"But I thought the idea of you know…getting worked over by a studded tongue…really turned men on."

"Well, yeah, but no man wants *other* people thinking that his woman is a blowjob machine. That just ain't right."

"I don't know…why else would all these young girls be doing it?"

"Cuz they're stupid little girls and not thinking about how ridiculous they're going to look when they're real women," he said, adding a silent but complimentary, *like you* with an appreciative eye caress of her glistening bare legs. "Look, if you don't believe me, let's ask him," he suggested, calling over the bartender. "I'll bet you the next round, that if given the choice, he'd pick nipple ring over tongue ring."

"You're on."

"Dude, could you settle a bet for us?"

"Sure."

"Tongue ring or nipple ring?"

"Depends. Girlfriend or one-nighter?"

The face with the uninhibited grin, sitting below a perfectly bald, domed head, erupted into a deep and rolling laugh that shook the cobwebs from her vagina. Lena joined in, her sing-song chuckle blending nicely with his.

"Bartender, another round please, on me," she requested, taking her loss with grace.

"Sir, what can I bring you?" the bartender asked over the hubbub of fans cheering the second half kick-off and the New York Jets' bullet train return to the New Orleans Saints' forty-yard line.

"Grey Goose, straight, on the rocks with a twist."

"You got it."

The cheers following the Jets' touchdown turned to boos as the snap was bobbled and the extra point drifted wide. Still, New York moved ahead of their rivals 20-7.

Lena raised her glass to his before tipping it to her lips.

No wedding ring. His eyes grabbed hers, electric interest flying between them, before lowering to check out her luscious, peach-stained lips wrapped around the rim of her drink. He exhaled the decidedly devious request for those same lips to be wrapped around his wakening dick, replacing them with a more apropos, stranger-friendly query.

"Jets or Saints?"

"Well, I'm definitely no sinner," she cooed, raising her eyes to meet his, while fingering the edge of her glass. Her looks, actions and words didn't match, leaving him wondering how much of an angel she could possibly be.

"I'll take that to mean that you're rooting for the Saints."

"You are correct."

"So you're a big Kim Kardashian fan?"

"What?" The out-of-left field quality of his question threw her. "Oh please, do explain," she requested with an amused chuckle.

"After she put Reggie Bush on her show, every woman in America became a Saints fan. They love her, so, by association, they love him, too."

"Women love her?"

"Yeah, they relate to her combination of innocent, but smoking hot, sex appeal. It's like she's saying, 'I'm a good girl, but I can be bad when I want to.' Beyoncé is the same way."

It's like he's reading me, Lena thought as she felt the good girl inside of her smile in agreement. Even at 42 years of age, she understood all too well the concept of being good while her bad girl was screaming to get out. But like most women she knew, she'd been taught from birth to be refined, respectful and mindful of her reputation, so she ignored the screams and carried that good girl mind-set in and out of the bedroom.

"No, I'm a Saints fan because I appreciate the skill and drive of Drew Brees. Given his foot agility, his release, his accuracy and the fact that he is smart as hell, he's got a skill set that makes him an amazing athlete and great quarterback.

"And, yeah, Reggie is a cutie, but he also can haul ass," Lena continued. "In just four seasons, he's rushed for nearly four thousand yards and scored twenty-four touchdowns. And let's not forget Garret Hartley. The boy has a leg on him. Deadly accurate inside of forty-five yards. He would have never missed that field goal like Feely did in the first half."

"Hey, it happens. But you're selling the Jets short. Mark Sanchez is just now coming into his own. He's got a strong arm, makes good decisions and is a leader on the field. His first year in the league, he led his team to the playoffs. How many rookie quarterbacks have done that and actually even won the first game?"

"Four," Lena offered, happily showing off her knowledge of sports.

"Really?" he asked, biting his lip and turning up the twinkle in his eye. "Damn, I think I'm looking at the perfect woman—a hottie who knows football."

And basketball, and baseball, and even a little hockey and NASCAR, she wanted to tell him, but didn't. You can't sit at the helm of one of cable broadcasting's first sports networks and not pick up a thing or two.

Lena gave him a wink and a tilted smile before turning her attention back to the Super Bowl. It was an exciting game; one that looked like it might go all the way down to the wire. The two watched as possession of the ball changed hands several times, neither team giving up enough yards for a score. On occasion, Lena could feel the stranger's eyes drifting away from the television and over to her. They never seemed to settle on one spot for long. Instead, his gaze roamed like a player in the backfield, weighing the options in front of him.

They jumped up with the rest of the crowd, brought to their feet by the running prowess of the Saints' Rickie Ross. His dodging and weaving brought New Orleans three yards shy of the Jets' thirty-seven-yard line and a first down.

"What do they say? Poetry in motion."

"Oh, so you're a Rickie Rosster?" he asked, referring to the player's legion of fans while trying to determine if she was just another groupie in town to get laid by a baller.

"He has skills." Lena downed the rest of her tequila, allowing the silky smooth liquid to coat her throat and loosen her tongue. "So skilled that he's about to take the lead. I will bet you another round that the Saints will *penetrate* the Jets' defenses and *score*."

He took in the body language that accompanied her offer—one heavily punctuated with sexual innuendo. She crossed her shimmering bronze legs and drew them closer to her body, all the while allowing one high-heeled sandal to dangle from her well-pedicured foot like a fishing lure. Was she fishing? He certainly hoped so, because between the foot, the flirting, and that woodsy floral scent that kept wafting over to his side of the bar, he was already hooked.

"You're on." He smiled, happily taking the bait.

"Bartender, another round on me," Lena requested with good-humored exasperation after the Jets stopped the Saints at the line of scrimmage with no gain.

"Here comes your boy," he teased. "Care to sweeten the pot?"

Her competitive nature, like the rest of her, was now aroused. Lena threw back her shot of tequila and smiled in response, secretly wondering if his chest was as smooth as his head. "Name your wager."

"If Hartly hits this field goal, dinner is on me. If he misses, it's on you."

There's that smirk again. Goddamn, this boy is good looking, she thought, while quickly visualizing the literal interpretation of his suggestion.

"That makes the assumption that we are having dinner together," she replied, adding a little cat to her mouse.

"But aren't we?" he asked. There was no challenge, just matter-of-factness in his eyes.

"It's on." *Who am I trying to kid?*

"Excellent."

"YES!!" Tequila and competitiveness combined caused Lena to stand up and cheer, and add a corny Cabbage Patch dance to her celebration. Thanks to Hartley's sure foot, Lena had dinner plans and the Jets lead was narrowed to seven points.

"Looks like I owe you. So I assume eating here at the Setai will work for you?" he asked, while in his head running down his room service menu, one that included everything *but* food. "I mean, I'd love to take you anywhere you'd like to go, but considering the fact that this town is crawling with Super Bowl fans, I don't think we're going to have much luck."

"Are you staying here?" Lena asked, not revealing that she was already a guest in one of the suites.

"Yes. I'm here on business. And you?"

"Same." *Though mixing in a little pleasure seems like a real possibility*, she thought, but didn't add. "And, yes, dinner here is fine."

Another round later, the two-minute warning sounded, leaving the Saints with possession of the ball. Lena and her mystery man watched as their quarterback led his team up the field and into scoring position. On the next play, with only twenty-six seconds left on the clock, the New Orleans fullback rushed past the New York defense and into the end zone, making the score 21-20.

"He's got to go for it. They need two points to win," he declared.

Tipsy and feeling flush, Lena leaned in close enough to breathe in his smell and with it, watered the seeds of arousal sprouting like wildflowers in her. "I'll bet you *anything* that they make this conversion."

"Anything?"

"Yep. Winner takes *all*."

"That's a hefty wager to make with a perfect stranger."

"I'm Pocahontas," she said, raising her empty glass to his. "Nice to meet you."

"Pocahontas?" he asked with a chuckle. "No last name?"

"Why be so formal?"

"True, and Disney characters don't tend to have last names anyway."

"Exactly." Lena smiled at him. When she upped the ante, she'd already decided to have sex with this stranger, but she had no intention of being herself while doing it.

"Well, in that case, Pocahontas, I'm Mr. Johnson." He smirked.

Lena giggled to herself, amused by not only his willingness to play her game, but his choice of moniker. She leaned in close to his ear. "As in Mr. *Big* Johnson?" she whispered coyly.

"Oh, I see you've heard of me," he said.